DRIVE BY

JiM CARRiNGTON

BLOOMSBURY

LONDON BERLIN NEW YORK SYDNEY

Bloomsbury Publishing, London, Berlin, New York and Sydney

First published in Great Britain in March 2012 by Bloomsbury Publishing Plc
50 Bedford Square, London, WC1B 3DP

Text copyright © Jim Carrington 2012

The moral right of the author has been asserted

A CIP catalogue record for this book is available from the British Library

ISBN 978 1 4088 2278 4

1 3 5 7 9 10 8 6 4 2

Typeset by Hewer Text UK Ltd
Printed in Great Britain by Clays Ltd, St Ives plc, Bungay, Suffolk

www.bloomsbury.com
www.JimCarrington.co.uk

For Sonja

Summer

The top deck of a London bus is definitely not the most pleasant place I could be right now. It's hot, it's crowded, it's noisy and it stinks of sweat and burgers and cigarette smoke. I'm struggling to find a seat, but I choose one over on the left-hand side, as far away from all the other passengers as I can manage.

I reach into my bag, grab my earphones and put them in. I get my book, take the bookmark out from where I'm up to and lodge it in the back of the book. *The Catcher in the Rye* by J. D. Salinger. My dad's favourite book. Mine too. I'm on to my third copy. I've read it loads of times – probably more than a hundred. I used to know exactly how many times I'd read it, but when I reached the fiftieth time, I decided not to keep count any more.

I start reading. And as soon as I do, I'm no longer on the bus. I'm somewhere else. The place in my head that I go to when I'm reading. Away from the rest of this world, where no one can get to me. Mum calls it my safety blanket. It annoys me when she says that, but I guess there's a bit of truth in it. Some days I'd like to be able to actually crawl inside a book and *live* there.

I've read *The Catcher in the Rye* enough times that I know *exactly* what each character is gonna say and what they're gonna do and how it's all gonna end up before it happens. I like it that way. I like knowing which word is coming next. I like knowing the characters so well they could be my friends. Rereading the book is like getting to hang out with them. Holden Caulfield's pretty good company too. I know he's messed up and he can be a total plum sometimes, but he's fun. He's complicated and interesting. He's the kind of guy I'd go for.

I feel the bus slow down at a stop. I look up from my book for a second. We're in Colliers Wood. I stare out of the window at the tube station. I hear the beep from downstairs as the bus doors shut. Then we're moving again. I reach into my bag and get myself some gum and then I look back at the book.

As I'm reading, I hear footsteps clomping up the stairs. I can vaguely see someone out of the corner of my eyes as I read. They walk up the bus and sit right next to me. Or, should I say, right *on* me. I put my book down and look across. It's a big guy in a grey T-shirt with big sweat rings spreading out from his armpits. I'm not sizeist or anything, but I hate the way his leg touches mine. Also, the way he talks loudly on his phone. I move up towards the window, so our legs don't touch any more. I turn my music up, bury my head in my book and try not to breathe in through my nose.

But I can't get back into it. Not with the guy sitting beside me, sweating all over me, basically shouting into his phone. So I put my bookmark back in and I look out of the window. I stare dumbly at nothing much, at the buildings and the people, as the bus flies along the roads towards Wimbledon, and ignore the guy next to me for all I'm worth.

Then, when we reach the other side of Wimbledon, I press the bell, say 'excuse me' and walk down the steps. I'm nearly a mile away from where I want to go, but so what? It's a sunny day. Mum's always telling me how I should get more sun on my face. A walk will be nice. Nicer than sitting next to the Before Guy in a deodorant advert anyway.

Johnny

At this very moment, at 3.23 p.m. on Tuesday 31st July, I'm lying, totally exhausted, on the playing field, checking my watch. I tug a tuft of parched grass from the field and let it fall to the ground. Even that feels kind of like an effort. It's *way* too hot today. My face feels like it's melting. I lie back on the grass and look up at the sky. It's perfectly blue, not a wisp of cloud in sight. The only blemish is a white vapour trail, high up in the atmosphere, left by an aeroplane. I close my eyes for a few seconds, feel the heat of the sun on my skin. I take a few deep breaths and get my puff back. Then I sit up and look at the others. Drac, Jake and Badger. Their faces are flushed and beaded with sweat, and their T-shirts cling to them, soaked through.

Drac sits on top of the ball. His ball. 'So, what was the final score, then?'

'Fifty-seven – forty-eight,' Jake says, leaning up on his elbow, 'to J and me.'

Badger, who's been leaning on his elbows up till now, sits up. 'No way,' he says. 'You never got fifty-seven.'

'Did,' Jake says. 'We kicked your sorry behinds.'

And they go on and on, arguing about the score of a meaningless kickabout on the playing field like it's the World Cup final or something. Ordinarily I'd join in, you understand, but it's way too hot and I'm way too exhausted.

'Who cares what the score was?' I say.

The three of them look at me blankly.

I get to my feet. My legs feel like they're filled with concrete. 'I need something to drink.'

Jake gets up as well. 'Good call,' he says. 'Let's go to the shop.'

We grab our stuff from inside the goal frame and walk slowly across the parched grass, past the rickety old pavilion and on to the little tarmacked road that leads out of the playing field to Exminster Avenue.

We walk down the centre of Exminster Avenue, not because we're trying to be clever or because we think we're hard or anything like that, but because the pavements are too narrow for the four of us to walk side by side. None of us says a word as we walk. Drac lazily bounces his football against the tarmac. The sound echoes back off the surrounding houses and cars. *Thwack. Thwack. Thwack.* As we walk, I watch Drac bouncing the ball and I have an idea. I smile and, as Drac bounces his ball again, I dart forward, get my foot in the way and poke the ball away.

Drac sighs. 'J! Don't be annoying.'

But I'm already dribbling the ball away from him, along the middle of the road. Badger and Jake laugh. They jog up to join me as though we're all still on the football pitch and not in the middle of the road.

'J, over here,' Jake calls.

I look up and pass the ball to him. He controls it with his first touch and then flicks it up into the air, starts playing keepie-uppie with it. He gets to about fifteen without the ball touching the ground before Badger nips in and knocks it off him. Badger tries some keepie-uppies himself, but seeing as he's hopeless at football, he loses control after three and smacks it as hard as he can instead. The ball flies like a cannonball towards a silver car parked by the side of the road. I try to get my leg in the way to deflect it, but I'm not quick enough. The ball hits the driver's door with a shallow *thunk* sound and immediately the car alarm goes off.

HONK-HONK-HONK-HONK.

I grab the ball and put it under my T-shirt, hiding the evidence. Then I look up cos I recognise the car. It belongs to the old woman with the screwed-up face and her husband. They live at number fifteen. I look up at their house just in time to see the blinds in the front room twitch. A couple of seconds later, their front door opens and the man comes out into the little glass porch. He unlocks the porch door and then steps outside in his vest and trackie bottoms, his white comb-over flapping as he moves. He opens the gate, but doesn't look at us, just marches over to his car and points his key at it. There's an electric *clunk* and a beep and then the alarm stops.

'Sorry,' I say to him. 'It was an accident.'

He looks at me and nods his head, as if to say, 'OK'. But he doesn't actually say anything. He marches back to his house, brushing his hair back over to the side as he goes. He locks the porch door behind him and then goes inside, leaving the front door open.

As soon as he's gone inside the four of us look at each other and laugh guiltily. I take the ball back out from under my T-shirt and chest pass it as hard as I can to Badger, trying to take him by surprise. He fumbles and it drops to the ground.

'You clumsy donkey,' I say.

7

Badger smiles. He controls the ball with his right foot though and starts dribbling it along the road, trying to do all the tricks. Jake robs it off his toes, flicks it up again and starts doing more keepie-uppies. He's a total show-off. He thinks that because he had a trial at a football club once, he's pretty much Pelé and Lionel Messi all rolled into one.

I glance over at the house. The old lady with the screwed-up face is standing in the porch. The Poisoned Dwarf, my mum calls her. She stands there, arms crossed. I'd say that she was scowling, but I don't remember ever seeing her without a scowl on her face – I think that's just the way her face is.

I think about grabbing the ball and walking away, but the others are well into it now. Drac's on the ball, dribbling it up the road. He controls the ball and looks up as though he's waiting to cross it. Jake's hand goes up straight away.

'On the volley, Drac,' he says.

Drac smiles. He takes a couple of paces back, then runs up to the ball and crosses it. We all watch the ball sail through the air. It comes down perfectly for Jake. He launches himself through the air and then volleys it. But he miskicks the ball and it flies high up into the air towards the Poisoned Dwarf's house, over her back gate, into her garden. It's gone.

'Jake!' Drac calls. 'That's my ball!'

Jake holds his hands up, protesting his innocence. 'It's not my fault. It was your lame cross that made me shin it!'

I look over at the Poisoned Dwarf's porch. She catches my eye and scowls even more than usual. She shakes her head, unfolds her arms and then disappears inside her house, shutting the door behind her.

'I'm not gonna get it back now, am I?' Drac says to Jake. 'That cost me ten quid. Idiot.'

'Don't worry. I'll get it back,' I say.

I walk over to the pavement and through the front gate of the Poisoned Dwarf's house. The others stand in the road, waiting, staring. I go up to the porch, ring the doorbell and stare through the glass at the front door. It stays shut. I think about how I'm gonna ask for the ball back if anyone answers. Should I apologise first or just ask for it back straight away? I hope the husband answers rather than the Poisoned Dwarf. I don't want to have to ask her.

But nobody answers the door. I ring the doorbell again, take a step back and peer through the blinds of their bay window. I can't see a thing though. I sigh. They're not gonna answer, are they? Drac's ball is gone. I knock on the glass part of the door just in case they didn't hear the bell. Still no one answers.

I turn and head back over to the others, who are standing on the pavement now. 'They're not answering. Sorry, Drac.'

Drac rolls his eyes. 'Thanks a lot, Jake.'

'You crossed it. It was your fault as well.'

Drac shakes his head and looks down at the ground. 'You should go and get it back,' he says to Jake.

Jake rolls his eyes. 'What? Why me?'

'Just go over the fence and get it,' Drac says.

Jake sighs, but he doesn't complain. Instead he looks around to check nobody's walking down the street or anything like that, then he walks over to the fence.

'Give me a leg up, then.'

I hold his right shoe, give him a boost. He gets up on to the top of the gate and drops down on the other side. I hear him land. Then we stand and wait. I take a turn back towards the road and keep an eye out, sneak a look into the porch. No one's there though.

I turn and walk back over when I hear the fence rattle. The whole thing wobbles as Jake's head appears at the top. He swings himself over and lands. The football is in his right hand. It's completely deflated. He shows us a large slit in the side of the ball.

'That witch has knifed the ball,' he says, passing it to Drac.

Drac looks at the ball for a second and then kicks

the ground in frustration. 'Jesus,' he says. He makes a kind of growling noise in his throat. 'It's ruined. You can buy me a new one.'

'Sorry,' Jake says.

'Come on,' I say. 'Let's go to the shop.'

Summer

It took way longer to walk here than I thought it would. Maybe I should have stayed on the bus. I'm now as sweaty as the blob that sat down next to me on the bus and my feet hurt like hell.

As I get to the turning towards Nan and Grandad's house, I get a text. I take my phone out and read it.

When you go to Nan's cld you stop and get her some flowers. I'll give you the money when I get home. Mum x

I sigh. Why did she have to send me the text now, when I've already walked along the high street, past two florists and a supermarket? Still, I send her a reply to say I'll do it. Then I look at the little parade of shops

12

that's just opposite. There's a general store. They might do flowers in there. Maybe. It would save me walking all the way back down the high street.

I'm about to push the door open when someone opens it from inside. A group of boys stand in the doorway. They look at me for a second. The one who's in front smiles kind of smarmily. He's holding a burst football. He turns to the others.

'Make way for the beautiful lady,' he says. And he holds the door open for me in a really exaggerated way.

I look at him for a second, trying to work out whether he's being kind or just taking the mickey out of me. I can't decide which it is. Both, I think. I raise an eyebrow at him suspiciously.

'Are you coming in or what?' he says.

I nod and walk in. 'Thanks.'

'My pleasure,' he says. Then he leaves the shop with the other three boys.

I smile to myself. And then I go and look for the flowers.

A few minutes later, I'm standing outside Nan and Grandad's with a lame-looking bunch of flowers. I get the key out of my bag and open the porch door. I shut it and lock it behind me. The front door's already open, so I go in.

'Hello? Nan? Grandad?' I call. 'It's me, Summer.'

As I walk through the hallway, Nan comes out of the kitchen. She gives me a kiss on the cheek.

'Hello, Summer,' she says. 'How are you?'

I smile. 'Good, thanks, Nan.' I hold out the flowers for her. 'These are for you from Mum,' I say. 'Happy birthday.'

There's a sparkle in her eyes. 'For me? Thank you, love,' she says. And she gives me another kiss on the cheek. 'Grandad's in the dining room,' she says. 'Go on through. I'll just put these in water and then I'll be in.'

I walk into the dining room and Grandad's sitting at the table, his toolkit spread out.

'Hello, Grandad.' I walk round to where he's sitting and give him a kiss.

'Hello, sweetheart.'

I sit down at the table and put my bag on the floor.

'What brings you out this way?' Grandad says.

I raise an eyebrow. Grandad is the king of asking stupid questions with blindingly obvious answers.

'Nan's birthday, of course,' I say. 'I wanted to see her.'

'Oh,' Grandad says, like he hadn't thought of that. 'Yes.' He goes back to fiddling about with his tools and the bits of wood in front of him.

'Do you want some lemonade, Summer?' Nan calls through from the kitchen.

14

I smile to myself. Lemonade. I love the fact that Nan hasn't come to terms with the fact that I'm no longer six years old. It's sweet. Besides, I do like lemonade. 'Yes, please.'

I sit and watch Grandad as he peers through his reading glasses at a sheet of instructions, shakes his head and then screws two bits of wood together. I can tell he's concentrating hard from the way his brow furrows and his tongue rests between his lips.

'What are you making?'

He doesn't answer right away. He waits until he's finished screwing the two bits of wood. 'Your great-aunt June bought your nan a bird table and some bird seed for her birthday,' he says. He studies the instructions again and he searches the table for the right pieces. 'Trouble is, these instructions are about as much use as a paper umbrella.'

I smile.

Nan comes in with the flowers in a vase. 'There. They look lovely. Thanks for bringing them, Summer.'

I smile at her.

Nan looks at the tools and bits of wood on the table. She shakes her head. 'Oh, Harry,' she says. 'Do you have to do that now? Summer's here. Can't it wait?'

Grandad sighs. 'You asked me to do it,' he says. 'It's your flipping birthday present.'

'But Summer's more important than a blinking bird table. I would have thought you'd have enough manners to clear your mess away when you know we have a guest. I want to put these lovely flowers on the table.'

Grandad puts his tools down. 'Yes, dear,' he says sarcastically. 'Right away, dear.'

Nan puts the vase down on the table and then goes back through to the kitchen. Grandad starts packing up the tools and bits of bird table. He gives me an exasperated look and I just smile back at him.

'There you go, Summer,' Nan says as she brings the lemonade out.

She takes a seat and looks at me. She breathes heavily for a few seconds and coughs – a deep, barking cough. She looks over at Grandad packing away.

'He can be such an antisocial so-and-so,' she says.

I say nothing. I'm not taking sides in this. Nan and Grandad are always on at each other like this. Always sniping. God knows how they've stayed together for nearly forty years.

'We got you a present,' I say to Nan. I reach down and get it from my bag.

'Oh, thank you,' she says as she takes it from me. 'Is it from you?'

I nod. 'And Mum. And Sky too, I think.'

Nan carefully undoes the sticky tape. 'I had a card from Sky,' she says. 'Came yesterday. I haven't heard

16

her voice for a while though. Is she coming home this summer at all?'

I shrug. 'Dunno,' I say. 'I hope so. It's not very exciting without her here.'

Nan opens the present. It's her favourite perfume. Mum bought it at the weekend.

'Oh, thank you,' she says with a sparkle in her eye. She leans over and kisses me again.

'That's all right,' I say. 'Mum knew it was your favourite, so . . .'

Nan folds the wrapping paper – because she wants to reuse it, I know – and puts it on the table next to the perfume box. 'So, where is your mum today?'

'At work, like always,' I say. 'She said to send her love and says sorry she can't see you on your birthday.'

Nan nods her head. She doesn't say anything for a while. I pick up my lemonade and have a sip. It tastes flat.

'Is your mum taking any time off over the summer?' Nan says.

I shrug. 'Not sure. She said she'd try to, but she only gets a few weeks' holiday.'

Nan makes a disapproving face. 'It's a shame though, isn't it?'

I don't know how to answer, whether to agree or to defend Mum. So I say nothing.

'You must be getting bored in the flat on your own.'

I shrug. 'A bit.'

Nan coughs again. 'Well, you're always welcome to come round and visit us, Summer.'

I smile. The idea of coming round here every day would do my head in. Don't get me wrong, I love my nan and grandad, but spending every day of the holidays with them? No thanks. I'd rather be with Holden.

'Your grandad could even come and pick you up. Couldn't you, Harry?'

Grandad, who's nearly finished packing away now, grunts. 'What?'

Nan tuts. 'You're so rude, Harry. I was just saying that if Summer gets lonely over the holidays, you'll pick her up and bring her here, won't you?'

'Yes, I suppose,' Grandad says. Then he catches sight of the clock and says, 'Isn't it time for your medication, Jean?'

Nan shakes her head and rolls her eyes at him.

Johnny

The two big plastic boxes of free newspapers are on my doorstep, waiting to be delivered. Seeing as Jake's here, I've convinced him to help me. We sit on the step and put the flyers into them, then load up the trolley. It's like one of those shopping trolleys that old ladies drag behind them in the supermarket, except it's fluorescent yellow and has the big blue logo of the local paper on it. It's embarrassing, but it beats the hell out of having to carry the newspapers around in a bag.

Jake sighs. 'You know, I think I may be overqualified for this job,' he says as he stuffs a handful of flyers into a newspaper.

'Really? I'm not sure about that,' I say sarcastically.

Jake flicks me the finger and looks at the headline on one of the papers: *RECYCLING PLANT PLANNED FOR MITCHAM*. 'Does anyone ever read this rubbish?'

I nod. 'My mum does – cover to cover every week.'

Jake shakes his head. 'She must be the only one,' he says. 'I reckon most of these just end up in the bin.'

In no time at all, the trolley's loaded and ready to go. We set off, delivering the newspapers down my street. With two of us doing the job, we manage to get through it much quicker than I usually do. We take a paper each and do alternate houses. Within five minutes the whole street's finished and we start on the next street, Exminster Avenue.

'How much do you get paid for this?' Jake says as he kicks a stone along the pavement.

'Tenner a week.'

Jake snorts. 'A tenner?'

I nod. 'It's all right. Usually it only takes about an hour to deliver the whole lot, so if you think about it, I'm getting ten pounds an hour. That's way more than the minimum wage, and there aren't many other sixteen-year-olds on ten pounds an hour, are there? It's way more than we get for the footy coaching.'

Jake doesn't answer. He takes a newspaper from the pile and goes to post it through a letter box.

'If I worked in a burger bar or something I'd only be on about six quid an hour,' I say.

'S'pose.'

I take a newspaper and post it through the letter box of number three, the house where the curtains are always drawn. Apparently an old recluse guy lives there, but I've never seen him. As I post the newspaper, I can't help but sneak a look through the letter box. I can't see anything much apart from a tatty old carpet and peeling wallpaper and loads of shadows though. I walk back along the drive to Jake and the trolley.

'Another good thing about this job is not having a boss,' I say as we walk along the road.

Jake looks at me with a face like he doesn't believe me. 'You must have a boss,' he says. 'I mean, who gives the papers to you?'

'Yeah. But he's not exactly my boss,' I say. 'I never see him and he doesn't follow me round telling me what to do. The papers just arrive on my doorstep each week. I've only ever met him once.' And then I think. 'No. Twice actually.'

Jake takes the paper to number five, then comes back over to me.

'I met him once when I applied to do the job,' I say, before taking the paper up to number seven and sneaking a look through the front window. A really fit woman lives there, but she's not in today.

'And the other time was when I got in trouble,' I say, when I get back to the trolley.

Jake laughs. 'You got in trouble? How can you get in trouble handing out free papers?'

I push the trolley along, listen to the squeaky wheels for a second. I've been thinking for months that I should put some oil on them.

'Every week I'd deliver the papers and wonder why I was bothering, whether anyone would notice if I didn't deliver them. So one week I decided not to bother. I mean, I did all the houses on my road but then, when it was dark, I took all the others down to the big recycling bins on the high street and dumped them.'

Jake laughs again. 'Seriously? Nice one. If this was my job, it's what I'd do every week. That's what we should be doing right now.'

I stop the trolley outside number nine. Jake stands and stares at me, waits for me to finish talking before he delivers the next paper.

'Anyway, it turns out the company that makes the newspaper has these people who get paid to phone houses on all the rounds each week to see if the papers have been delivered or not. When they phoned people on my round that week, they found out I hadn't delivered them. First I knew of it was when I got a phone call from the boss.'

Jake sniggers. He grabs a paper, but he doesn't go and post it. 'You idiot,' he says. 'So what did he do?'

I shrug. 'Deliver that paper to number nine and I'll tell you.'

Jake runs up the drive of number nine and posts the paper. He comes back and looks at me expectantly. We carry on walking.

'Not much really. He didn't shout or anything. He just told me that if it happened again, he'd find someone else to do my job. Gave me a replacement set of papers and made me deliver them. That was it.'

Jake laughs. 'You deserved it – and more. He should have sacked you.'

I look at him, eyebrows raised. 'What? You said you'd do the same thing if this was your job!'

He laughs. 'Whatever, J.'

We deliver papers to the next couple of houses without saying anything. I take a paper out for number fifteen and then look up. I freeze where I am.

'Look,' I say, nodding my head towards the house.

'What?'

'In the porch. The Poisoned Dwarf.'

Jake looks. He turns to me, a wicked grin on his face. 'That's the old witch that slashed Drac's ball, isn't it?'

I nod. I glance at her again. She's staring at us from the porch of her house, that same scowl on her face, lips pursed, brow furrowed. She looks like she's spent so much of her life scowling at people that all the other muscles have stopped working properly.

'Gimme that paper,' Jakes says, and he grabs it from me and marches towards the house.

As soon as she sees him coming, the Poisoned Dwarf goes back inside and closes the door.

I wheel the trolley closer, to the end of the drive, and watch Jake. He doesn't fold the paper, but just shoves it roughly through the letter box. Even from five metres away I can see the paper shredding into pieces as he forces it through. A smile forms on my lips, even though I don't want it to. The paper drops into the porch in a mess. Jake turns and smiles. Then he rings the doorbell. Not once, but over and over again. When he's finally done with that, he opens the letter box and shouts through.

'Football killer! Psycho! We're gonna call the police if you ever do that again!'

He lets go of the flap on the letter box. It closes with a snap. He stands up and rings the doorbell again for good measure. Then he turns and runs back down the drive towards me, laughing.

'You idiot,' I say as he gets close. 'We could get into trouble for that! What if she rings up the paper and complains? I could lose my job!'

We walk along the pavement and Jake shrugs. 'So

what?' he says. 'You can do better than this job, J. She'd be doing you a favour. Besides, if she grasses on you, we grass her up to the cops for killing Drac's ball. That's criminal damage, you know.'

Summer

I pick up the phone and dial Sky's number. I hold the phone to my ear and listen as it rings. The same monotonous sound over and over again. Nobody picks up. I imagine her flat, the phone in the tiny lounge ringing and nobody picking it up. I wonder for a second whether they're all out, but then I catch a glimpse of the clock. It's nearly eleven. They're students; they're probably all still asleep.

I put the phone down. And I feel lonely. I feel alone. I think of what Nan said yesterday. *'Phone us if you're lonely.'* I smile to myself. I'm not *that* lonely. I pick my mobile up and text Sky.

R u in? I'm bored — I want a chat. X

I go back to my room. Petal, our cat, is lying on my bed, legs outstretched. She looks up as I come in. I bend down by my bed and reach underneath it. I pull out a cardboard box – my memory box – and put it on my bed. I climb on to my bed and sit down, pick up Petal and drape her across my legs.

I say it's my memory box, but in a way that's a lie. It's Dad's stuff. One of his diaries. A Wimbledon scarf. His battered copy of *The Catcher in the Rye*. And there are some of his old records and CDs in there. His favourites. All stuff from before I was born.

Dad died four months before I was born. I never met him. He never met me. He never saw me or held me. I never heard him talk, except I guess maybe when I was in the womb. But I have no memory of that, obviously. I have no actual memories of my dad at all. Nothing. Everything I know about him is from what other people have told me, so I can't be sure that it's true. And some things about him I think I've made up myself.

I can't help but imagine what he would be like if he was here today: what he'd be doing, what he'd say, the things we would have done together if we'd had the chance.

I pick up his copy of *Catcher* and look inside the cover, where his name is written. *James Hornby*. It looks like he wrote it with a fountain pen. The

handwriting is different in his diary. Mum says it's his copy from when he was at school, which explains the handwriting.

My mobile rings. I put the book back into the box and put the lid on. It's Sky calling. I smile and answer.

'Hi, Sky,' I say.

'How you doing, little sis?'

'OK,' I say. 'Bored.'

'Mum working?'

'Yeah. Always.'

'That's a bummer,' Sky says.

'Yeah,' I say. I pause. 'Are you coming home at all this summer?'

Sky doesn't answer right away. I can hear other voices at the other end of the phone, talking in the background. 'I'm not sure, Summer.'

I sigh. 'Really?'

'I'm busy up here,' she says. 'I have to work to pay the rent.'

'Oh.'

'And Dougie's up here too. Things are a bit complicated right now.'

'I'd love to see you though.'

Sky is silent for a couple of seconds. 'Look, I'll see if I can come back for a weekend or something soon.'

'That'd be good. I miss you and I'm so bored here.'

'I miss you as well,' Sky says. 'You know, you're welcome to come up here and stay if you want.'

'Really?'

'Yeah, why not,' Sky says. 'It'd be fun. We could get you into some clubs and pubs and stuff.'

'That'd be awesome,' I say. 'Can I?'

'Yeah,' Sky says. 'As long as Mum says it's OK.'

And then I hear more talking in the background. It sounds like someone is talking to Sky.

'Are you still there?' I say.

'Yeah. Sorry, Summer,' Sky says. 'Gotta go. I'm meant to be at work in a minute. Listen, I'll give you a call later and we can chat properly.'

'Promise?'

'Promise,' she says.

And then she's gone.

Johnny

It's one of those summer days where it feels like the whole world's starting to melt, where the air feels hot and moist and heavy, and the tarmac sticks to your feet as you walk along the pavement. We're sitting on the wall of the little castle on the seventeenth hole of the weed-choked crazy golf course in the park. We're all soaked to the skin. Our water pistols lie on the parched grass.

I look out across the park, idly swinging my legs and kicking the castle wall with the heels of my trainers. Next to me, Jake still has a hold of his water pistol. He takes aim and shoots a jet of water at the eighteenth hole. The water sprays straight through the tunnel you're meant to hit the ball through. I say it's a water pistol, but to be honest it's more like a water pump-action shotgun. The thing has a range of fifteen metres. It's deadly. A total beast.

'Oh, mama,' Drac says all of a sudden. 'Pretty ladies at nine o'clock.'

We all look round. Two girls walk along the fence of the crazy golf course, chatting. They're good-looking all right. I'd say they're a year or two older than us. Wearing vest tops and tight cut-off jeans. We stare as they walk past. They don't give us so much as a glance, but they do that thing where they smile to each other as they pass us, like they know we're looking at them.

Jake looks at them and then at the rest of us. He grins. He holds up his water pistol and I can almost see the cogs going round in his head. After a second he pumps his water pistol.

'I'll aim at their tops,' he says, taking aim. 'Know what I mean?'

I laugh. 'Don't do that, Jake,' I say. 'They'll think you're a pervert.'

Jake's smile gets wider. Me, Drac and Badger laugh. My eyes dart between Jake and the girls. Jake tracks them with his water pistol. He gets them in his sights and squeezes the trigger. A jet of water flies across the crazy golf course, over the fence and hits one of the girls smack bang in the back of her head.

The instant it hits her, both girls scream and cover their faces with their arms. They look all around, trying to work out what just happened, and see us, laughing like idiots. Jake waves and smiles at them. They just stare back at us, looking moody. Jake looks down the barrel again, aims and shoots before they have time to move. This time he hits their faces.

'Get lost, freak!' one of them shouts.

Jake ignores them, grins and takes aim again. But as he's sizing the shot up, the girls scream and run away across the park. He shoots anyway. The jet of water hits them in their retreating backs. But in another second they've run well out of range.

'Man, I'm deadly with this thing,' he says as he swings back round and puts the water gun down on the grass. 'I should be a hitman or something.'

Drac shakes his head. 'You're a tool, you mean,' he says. 'You've gone and scared off the only decent-looking girls we've seen all afternoon.'

Jake laughs. 'Girls love that stuff, Drac, man,' he says. 'They couldn't get enough of it.'

'How would *you* know what girls like?' Drac says.

I nod my head. 'They've run off, Casanova. We won't see them again.'

'Yeah, so what,' Jake says. 'There were only two of them, and there's four of us. It would never have worked out.'

We sit in silence for a bit. I stare past the fence into the park, at all the kids running about, chasing balls, playing cricket. I stare at the heat haze, shimmering above the grass. I'm too hot. My mouth feels dry and my face feels like it's starting to melt.

'I need to cool off,' I say. 'Anyone else coming to the shop?'

The other three nod their heads. We all get up slowly from the seventeenth hole and pick up our water guns. My shorts and T-shirt stick to my body as I walk over to the fence and grab my bike.

A minute later, we're cruising along the streets, back towards the parade of shops at the top of Jake's road. The smell of melting tarmac fills the air. We cycle past some young kids playing football in the street, kicking their ball against people's walls. I smile as their ball smacks into the side of a parked car. If the Poisoned Dwarf saw them doing that she'd have a fit. She'd have something to say about it, that's for sure. She'd knife their ball, like she did Drac's.

We turn left at the end of the street, on to the main road. I cycle in front, one handed, my other hand clutching my water gun. Cars flash by us. A couple of them honk their horns cos we're riding in the road instead of in the cycle lane. Behind me, I hear a car stereo. The road shakes with each boom of the bass drum. The car cruises past us, windows open. It's a

33

black car with lowered suspension, darkened windows and all that kind of rubbish. There are two blokes in there: a white guy with a shaved head, driving, and a black guy with dreads sitting next to him, smoking. As the car passes, I get a waft of the bitter smell of spliff.

We cut out the traffic lights at the top of the main road by nipping through a gap in the traffic and going up on to the wide pavement on the other side of the road. From the pavement, I can see the parade of shops up ahead. I try and work out how much money I have in my pocket and how much I'll be able to afford. Should be enough for a can of drink and an ice cream, I reckon, which will do the trick nicely.

As we get closer though, I see something which takes my mind off drinks and ice creams. One of the cars parked on the double yellow lines outside the shop is the silver car. The one we hit with the football the other day. The Poisoned Dwarf's car. And what's more, she's sitting in the passenger seat with the window wide open, looking hot and bothered. I put my feet down and stop my bike. The others stop beside me.

'What you doing?' Jake says.

I smile at him. 'I've just had an idea,' I say. I point over at the Poisoned Dwarf's car. 'You see who it is?'

They all narrow their eyes and stare, not sure what

they're looking at. All except Jake, who smiles as soon as he sees her.

'It's the old bag that knifed Drac's ball. The Poisoned Dwarf,' he says. 'Ah. Perfect. We have to get our own back on her.'

Drac nods his head. 'Too right.'

We all look at each other and smile. I raise my water pistol ever so slightly. Jake and Drac nod their heads, like they're thinking the same thing.

'What if someone sees?' Badger says. 'We'll get in trouble.'

'We're not gonna do anything illegal,' I say. 'We're just gonna cool her off a little.'

'Besides, she's not gonna know who did it,' Jake says, 'cos by the time she realises what's happened, we'll be long gone.'

Jake pumps his water gun up. Me and the others do the same. Then we start pedalling really slow, really casual, holding our guns in one hand, keeping our handlebars straight with the other. She doesn't look at us as we approach because she's too busy scowling across at the other side of the road where the new supermarket is being built.

When I'm level with the car window, I stop, put my feet on the ground, hold my water gun with both hands, take aim and fire. I hit the Poisoned Dwarf in the back of the head. She jumps in her seat and screams in terror. The others catch up and they do the same. They get her full in the face. We shoot for a second or two till she's completely soaked.

We ditch the idea of going to the shop and pedal away from the Poisoned Dwarf as fast as we can. It's only when we're out of sight of her car that we slow a little. We'll go around the block or whatever, give her time to drive off. We grin like idiots as we pedal.

'That was brilliant,' Jake says. 'That was without doubt the most satisfying moment of my entire life.'

Drac nods. 'That'll teach that witch to mess with my football!'

We cycle to Jake's house because it's the closest.

'We should get rid of the water pistols,' he says, 'just in case she sees us holding them.'

We leave our bikes in the front garden and go round to the back, chuck the water pistols in the garden and then get back on our bikes. We head in the direction of the shops. But as I reach the end of the road and look over at the shops, I see something that makes me stop dead. The Poisoned Dwarf's car is still parked in exactly the same spot, and kneeling on the pavement, leaning into the car, is one of those volunteer police officer people. He looks like he's talking to the Poisoned Dwarf – probably getting our descriptions. Her husband stands by the open passenger door, running his hands through his comb-over, looking worried.

'Jesus,' I say. 'Let's get out of here. Quick.'

We turn our bikes around right away and pedal like crazy back down the road, back to Jake's house.

'Take the bikes round into the back garden,' Jake says as he jumps off his bike.

We leave our bikes at the back of the house and then silently walk round to the front door and wait for Jake to open up. There are no smart comments. No taking the mickey. No laughing. Nothing. All I can hear are the sounds of the trains rumbling along on the tracks nearby, the cars on the main road, a siren, kids playing somewhere in the distance.

We all go inside the house, into the dark, shady hallway and then through to the lounge. We slump into the sofas. The leather feels cool against my clammy skin.

'Do you think she was giving the police officer our descriptions?' I say.

The others shrug.

'She must have been,' I say. 'Why else would she have been talking to a policeman?'

'That wasn't a policeman,' Jake says. 'That was one of those community support people. A plastic policeman. They don't have any more powers than you or me. He was probably lending her his hankie to dry her face or something.'

I nod, but I still think we might be in trouble.

37

'Do you think she saw us properly?' Badger says. 'Do you reckon she'd be able to describe us to the police?'

I try to play back in my head the bit when I aimed my water pistol at her and fired, to work out whether she looked at me or not. But I can't remember it clearly. It's all a blur.

Jake shakes his head. 'No way she saw us properly,' he says. 'It was all over in about two seconds. She didn't have time to see us.'

'But she turned round,' Badger says. 'She must have seen us. She's not blind.'

Drac shrugs. 'As soon as she turned round, we got her right in the face. She would have had, like, a millisecond at the most before we got her. Besides, she doesn't know who we are. Relax, will you.'

'She knows who me and Jake are,' I say. 'We live on the roads next to hers. She sees me almost every day of the year when I walk to school. And she watched all of us the other day when we set her car alarm off.'

'Who cares if she saw us,' Jake says. 'What's she gonna do? Get us in trouble with the cops? For what? Using a water pistol? A drive-by soaking!'

Drac nods his head. He straightens up in the sofa. 'Jake's right, man. It's not illegal to use a water pistol, is it?'

I shrug. I guess he's right. All we need to do is stay out of the way for a bit, make sure the policeman doesn't see us.

It's silent for a while, till Jake stands up. 'Anyone want a drink?'

We all murmur that we do and he comes back a minute later and hands glasses of squash to everyone.

Outside, I hear a siren. You hear sirens round here all the time, day and night. But all of a sudden I feel paranoid. What if this one's for us? For me – it was my stupid idea to soak her. What if the Poisoned Dwarf *has* grassed us up to the community support officer and the police are heading here this second to come and get us? The seconds tick slowly past and the siren sounds like it's getting closer and closer, heading this way. The thought strikes me that if the siren is coming for us, we should hide. Maybe we should get rid of the water pistols too. I wonder whether I should say something to the others, warn them. But I don't. They'd probably think I'm stupid.

They're all silent. They all look like they're doing the same as me: listening to the siren, waiting for the police to skid to a halt in front of Jake's house, making up excuses in their minds, wondering what their parents will say when they have to come down to the police station to bail them out. The siren keeps on and on, getting closer and louder, so loud that it sounds like it must be on our road. Then it stops.

We all look at each other. No one says a word. I go over to the bay window and nervously look up and down the road. I can't see a police car. Maybe it *was* going somewhere else. Maybe I *was* being paranoid. Why would the police come after us for using water pistols? They have way more important things to do with their time.

'The look on her face was funny though, wasn't it?' Jake says.

We all laugh quietly as we remember it.

'She deserved it too,' Drac says.

Jake nods his head. 'Too right she did. If she'd done that to *my* football, I'd have used bullets instead of water.'

I laugh.

Jake goes over to the TV cabinet, switches the games console and the TV on and grabs the controllers.

'Right, then,' he says. 'Who wants their backside kicked at football first?'

Before anyone else can answer, I get up and grab a controller from him.

'Prepare to lose, ginger nuts,' Jake says to me.

Summer

I turn the page, to the last chapter of the book. Not Dad's copy, but my own. A while back, I realised that if I kept reading Dad's, I was gonna wear it out – the cover is already starting to come away from the binding.

As I start reading, Petal raises her head and her ears kind of prick up. A couple of seconds later, the phone starts to ring. She always does that – reacts to something before it's even happened – like she's psychic. It used to freak me out, but I think it must be something to do with the way cats hear.

I think about whether I can be bothered to get up and answer the phone for a second. I should. Mum gets peed off if I don't answer the phone for her when she's at work. But then maybe she should get an answerphone service like the rest of the twenty-first century.

I decide to ignore the phone and carry on reading instead. After a minute or so the phone stops ringing, then almost immediately my mobile starts to ring. I mark my page with a bookmark and pick it up. It's Mum calling.

'Hello, Mum.'

'Summer,' Mum says. 'Are you at home? I've just tried the home phone.'

'Yeah,' I say through a sigh. 'I know. Sorry.'

'Why didn't you pick up?'

'I didn't get to the phone in time.'

Mum doesn't say anything right away. She takes a breath. 'I've got some bad news, I'm afraid,' she says. 'Your nan's gone into hospital.'

My mouth opens to say something, but all that comes out is 'Oh'.

'I'm going to go to the hospital, so I'll be home late tonight. Can you get yourself some tea,' Mum says. 'I'll get myself something when I come back.'

'Right,' I say. I feel shell-shocked. 'Can't I come too?'

There's a pause at the other end of the line. 'Not right now. I don't think she can have visitors at the moment.'

I think about asking why Mum's allowed to go in then, but I don't say anything.

'Maybe we can go in and visit her tomorrow,' Mum says. 'If she's up to it.'

I sigh. 'What's happened? Why's she in hospital?'

There's another pause. 'I don't really know yet. Harry just phoned to let me know.'

I tut. I hate it when Mum calls Grandad Harry. He's not Harry, he's Grandad.

'He didn't say much,' Mum goes on. 'He was in a bit of a state. He wasn't really thinking straight. I'll phone you when I know anything, OK?'

'Yeah, all right,' I say. But I don't feel OK.

I hear Mum sigh. 'Don't worry about her, Summer, love. You know your nan – she's as tough as old boots. She'll be fine.'

'Right,' I say. I feel like I want to cry.

'I'll be back as soon as I can,' Mum says. 'Love you.'

'Love you.'

And the phone goes dead. I put my phone down and lie on my bed, stare at the ceiling.

Mum didn't call back. I've spent most of the time since she rang thinking about what might have happened to Nan. It's not the first time she's been in hospital. She's been in with her hips and her knees and her heart and her breathing. Grandad says she's on so many pills that she rattles when she walks. He's right – whenever I've seen her take her pills, she lines them up and there must be about ten of them. All different sizes and different colours.

When I finally hear Mum's key in the lock, I'm sitting on the sofa, watching TV. I switch it off as she comes into the lounge. She comes straight over to the sofa and sits down. She puts her arms round me and gives me a hug. I hug her back and try to stop myself from crying. But I can smell the hospital – the disinfectant smell – on Mum's clothes, and that makes me think of Nan. Against my will, tears start to form in the corners of my eyes. After a while Mum pulls away from the hug and looks at me, her hands on my arms.

'Hey, don't cry, Summer,' Mum says. 'It's OK.'

She wipes a tear away from my eye with her fingers.

'Is Nan all right?' I say, sniffing away the tears. 'Is she gonna be OK?'

Mum nods. 'She's all right. I told you, she's as tough as old boots.'

I wipe my eyes on the sleeve of my top. Mum looks in her handbag and takes out a tissue. She hands it to me.

'What's the matter with her?'

Mum sighs. 'She's had a heart attack.'

I start crying again.

And Mum's face folds, as though she's going to cry too. 'She's all right now though. The doctors say she's stable,' she says. 'She's just very weak. We'll know more in the morning. They seem to think she'll recover OK.'

'Is Grandad all right?'

Mum nods. 'A bit shaken up, but he's fine. I took him home and got him some food.'

'Can I see Nan?'

Mum makes a face like she isn't sure. 'We'll see in the morning,' she says. 'I'm going to take the day off tomorrow. If your nan's up to it then of course you can.'

Mum's been up for ages, since seven at least. I heard her moving around, making breakfast, making phone calls. I'm still in bed though.

There's a knock on my door. I sit up in bed and look at the clock. 9.43 a.m. I get a feeling of foreboding, like Mum's come to tell me something happened to Nan in the night.

'Come in,' I say quietly.

Mum pops her head round the door. She smiles. That must be a good sign.

'Morning, Summer,' she says. 'I brought you a cup of tea.'

I smile at her.

45

She puts the tea on my bedside table and plonks herself down on my bed. 'How are you?'

I ruffle my hair and yawn. I feel pretty awful. I have a knot in my stomach and a headache. But Mum doesn't need to know that.

'OK, I think,' I say. 'How about you?'

Mum smiles again. 'I'm all right,' she says. There's a pause. The smile goes from Mum's face. 'I called the hospital just now. They said that your nan's doing well. She should be up to having visitors later on today.'

I smile. The knot in my stomach loosens a little. 'Oh,' I say, because I can't think of what else to say. 'That's good.'

'I'm just going over to your grandad's now to make sure he's all right,' Mum says. 'I'll come over this way later if you want and pick you up to go to the hospital.'

I nod.

'OK, then.'

Mum plants a kiss on top of my head.

Johnny

I stretch my arms and look at the clock. It's after nine. I think about turning over and going back to sleep, but I can't – I have to be at footy training by ten. I climb out of bed, grab my dressing gown and leave my room. After taking a leak, I go downstairs into the lounge, where my little brother, Mikey, is lying across the sofa, watching TV.

'Shift up,' I say.

Mikey slowly turns his attention away from the TV and looks at me. He raises an eyebrow and lifts his right hand, middle finger raised.

'Don't be an idiot,' I say. 'Shift your backside.'

Mikey stays sprawled across the sofa. 'Go and find somewhere else to sit,' he says. 'I was here first.'

I take a deep breath, coolly run through my options before I do something that we'll both regret. I could always rise above it all, go through to the kitchen and get myself some breakfast. I could be the mature one here and ignore Mikey's childish behaviour. I could even let him have the upper hand and go and sit on another seat, like he said. But, let's face it, none of those things is gonna happen. Instead I shrug my shoulders.

'You've got five seconds to shift your scrawny, unwashed backside,' I say. 'Five . . . four . . . three . . .'

Mikey stays where he is, ignoring me.

'Two . . . one . . . zero . . .' I sigh. 'You asked for it!'

I sit down hard right on top of Mikey's legs. And as I sit, I squeeze one out.

'Ow!' Mikey squeals. 'Jesus. You freak.'

'I warned you,' I say.

Mikey pulls his legs from underneath me. He adjusts himself on the sofa, so he's sitting instead of lying. All of a sudden his face folds into a look of absolute disgust. 'Oh God,' he says, holding his nose. 'Did you fart on me?'

I smile. 'D'you know what, I think I might have done.'

Mikey aims a punch at my arm, but I catch his fist before it lands.

'Now, now,' I say.

He gives up trying to get back at me and looks at the TV, ignoring me. I watch it as well. It's a repeat of some lame American sitcom.

'Pass me the remote,' I say.

Mikey shakes his head without taking his eyes off the TV. 'No way. I was in here first.'

'So?'

'That's the rule. Whoever's in here first gets to choose what to watch.'

I shake my head. 'Says who?'

'Mum and Dad,' Mikey says.

'Mum and Dad aren't here right now, are they?' I say.

Mikey doesn't say anything, just gawps at the TV.

I look at the remote control in his hand. I could just snatch it now. He's not strong enough to stop me or to get it back.

'I'm gonna ask you nicely,' I say. 'Please can I have the remote control?'

He shakes his head.

'Fine,' I say. 'Have it your own way.'

I lean across and grab the remote. Mikey strengthens his grip on it, so I grab his wrist with my other hand and twist it till he weakens. I grab the remote, switch channels and sit back on the sofa.

'What did you do that for?' Mikey says, massaging his wrist.

'Do what?'

'Give me a Chinese burn.'

I look at him, pretending to be confused. 'I don't know what you're talking about. I didn't do anything.'

Mikey sighs. He gets up from the sofa and walks towards the door. 'I'm gonna tell Mum and Dad about this.'

I shrug. 'About what?'

'You're a loser, Johnny.'

I smile at him. 'Make me a cup of tea while you're up, Mikey.'

Mikey flicks me a V-sign and leaves the room.

Summer

We get out of the car at the hospital. While Grandad goes and pays for a parking ticket, Mum looks me up and down disapprovingly.

'What?'

'You're dressed all in black, Summer.'

I shrug my shoulders. 'And?'

'Your nan's in hospital, Summer. Don't you think it seems a bit wrong to be dressed like you're going to a fune—'

Mum stops herself as Grandad walks back over with the parking ticket.

'Let's not argue about this right now,' she says. 'Visiting time starts in a couple of minutes so let's get going.'

We walk towards the hospital. Mum carries a big bunch of flowers with her. They're way nicer and posher than the ones I got for Nan's birthday the other day.

I start imagining what Nan's going to look like in the hospital bed. In my head, I can see her lying there, pale and ghostly, hooked up to machines, tubes coming out of her mouth and her nose and her hands and her chest, clinging on to life. I imagine the machines beeping as they keep her alive. I imagine her in her nightdress, looking wrinkled and grey-skinned.

The automatic doors swish open in front of Mum and Grandad and they walk in. I follow behind. And as soon as I get inside, the hospital smell fills my nostrils. It takes me right back to the first time I went to hospital to see Nan. I'm still the same scared little girl, still creeped out by everything around me. I want to go somewhere else and pretend this isn't happening.

I feel a hand on my shoulder and almost jump out of my skin. I turn to see Grandad. He smiles at me.

'Are you OK?' he asks in a quiet voice.

I nod.

Grandad sweeps his hair over his head and sighs. 'Funny places, hospitals, aren't they?' he says. 'Never liked them myself.'

I smile. Or at least I try to. It doesn't feel like a proper smile.

'Don't know what we'd do without them though.'

I nod. He has a point. I just wish I didn't have to be here. I wish Nan wasn't here.

We take the lift up to the third floor in silence and then walk out into a smelly corridor, past the nurses' station and on to a ward. We see Nan before she sees us. She's lying on her bed at the end of the ward. She looks up as we get there. She doesn't smile, but I see a little sparkle in her eye. It's there for a second and then it's gone. It makes me feel a bit better.

'Hello, Jean,' Grandad says. He leans across the bed and kisses her on her dry-looking lips.

Nan hardly moves at all. She doesn't say anything either. Her mouth doesn't move. She just looks at us.

'How are you feeling today?' Grandad says.

Nan coughs a little. She opens her mouth to speak and nothing comes out for what seems like ages. Then a croaky, tiny voice – not Nan's voice – comes out.

'Better.'

And that's it. Everybody pauses, like they're waiting for her to say something else, but she doesn't. She just carries on looking at us. And then, as though she's just been jerked awake, Mum steps forward and kisses Nan on the cheek.

53

'Hello, Jean,' she says. She steps back and holds up the bunch of flowers she bought. 'I got you these.'

Nan nods her head slightly to say thanks.

And everyone is silent again. After a while, Mum turns to me and says, 'Summer, do you want to help me get something to sit on?'

We go over to the corner of the ward and bring back chairs for me, Mum and Grandad. Before I've even had a chance to sit down, Mum tells me to go and ask the nurses if they have a vase for Nan's flowers. When I get back with it, Mum takes it and sorts the flowers out.

I sit down and look at Nan. She doesn't look as bad as I imagined earlier. But she doesn't look like herself either. Her hair looks different – wild and bushy and unbrushed. Her face looks drained and her skin is a kind of bluey grey colour. She's always had a wrinkled face as long as I can remember, but now I see wrinkles that I've never noticed before. At least she's not as full of tubes as I thought she might be.

She just lies there, propped up in bed, listening as Grandad babbles on and on about nothing in particular. He tells her all about the fan belt on Mum's car, which I can tell winds Mum up even though she smiles and says, 'I'll get it fixed, Harry. I told you.'

Then Grandad goes on about what time the postman came this morning and how we still haven't had any rain and the lawn is crying out for it. Nan doesn't say more than two words in a row the whole time.

I just sit and listen and think about her. I wonder how she's feeling, whether she's scared. I would be if it was me lying there in a hospital bed. I wonder if she's gonna get better as quickly as she did last time, or whether the more times you have a heart attack, the worse you become. I wonder whether she knows the answer to that question.

After a while, Mum stands up and says, 'Right, who wants a drink? Jean? Tea? Coffee?'

Nan slowly shakes her head. She shakily lifts her arm and points towards the bedside cabinet.

'Water?'

'Please,' Nan croaks.

Mum walks over to the cabinet beside Nan's bed. She takes a glass and a jug of water.

'Is this water fresh?' she asks Nan.

Nan nods her head ever so slightly.

Mum pours the water and then puts it on the tray thing that goes over Nan's bed. Nan picks it up unsteadily and drinks. Some of it misses her mouth and dribbles down her chin. Nan wipes at it with her wrist. I look at the tube that's been taped on to her hand and I wonder why they haven't taken it off, seeing as there's nothing going in or out now.

'Harry? Drink?'

Grandad nods. 'Coffee, please. I'll give you the money.'

Mum shakes her head and looks over at me. 'Come on, Summer. You can help me.'

When we're over by the drinks machine and Mum is making Grandad's coffee, she says, 'Summer, you don't have to stick around if you don't want to. Why don't you scoot off?'

I don't know what to say. There's a part of me that desperately wants to get out of here right away. This place gives me the creeps, especially seeing Nan like that. But there's also a part of me that feels like I should stay for Nan.

'Are you sure?' I say.

Mum smiles and nods. 'Yes. You've made your nan's day by coming, but she won't expect you to stick around. I don't think she's up to too much today.'

'OK, then. If you're sure.'

'Just come over and say goodbye, won't you?' Mum says.

We walk back over to the ward. Grandad's sitting up really straight in the uncomfortable plastic chair, looking sort of awkward. When we get close up I can hear that he's talking about putting weedkiller on the path down the side of his and Nan's house. Nan stares into space, like her mind's somewhere else entirely. I

56

stand at the side of the bed, waiting for Grandad to take a breath so that I can say I'm gonna go.

But before I get a chance, Mum butts in and says, 'Summer's going to go now, Jean.'

I look at Mum, give her a look to say she didn't need to speak for me. Then I turn back to Nan. I look in her eyes, searching for that familiar sparkle, and I want to cry. But I smile instead.

'Bye, Nan. Love you.'

I lean over and kiss her gently, nervously, on the cheek. I've kissed my nan goodbye a million times, but I've never felt so nervous doing it before. It feels like if I kiss her too hard, she'll break.

As I'm bent over, kissing her, she whispers something really quietly in my ear. 'Take care, love,' she says. And then she says something else that I don't get, cos it's too croaky and quiet. And I don't like to ask her to say it again, so I stand back up and smile. I go and say goodbye to Grandad and Mum and then I leave the hospital.

As soon as I get outside I feel better. It feels like I can breathe again. I look in my bag, get my earphones out and put some music on, then get some gum. I head for the bus stop.

Johnny

We're sitting on the metal bench at the bus stop in Kingston. I see the 57 approach so I nudge the others and get up. Once we're on, we head straight to the back seat on the top deck. The bus crawls along, stopping every couple of seconds either for traffic lights or at a bus stop or for a taxi that's pulled out in front of it.

'You know, Jake,' Drac says as he tries to spin his new football around on his index finger, '*you* should have paid for this ball, seeing as you were the one that lost the last one.'

Jake sighs. 'You're not still on about that, are you? I went and got it back for you. It was the mad old Poisoned Dwarf that knifed it – she should be paying.'

Drac's ball spins off his finger as the bus brakes sharply and stops at a bus stop. The ball falls to the floor and rolls away along the central aisle. Drac scrabbles up from his seat to get it. He comes and sits back down, his face slightly flushed. 'I'm just saying, a contribution might have been nice, that's all. This ball cost me ten quid.'

Jake shakes his head and sighs. He puts his hand in his pocket and pulls out some change. He sifts through it and passes some to Drac. 'There. Maybe that'll shut you up,' he says. 'Happy now?'

Drac takes the money and looks at it. He adds it up in his head and smiles. 'Yeah, that'll do nicely. Thanks.' And he pockets the money.

'Half of the ball is mine now though,' Jake says. 'So you need to get my written permission whenever you want to use it from now on.'

Drac gives Jake a sarcastic raised eyebrow and then sticks his fingers up at him. Jake laughs.

The bus moves away from the stop. A branch from a tree at the side of the road brushes against the window with a cringy screeching noise. And I notice someone walking up the stairs. A girl, chewing gum like crazy, dressed all in black, black fingernails and all. She's got a pretty face even though she's trying to hide it behind a load of make-up and hair. She looks vaguely familiar, but I can't think where from.

She flicks her hair out of her eyes as she gets to the top of the steps and looks for somewhere to sit. I stare at her, hoping that she'll look at me. She doesn't though. She sits down about five rows in front of us, takes a battered book out of her bag and starts reading.

I feel a nudge in my ribs. Drac. He grins at me. 'What you gawping at?'

'Nothing.'

Not that I'm fooling Drac. He grins even wider. And he looks over at the girl. 'She's fit.'

Jake overhears and leans over Drac. 'What?'

I shrug. 'Nothing.'

Drac laughs and says, 'Johnny-boy was just saying how he fancies that girl over there.'

I shake my head. 'No, I wasn't. Shut up, Drac.'

Jake looks over at the girl. Not that you can see much of her – just the back of her head. 'Yeah, she's all right. Probably a seven. Maybe an eight at a push,' he says. He sits forward in his seat a little and calls down the bus, 'Excuse me.'

But she doesn't look round – for one thing because she doesn't know that Jake is talking to her and for another she has her earphones in.

I squirm though. 'Shut up, Jake.'

He looks at me and smiles. The bus lurches to a halt at another stop.

'Excuse me,' he calls again. 'Pretty girl dressed in black . . .'

She still doesn't look round.

'Stop acting like a three-year-old,' I tell Jake.

Drac just laughs.

Over on the end of the back seat, Badger flicks through his comic, acting like he's not with us at all.

'What? I'm helping you out,' Jake says.

I lean across Drac and try to give Jake a dead arm to shut him up. He laughs it off. Then, as I'm expecting him to start it up again, he leans back into his seat and sits quietly.

The bus pulls out into the traffic again. I sneak a glance at the girl. She's totally engrossed in her book and her music. She looks cool. Way too cool for me. She isn't even aware of my existence.

And then, out of the corner of my eye, I see something fly towards her. It comes from beside me and smacks her in the back of the head. A screwed-up bit of paper, I think. I see her tense up. After a second or so she turns round. She sees us all on the back seat and figures that it must have come from us, which, judging by the way Jake and Drac are chuckling, is a pretty good guess. She rolls her eyes. She picks the ball of paper up and throws it back. It lands on a seat a couple of rows in front of us. And then she turns back to her book.

I look at Jake. 'What did you do that for?'

Jake smirks. 'What? I didn't do anything.'

I shake my head and look out of the window. We're just coming up to the station – nearly home. Which is just as well cos I want to get off now, before Drac and Jake can do anything else immature.

But over to my right, I sense more movement. Another screwed-up paper ball. It flies through the air and hits the girl on the back of the head again. She puts her book down.

Next to me Drac and Jake crack up laughing. The girl turns round. She sees them and rolls her eyes.

'Excuse me,' Jake says. 'But my friend there fancies you.' He points to me.

I shrink down in my seat. I can't believe he's said that. Why's he acting like a total numbskull?

The girl looks angry. She narrows her eyes. But I'm not sure if she heard what Jake said or not because she's still got earphones in. She looks like she's ready to come and give Jake a good slap though. She doesn't even look at the rest of us. She raises an eyebrow at him, chews her gum and then blows a bubble about half the size of her face. She gives Jake the middle finger. The bubblegum pops. She turns back round and reads her book. Next time the bus stops, she gets off without looking back at us.

*　　*　　*

Dad's been home literally minutes when I hear him call up the stairs, 'Johnny, can you come down here?'

I sigh. I know exactly what this is gonna be about.

When I get downstairs, Mum and Dad are both in the kitchen holding cups of tea.

'What happened while we were at work?' Dad says.

I shrug. 'Dunno. I was at football training most of the time and then I went into Kingston.'

Dad raises an eyebrow. 'Let's not play silly games,' he says. 'Are you going to tell me or not?'

'Tell you what?'

'Mikey's arm . . .' Dad says.

'Oh,' I say. '*That*.' I smile involuntarily.

'Yes, that.'

'He was being an annoying little idiot,' I say. 'He deserved it.'

Dad shifts about. I can tell he's annoyed with me.

'He's thirteen, Johnny,' he says. 'Thirteen-year-old boys *are* annoying. But you're sixteen, for God's sake. You're supposed to be a man. You should be a bit more mature than to do something like that.'

I sigh. 'Is that it? Can I go now?'

'No,' Dad says. 'We haven't finished talking about this. There was a mark left on Mikey's wrist, Johnny.'

I don't say anything. Mikey deserved a mark on his wrist. Mum and Dad don't see half of the stuff that

Mikey does to me, mainly because I'm not a grass like he is.

'Your mother and I should be able to trust you when we're not here,' Dad says.

Again I don't say anything. What am I meant to say to that?

'Maybe we can't trust the two of you to be left together when we're out.'

'Suits me,' I say. 'Why doesn't one of you take Mikey to work with you?'

Dad gives me a look and I can tell that he's on the verge of losing it with me. 'I want you to go upstairs and say sorry to him,' he says.

'What?'

'You heard me. Now.'

I sigh. I turn, go back up the stairs and walk straight into Mikey's room without knocking.

'Hey! What do you think you're doing?' he says angrily.

'Dad said you grassed on me. He made me come and say sorry to you,' I say, trying to get as much contempt into my voice as I can possibly manage. 'So here I am. Sorry, you grass.'

Mikey sniggers at me.

'Freak,' I say as I leave his room.

Summer

'Mum?'

Mum doesn't look up from the paper. 'Hmm?'

I can tell she's not paying any attention. Maybe this is the right time to ask her – she might give me the answer I want without thinking about it properly.

'Sky said that I could go and stay with her up in Edinburgh.'

Mum nods without looking up.

'So, can I?'

No answer. I don't think she heard what I said. Maybe I should just take her silence as a yes and start making arrangements with Sky. I could go and write it in the calendar. Mum probably wouldn't notice until it was time for me to catch the train and by then there wouldn't be much she could do about it. I wouldn't be lying if I said I'd told her about it. She wouldn't have forbidden me from doing it.

But just as I'm about to go to the kitchen and add it to the calendar, Mum finally responds.

'Did you say something, Summer?'

I sigh. 'Yes,' I say. 'Can I go and stay at Sky's house?'

Mum puts her paper down and turns to me. She doesn't say anything right away, but I can tell from the look on her face that she doesn't think it's a good idea. I knew she'd react like this.

'Please.'

She shakes her head. 'I'm not sure I like the sound of this.'

I sigh and sit forward in my chair. I knew I should have taken her silence as a yes before. 'Please, Mum.'

She doesn't say anything.

'All I'm doing is sitting around the place getting bored,' I say. 'You're at work every day . . .'

'But Sky has a summer job – she'd be working every day as well,' Mum says.

'I know,' I say. 'But she has flatmates, doesn't she? And when she's not working, she might actually spend time with me.'

Mum raises an eyebrow. 'I don't think so, Summer.'

I sigh. 'But I'm going out of my mind with boredom.'

'Why don't you see if any of your friends want to do anything, then?'

I can't believe this. I've told her a million times. She never listens to me. 'Because they're not here, Mum,' I say. 'Jodie's moved and Lauren's away for the whole holiday.'

Mum sighs and picks her newspaper up. 'Sorry, Summer. The answer's still no.'

I go to my room, slamming the door behind me.

Johnny

I don't hate Mikey. Well, not completely. If I saw someone giving him hassle or beating him up, I'd come to his rescue. He is my brother after all. And I don't think he hates me. But we don't like each other much either. It's just one of those things. It's a brotherly thing, I s'pose. I can't imagine getting on nicely with him. That would be weird.

Basically, Mikey is like an annoying little parasite. Or an insect bite – always there, always in the back of your mind, trying to get a reaction, trying to get you to scratch and make it worse. He gets his kicks by winding me up every day. It's what he lives for. And do you know what? It'd be weird if he didn't act like that. If, all of a sudden, one day, Mikey just came out and started being nice, I'd think he'd lost it. I'd probably punch him because I'd suspect that his niceness was part of a bigger, elaborate plan to annoy me.

Not that I'm innocent. I have to admit that I get pleasure from taking the mickey out of Mikey. I like being older and bigger than him because it means I can give him a slap if he steps out of line and there's nothing he can do about it. Apart from grass on me – something that he's an unashamed expert at.

It's harmless though. Mostly. I guess it's a bit like lion cubs, the way they fight with each other, not so they actually hurt each other, but so they toughen up, hone their fighting and hunting skills. That's what me and Mikey are like.

When we were younger, we used to be a right pain when we were in the back of the car together. We'd fight and argue and wind each other up something chronic. And a lot of the time, because Mum and Dad's backs were turned, we'd try and get each other in trouble.

There was one time – we were coming back from visiting Grace, our great-aunt – when Mikey and me were going out of our heads with boredom. So I did what Mikey hates me doing – God knows why – I pointed at him. I just put my hand close to his leg and extended my index finger so that it almost, but not quite, touched his leg.

As soon as he noticed, Mikey wailed, 'Mum. Dad. Johnny's annoying me!'

Mum and Dad tried to ignore him, so I kept my finger there.

'Mum! Dad!' Mikey said. 'He's doing it on purpose. Make him stop.'

Mum sighed in the passenger seat. 'Johnny,' she said without looking around. 'Give it a rest, please.'

'What?' I pleaded. 'I haven't done anything! I'm not even touching him.'

Mum turned round. She saw my finger millimetres from Mikey's leg, pointing. 'Johnny, please,' she said. 'You're supposed to be the older one. Can't you set a good example?'

I rolled my eyes and tutted. I took my finger away.

As soon as Mum had turned to look out of the car window again, Mikey stuck his tongue out at me.

I bided my time, pretended to look out of the window at the rainswept road for a bit. But then, when I could see that Mikey wasn't looking, I reached my hand across again, extended my index finger, pointed and waited.

There was another squeal. 'He's doing it again, Mum! Make him stop.'

Mum sighed again. She slowly turned in her seat and looked at me. She raised an eyebrow. 'Johnny. Stop it, please,' she said, trying to sound calm, but looking stressed.

I raised my eyebrows in mock astonishment. 'What? I'm not doing anything. I'm only pointing my finger. I'm not even touching Mikey.'

'You know what you're doing, Johnny,' she said. 'Stop winding your brother up, please.'

I rolled my eyes and shook my head. 'It's a free country,' I mumbled under my breath.

Mum chose not to hear me as she turned back.

Mikey and I exchanged rude gestures. And then we were quiet for a while, each looking out of our windows. We were nearly home – coming up to the Shannon Corner junction, where we always leave the A3.

I looked around to check Mum wasn't watching, then I extended my hand once more. I couldn't help it. It's like a reflex to boredom.

This time, when he noticed my finger, instead of crying to Mum and Dad, he grabbed my finger and yanked it as hard as he could.

'Ow! Jesus!' I said, pulling my finger from his grasp and aiming a punch at his arm.

'Stop it now!' Mum shouted. She turned in her seat once more and scowled at me. 'I've been very disappointed with you on this journey, Johnny.'

'One more thing and I'll stop this car and you can get out and walk home,' Dad said.

As soon as Mum's back was turned, Mikey looked at me and held his sides, pretending to laugh at me. And I lost it. My right hand formed into a fist and I punched him twice on the leg.

'OW!' From the noise Mikey made, you would have thought he'd been shot. He even managed to summon some tears from somewhere.

Dad pulled the car over straight away, in the car park at the front of a timber yard. He pulled the hand-brake on and turned in his seat. 'Out!' he yelled at me.

I didn't move. 'What?'

'Out, Johnny. Now! You're walking the rest of the way home.'

Again I didn't move.

Dad sighed. And then he unclicked his seatbelt and went to open his door. At that point I decided it was probably better to get out myself rather than wait to be hauled out of the car.

Thirty seconds later, I stood on the kerb about ten minutes' walk from home, and I watched as Dad indicated and then pulled out into the traffic. As the car went, Mikey waved at me and gave me two fingers.

That's the way it's always been. Always.

Summer

I climb the stairs up to the top deck of the bus. I stop a couple of steps before the top and look around for a seat. My heart sinks. It's full up. No seats anywhere. For a second I think I'm gonna have to go back downstairs and stand, but then I spot the last spare seat on the bus. Next to a boy. Well, I say boy, but I mean a guy, man, whatever. He's my sort of age and he looks pretty cute. He looks familiar too. I'm sure I've seen him somewhere before. I climb the last couple of steps and walk towards the seat. The boy looks out of the window as I get there, earphones in. He doesn't notice me sit down.

'Do you mind if I sit here?'

The boy looks round at me, a startled expression on his face. He takes one of his earphones out. 'What?'

'Do you mind if I sit here?'

He shakes his head. He blushes slightly and shuffles up in his seat. 'Help yourself,' he says. Then he looks out of the window again.

'Thanks,' I say and I sit down next to him.

Out of the corner of my eye I look at him to see if he's sneaking a look back at me or anything like that. But he isn't. He's staring out of the window, still holding the earphone he took out. And I wonder whether that's because he secretly wants to talk.

'What you listening to?' I say.

He turns, looking startled again. 'Me?'

I nod. I smile. 'Yeah. Of course you. What are you listening to?'

He looks down for a second. He looks kind of sheepish, like he doesn't want to tell me. 'Oh, it's just an old band. You probably haven't heard of them . . .' he says. He sounds apologetic about it.

'Go on. I might know them.'

He shakes his head. 'I doubt it,' he says. 'They're called The Cure.'

My heartbeat quickens. 'No way,' I say. 'Seriously?'

He nods. 'Have you heard of them, then?'

I nod. 'Yeah, totally. I love them. They were my dad's favourite band. I've got all his records and CDs.'

The boy raises his eyebrows and smiles. 'Oh. Right.'

'I'm always going on about them and no one ever takes any notice. I've never met anyone my own age who's heard of them before.'

He smiles again. 'What can I say?'

'You must have good taste,' I say. 'Which album is it?'

He shrugs. 'Just the greatest hits.'

He looks at me for a second before staring back out of the window.

I hear the beeping noise as the bus doors shut downstairs and then the bus moves off. I think about getting my earphones out of my bag and putting them in, getting my book and burying myself in it. But then I notice the boy turning.

'Um, this is gonna sound a bit weird,' the boy says, 'but were you on this bus the other day?'

I look at him. He's taken both of his earphones out now. 'Um, yeah,' I say. 'Why?'

He smiles, embarrassed. 'I recognise you.'

'Oh? Really?' I don't know what to think. Should I be flattered or scared?

'I was on the back seat with my friends. They were being childish and they threw some paper balls at you,' he says. 'It was you, wasn't it?'

I feel a bit bit embarrassed now. 'Yeah,' I say reluctantly. 'That was me. They were idiots.'

'I know,' he says. 'I cringed when they did that. I'm sorry. They're a bit immature sometimes. They're not always like that though.'

I raise an eyebrow. 'Were you throwing them as well?'

He shakes his head. 'No way. I was willing them to stop.'

The bus pulls into a stop. I stare into space and think. I don't know what to say to him now. I feel like a bit of an idiot.

'I thought it was cool though,' he says. 'I mean, the way you threw the paper ball back at them and then gave them the finger. That was a good way to deal with it.'

I don't say anything, but I smile to myself. That was a compliment, I think. Maybe he likes me. I kind of want to find out more about him. There's something intriguing about him. He's sort of awkward and weird. But I like awkward and weird.

'My name's Summer,' I say, turning to him.

'Johnny,' he says.

And then we're both quiet. The bus speeds along the road. I rack my brains for something to say. I could ask him what other bands he likes. I could ask him what his favourite film is. Or . . . What do people talk about in situations like this? I never do this kind of stuff.

'So do you always wear black?' he says, taking me by surprise.

I turn to him. 'Pardon? You sound like my mum!'

'What?'

'That's what my mum always says. She's always on at me for wearing black. She thinks I always look like I'm going to a funeral.'

'Oh,' he says. 'Sorry. I didn't mean it like that. I . . .' He pauses. He's going red. 'I was just asking cos you were wearing black last time I saw you as well. Anyway, I think it looks good. Black suits you. Keep wearing black.'

'Thanks,' I say. 'I think.'

He laughs to himself. 'Sorry. I'm not very good at talking to people. They don't let me out in public very often.'

I smile. 'They should. A little more practice and you'll be fine.'

He smiles at me. But then he looks out of the window and straight away reaches across and presses the bell. The bus starts to slow.

'My stop,' he says.

I stand up to make room for him. As he passes me, he looks at me, right into my eyes. We hold the eye contact. And it feels great.

'Nice talking to you,' I say. 'Don't forget to tell your friends to stop acting like monkeys.'

'Sure thing,' he says. 'See you around.'

The bus stops and he clumps down the steps. As it moves off again, I look out of the window. Johnny's looking up at me. He smiles. And in a couple more seconds he's too far away to see. I get my book and my earphones out of my bag. I put my earphones in and switch the music on. I take my bookmark out and start reading. But I don't take a single word in.

Johnny

I grab a handful of newspapers, stuff them with flyers, then start to load up my trolley. When I'm done with the first box, I take the scissors out of my back pocket and open the second box to cut the plastic ties. But I stop because I notice something. The front of the newspaper. There's a picture of the parade of shops at the end of Jake's road and next to that the headline, *LOCAL WOMAN SUFFERS HEART ATTACK IN UNPROVOKED WATER PISTOL ATTACK BY YOBS*.

The world folds in on me. The scissors fall from my hand, hit the pile of newspapers and then clatter down on to the front step. I just can't help but stare at the headline. It can't be. Not us. Jesus. Please. No.

I close my eyes, try to keep calm and think rationally. It can't be anything to do with us. It must be a coincidence. All we did was shoot a bit of water through a car window. We couldn't have done any damage. We couldn't have given the Poisoned Dwarf a heart attack. Could we? We'd have heard about it by now if we had, right?

I open my eyes, sit on the step and pick the scissors up from the ground. I snip the hard plastic ties, take the top newspaper from the pile and start reading.

An elderly Raynes Park resident suffered a heart attack last week after being shot at by local yobs with water pistols. Jean Hornby, 72, of Exminster Avenue, was waiting in her car for her husband to come out of a newsagent when yobs on bikes shot at her through her open car window. Mrs Hornby, who is on medication for heart disease, suffered a heart attack at the scene. When her husband, Harry Hornby, came out of the shop on East Barnards Lane, he discovered Mrs Hornby and immediately beckoned over a passing Police Community Support Officer, who administered first aid and called an ambulance.

Mrs Hornby was taken to St Matthew's Hospital, where medics worked to stabilise her condition. She remains in hospital and is in a serious but stable condition.

Police are appealing for witnesses who may have seen the incident to come forward with information.

I look up from the newspaper with clammy hands, a dry mouth and my heart thumping. I put my head in my hands. This is bad. This is worse than bad. I don't know what to do about this.

No.

No.

NO.

Jesus Christ, no.

I take my phone out of my pocket and write a message to Jake and Badger and Drac. **Come over to mine now. We r in trouble.** I send it and then go inside the house.

Mikey comes out of the kitchen just as I get in the door.

'All right, loser?' he says.

I don't have time for his stupid games right now though. I head straight up the stairs without a word.

Ten minutes later, Drac, Jake and Badger are all at mine, up in my room, reading the front page of the newspaper. It doesn't take long for it to dawn on them, to realise who's to blame. The colour drains from their faces and their expressions turn to shock and guilt.

The room is silent for ages.

'Oh, Jesus,' Jake says eventually.

'No way!' Drac says. 'That was us. Far out.'

Badger doesn't say anything, but the look on his face says it all. His eyes have gone bulgy as he stares at the front page. For a second he looks like he's gonna cry. He looks away from the newspaper, gets up and goes over to my bedroom window and stares out of it without a word.

'What do you think we should do?' I say.

No one answers. No one makes eye contact. Jake reads the newspaper again.

'Do you think we should tell the police it was us?' I say.

Badger sighs. He moves away from the window and comes and sits on the floor.

Jake puts the paper down. 'No way,' he says. 'We do that and we're in trouble.'

'But won't it count for something that we told the truth?' I say.

'I don't know,' Jake says. 'And I don't want to find out.'

'We didn't mean to do it,' I say. 'It was an accident.'

Drac snorts. 'It wasn't an accident though, was it?' he says. 'We shot at her with our water pistols. We didn't do that by accident cos we aimed at her on purpose.'

'You know what I mean. We didn't mean for her to have a heart attack, did we? We didn't know she had heart disease.'

Badger nods. 'J's right.'

Jake looks over at Badger. 'So what? You wanna go to the police? You think we should confess?'

Badger shrugs. He looks down at the carpet. Then he shakes his head. 'I don't know what I think right now.'

'I say we keep quiet,' Drac says. 'If the police knew it was us, they'd have arrested us already, wouldn't they?'

I don't say anything, but I guess that makes sense.

'Drac's right. We shouldn't tell the police. No way. We should keep quiet,' Jake says. 'Badger? Do you agree?'

He shrugs again. 'I s'pose.' He doesn't exactly look thrilled with the choice.

'J?' Drac says.

Jake and Drac stare at me. I don't like the looks on their faces. They look intimidating, like I should be agreeing with them whatever I think. I look at Badger. He's still staring at the carpet, picking bits of fluff from it, letting them fall back to the floor. I sigh. I really have no idea what we should do. Neither answer is the right one.

'OK,' I say. 'I agree. We keep quiet.'

No one speaks. It feels weird. I don't want this to be happening. I suddenly get an image of the Poisoned Dwarf in my mind, of her sitting, unsuspecting, in her car as we approached. And I get a guilty, stabbing feeling in my guts. I imagine her now, in hospital, stuffed full of tubes, hooked up to machines that beep. All because of one moment of madness.

'So what do we do now?' Drac says.

'Nothing,' Jake says. 'That's the point. We just act normal, wait for all the fuss to die down. Don't mention it to anyone. Try not to think about it. She'll get better. And then it'll all be forgotten in a couple of weeks.'

'What about the newspapers?' I say.

Jake looks at me. 'What about them?'

'What do I do with them?'

'Deliver them, of course,' Jake says. 'Just like everything's normal.'

We're almost entirely silent as we deliver the newspapers. We all help each other out, taking it in turns to take a paper from the trolley and post it through a door. We have my road done in a couple of minutes. But each time a newspaper is pushed through a letter box and I hear it plop down on to a carpet, it feels wrong. It feels like we're shoving a letter confessing our guilt through every letter box in the area. Any one of the people in the houses we're delivering to could have seen us messing about with our water pistols that day, could have been passing the shop when we gave the old lady the fright of her life. Maybe we should be shoving the newspapers into a recycling bin instead. All gone, all done with. Who cares if I lose my job?

But I know why we have to do this. Jake's right. We need to keep everything the same as normal so we don't attract any attention. If we keep our heads, if we're lucky, no one will ever know what we did. It will all blow over and we'll be able to forget it and the Poisoned Dwarf will be OK. So I keep silently taking my turn, posting the newspapers through letter boxes, trying to get this over with as soon as I can.

We turn on to Exminster Avenue and my stomach lurches immediately because it dawns on me that we're gonna have to push one of these newspapers through the letter box of number fifteen. The Poisoned Dwarf's house.

We do the first couple of houses. Drac takes the first one, Jake posts the next, then Badger. Then it's my turn. I take a paper from the trolley, fold it in two without looking at the front cover, and I walk up the front path of number seven, up the step and open the letter box. I push the paper through. It resists for a second, makes a scraping noise as I push it, but then I feel gravity take over. I hear it hit the mat and then the letter box snaps shut. I rush back along the path as Drac takes the next one and delivers it to number nine. In no time at all Jake and Badger have delivered to numbers eleven and thirteen.

I pause before I pick the next newspaper up from the trolley. I stare at number fifteen. The blinds are closed in the living room. There's no one standing in the porch. But still my heart beats like mad.

'Come on, J, get a move on,' Drac says.

I look round at him. I nod my head. 'It's her house,' I say quietly.

Drac stares back at me.

I take a deep breath and I start walking towards the house. I fumble to get the front gate open. It squeaks as it swings open. I walk along the crazy-paving pathway, staring ahead at the porch and at the blinds, praying no one will come to the door as I deliver the paper, that no one will see me. I look down at the newspaper as I fold it in two. As I catch a glimpse of the headline, I think about just making a run for it back along the pathway and carrying on delivering to the other houses. My boss would never find out that I didn't deliver to 15 Exminster Avenue.

But my legs carry me forward. And as I reach the glass porch, I find my hand opening the letter box almost against my will. I pause. My hands feel clammy. This feels wrong. It feels cruel. They're not gonna want to read this. This is the last thing they're gonna want shoved through their door.

'Hurry up, J,' Jake calls from the pavement.

I lift the paper, rest it in the letter box. I push it

slowly, inch it inside. It falls. It hits the mat, lands headline side up.

'What was that all about, then?'

I look at Mikey, but don't say anything. I go and sit on the sofa and point the remote control at the telly. When the telly comes on, it's the lame channel that he spends all day watching. I switch over.

'What was the big powwow for?' Mikey says, sitting down on the sofa next to me.

I look at him, raise an eyebrow. There's something in his voice that I don't like – it sounds as if he's taunting me. 'What are you on about?'

'You and your boyfriends,' he says, smirking.

I shake my head, look over at the TV. 'What? I had my friends round, so what? Just because you don't have any friends, doesn't mean that no one else does.'

Mikey lets out a sigh. 'You all looked like you were bricking yourselves to me,' he says. 'Have you done something naughty?'

'Go and play in the road, Mikey,' I say.

Mikey sniggers. 'Your secret's safe with me.' He winks and gets up and leaves the room.

I stay on the sofa, the uneasy feeling in my stomach growing.

*　　*　　*

It's the end of football training. Me and Jake stand around and exchange a look as our coach starts his car. It splutters and coughs, just like he does half the time. He slams the old banger into reverse, turns it around and then chugs out of the car park. We get on our bikes and head home.

We ride along the pavement quietly, dodging in and out of all the people who are walking towards the supermarket.

'You OK?' Jake says after a bit.

I slow down a little, look round at him. 'Yeah. Why? What do you mean?'

'You just seem quiet today.'

As if that should be a surprise to him given what we found out yesterday.

'Just thinking about stuff,' I say.

Jake doesn't reply. He hasn't said anything about yesterday. I don't know whether he just doesn't think it's important or whether he doesn't want to think about it. Me, I can't help but think about it.

'About the old lady. The Poisoned Dwarf,' I say. 'I feel bad about what happened.'

Jake still doesn't say anything. We get to the railway bridge where the pavement narrows. There's someone coming the other way, so we jump down off our bikes and wheel them through.

'You need to relax about all that old lady stuff,'

Jake says quietly. 'We didn't mean to give her a heart attack. How were we to know she had a heart condition?'

'Do you think she'll be all right though?'

'How should I know? Probably.'

I think about the old lady, wondering whether she's still in hospital, whether she could have died and we don't know about it. Jake has a look about him like he doesn't have a care in the world and I can't understand it.

'Don't you even feel a bit guilty?' I say.

He turns to me. 'A bit,' he says. 'Course I do. But I'm not gonna waste the rest of my life worrying about it. There's nothing I can do about it now, is there?'

I sigh. 'But if we hadn't shot at her with our water pistols, she probably wouldn't have had a heart attack, which means it is our fault.'

'Look. The old lady had a heart condition, right? It said that in the newspaper. If it hadn't been us shooting her that gave her a heart attack it would have been something else. It sucks that she had a heart attack, but . . .'

'What?'

'Unless you've got a time machine, there's nothing you can do to change what happened.'

I wish I did have a time machine. There's no way I would have shot at her if I'd known. Maybe I should have known. You only need to look at her red, screwed-up face to know that she's a heart attack waiting to happen.

'Besides, she wasn't exactly innocent herself,' Jake says. 'She slashed Drac's ball.'

An angry reply flashes into my mind, but I don't say anything. I have my eyes set on what lies ahead – the parade of shops where it happened. I feel shaky and nervous. I look at the parking space where the Poisoned Dwarf was parked last week. It's empty right now.

The whole incident replays through my mind in slow motion. Aiming in through the car window and firing water at her. Her scream. Her shocked face. Us pedalling away, laughing.

I wheel my bike along and try to get home as quickly as possible. I feel my cheeks flush as I pass the spot.

'You wanna go and get some chips for lunch?' Jake asks.

I shake my head. How can he think about that right now?

'No,' I say. 'I think I'm gonna go home.'

But then I see something that takes my mind off everything, makes my heart stop for a second and then race at about a million beats per minute.

It's the girl from the bus. Summer. I'm sure it is. She's walking towards us on the same bit of pavement. Her head is down at the moment. She hasn't noticed us. I glance at Jake, hoping he hasn't noticed her, that he doesn't say anything childish like he did the other day. But he's too busy looking across at the building site on the other side of the road to notice anything.

I look back at the girl. It is Summer, definitely. She's dressed all in black again, earphones in, blowing bubbles with her gum as she walks. As she approaches us she looks at me. I stare back at her, not sure whether she's recognised me or not. But then she smiles, so I smile back. I wonder whether I should stop and try and have a conversation with her, or whether Jake will butt in and ruin it all. As I'm trying to work out what I'm gonna do, she reaches into her bag and takes out her phone, which is ringing. She pulls her earphones out and puts the phone to her ear.

'Hello, Mum,' I hear her say.

I see something fall from her bag and hit the pavement. In a second, she's passed us, gone towards the shop.

I put my bike down. 'Watch my bike for me,' I say to Jake.

I go over to what Summer dropped on the ground. As I get close, I realise it's her bus pass. I bend down and pick it up and then I run along the road after her.

'Hey,' I call. 'Summer.'

She doesn't hear me.

'Summer!'

Again she doesn't look round. She opens the shop door and goes inside. I follow her in and up an aisle to where the milk is kept. I stretch out my arm and tap her on the shoulder. She kind of jumps and then turns round. She stares at me. She looks scared to begin with. Then she sees it's me and she smiles.

'Hi,' she says, taking her phone away from her ear for a second.

I hold out her bus pass. 'You dropped this.'

She stares at it for a second. Then she reaches out and takes it from me. She looks at me again and my heart skips a beat. 'Thanks,' she says. 'Johnny.'

We stand and look at each other and I think that I should say something. I should talk to her. I might never see her again in my life. But after a couple of seconds she puts her phone back to her ear and says, 'Sorry, Mum . . .'

I start trying to say 'See you around', but it kind of catches in my throat. I turn and head back out of the shop.

I pick up my bike.

'Who was that?' Jake says.

'Uh?' I say. 'Oh, just a girl. She dropped something, that's all.'

Jake doesn't say anything more and we carry on walking, pushing our bikes. As I walk, I wish I'd thought of something to say to start a conversation other than 'you dropped this'. I'm hopeless.

*   *   *

'Johnny?' Mum says as she walks into the living room.

I ignore her and stare at the TV.

'Johnny, do you know what happened to this week's paper?'

I look up straight away. 'What do you mean?'

'I can't find it anywhere. Did you deliver one to us or not?'

I don't say anything. I didn't deliver one, no. I didn't want Mum or Dad to read about what me and my friends did. I know our names weren't in the paper, but I just felt weird about it. They can always see through me when I'm lying or trying to keep a secret, and I thought they'd do the same this time.

'Um. I think so, yeah,' I say.

Mum looks confused. 'I asked your dad and he said he hasn't seen it though.'

'I've seen it,' Mikey pipes up. 'In the recycling bin in the front garden.'

'Really?' Mum says. 'Did you put it there, Johnny?'

I shake my head and hope that my cheeks aren't starting to flush.

'Mikey?' Mum says.

Mikey shakes his head. 'Why would I do that?'

Mum leaves the room to go and retrieve the newspaper from the bin.

Summer

Mum walks into the kitchen and puts her handbag down on the table. She comes over and kisses me on the top of my head.

'Good day?'

I nod. 'Yeah, OK.'

'Good,' she says. She goes straight to the kettle and fills it at the sink. 'Drink?'

I shake my head. 'I went over to see Grandad for a bit today,' I say.

Mum plugs the kettle in. Then she stops and looks at me. 'Oh, yes. How was he?'

'Fine, I think,' I say. 'He was doing some gardening.'

Mum nods. She starts looking through cupboards for a mug and a tea bag.

'He didn't mention Nan,' I say.

'Really?' Mum says without looking at me.

'Nope. I even asked him how she was and he didn't say a word. He just gave me her library books and asked me to take them back to the library for him.'

'That sounds like a typical man,' Mum says. 'Totally emotionally retarded!'

'Mum!' I say. 'Don't say that.'

'Sorry, love,' she says. 'That came out wrong.'

Neither of us says anything for a bit. Mum busies herself making a cup of tea and I sit and think. When she's done making her tea, Mum comes and sits at the table with her drink.

'Do you think Nan's gonna be all right?'

Mum looks deep into my eyes and smiles. She puts her hand on top of mine and rubs it. She nods. 'I'm sure of it,' she says. 'She's a tough cookie, your nan.'

I smile back, but I wonder whether that's just the kind of thing that you say to make someone feel better or whether Mum really does think she's gonna get better.

'We could go and see her if you like,' Mum says. 'The ward is open to visitors in a bit.'

I shake my head. I don't want to see Nan in the hospital again. It makes me feel weird. It makes me feel nervous. I want to see her back at home.

'Well, I could phone the hospital,' Mum says. 'They could tell us exactly how she is.'

'Can you? Please.'

Mum sits for a while, sipping tea. She must be able to sense something from me, because after a few seconds she says, 'You want me to phone them now, don't you?'

I nod. I feel like a little girl again.

Mum gets up from the table and goes through to the lounge. She takes the phone and dials the number for Nan's ward. I hang around close to her, desperate to hear the news. But I can't work anything out just from Mum's side of the conversation, because all she says is 'yeah' and 'OK' and 'oh'. At the end of the conversation, she puts the phone back in its cradle. It seems to take an eternity for her to look back at me and open her mouth.

'She's doing well,' Mum says.

A wave of relief washes over me.

'She's not one hundred per cent, obviously, but she might be able to come out of hospital soon.'

'Really?'

'They did say that she's very weak though,' Mum

says. 'She's going to need a lot of rest and recuperation.'

I'm so relieved.

'Feel better now?'

'Yes. Thanks, Mum.'

Johnny

Instead of relaxing at home like I should be, I'm heading down the high street at two thirty in the afternoon. I have my earphones in and I'm carrying a plastic bag full of milk and bread and all the other stuff Mum put on the shopping list for me to get. The sky overhead is starting to look nasty. The clouds have rolled in and it's almost dark. It feels like it's gonna chuck it down any second now. I start walking faster, hoping I can get home before it starts cos I'm in just my T-shirt and shorts.

I turn left at the lights and then cross the road, hurrying along, swapping the carrier bag from hand to hand to stop it digging in and leaving a mark in my skin. I walk on, take the road on the right before the parade of shops, try not to look at them or think about what happened there, and then I'm on Exminster Avenue. I cross straight over, so I'm on the side where all the even-numbered houses are. I've started doing it every time I walk down this road. I don't want to walk past the Poisoned Dwarf's house. I feel guilty every time I see it.

As I'm walking along the road, it starts raining – big, plump drops of rain – slowly at first, just one or two drops, but within seconds it's absolutely tipping it down. I hurry even faster, cursing.

A car swishes along the road through the rain. I look up at it. It's the silver car. The one we hit with the football the other week. The one whose window we fired through. The Poisoned Dwarf's car. I walk on quickly, keeping my head down but watching it. The brake lights come on just before it gets to number fifteen. The passenger door opens. I stop still and stare as the raindrops soak me. A lady gets out of the passenger side. Not someone I recognise.

The lady jogs round the front of the car to the parking space in front of the house and moves the traffic cone they always put in their space. It's usually the Poisoned Dwarf that does that. At least, it used to be her. As she's doing that, the car pulls into the parking space. I move a few paces forward so I can see better.

The driver's door opens as the lady goes to the porch and unlocks the house. The Poisoned Dwarf's husband gets out of the car. He sweeps his comb-over back into place, then he goes to the rear door of the car and opens it. He bends down as though he's speaking to someone in the back while the lady from the passenger seat comes back outside with an umbrella. She holds it above the back door of the car. The Poisoned Dwarf's husband moves back, and as he does someone slowly gets out of the car.

It takes the person a while to get out, but when they have, my stomach churns. It's the Poisoned Dwarf. She stands unsteadily underneath the umbrella and looks around. She starts to shuffle slowly along the pavement, through the gate and to her house. I just stand and stare. She looks pale. She looks skinny and frail, like a ghost or something. She takes a while to get up the step – her husband and the other woman (her daughter or a social worker maybe) help her up. They all go slowly inside the house and shut the door behind them.

I feel relieved. I'm so glad she's all right, that she's not dead or anything. But . . . Well, she looked really awful. She looked about ten years older than before. Did we do that to her? Will she get better? How should

I feel – relieved she's out of hospital or guilty because she looks like a ghost?

Then I realise that I'm standing in the pouring rain, getting soaked, and I rush home.

Summer

Nan comes shuffling slowly into the house. Grandad holds her elbow as he guides her in through the front door and then the hallway. Nan looks up at me. I smile at her.

'Hi, Nan,' I say.

Nan takes a couple of deep breaths, like she's just run the hundred metres or something. 'Hello, Summer, love,' she says. She sounds a bit better than when I saw her in hospital, but not much.

'Good to have you back,' I say. 'Welcome home.'

Nan looks at me again. She doesn't smile, but I see something in her eyes – something like her old sparkle – and I know that inside she's smiling at me.

She continues to shuffle through to the lounge, right over to her armchair. Grandad keeps hold of her arm the whole way, keeping her steady. When Nan gets to her chair she kind of backs towards it and slowly lowers herself down. Grandad only lets go when she's sunk into the chair.

'Right, I'll get your bag out of the car, Jean,' he says. 'And let's get the kettle on while we're at it, shall we. Summer . . .'

'Of course,' I say. 'What does everyone want to drink?'

Once everyone's decided what they want, I go through to the kitchen. Mum, who's taken the afternoon off work especially, comes with me.

'It's good to see her back, isn't it?' Mum says.

I nod. I take the lid off the kettle and turn the tap on.

'Do you feel relieved?'

I don't say anything, don't look at Mum. I feel weird now I've seen Nan. It's great to see her back, but she seems frail. She doesn't seem like Nan. I look for mugs and tea pots and coffee and everything else to avoid having to look at Mum.

'Are you OK, Summer?' Mum says, watching me fuss around the kitchen.

I nod my head again. I don't look at her. I can't. I'm not OK. I don't know what it is. I walk over to the fridge and take the milk out.

'Summer?' Mum says. She comes over and puts her hands on my arms, tries to turn me round so she can look into my eyes.

I avoid her eyes for as long as I can, but after ten seconds or so I crumble. I look at her and the tears start immediately.

'Oh, Summer, come here,' she says.

I sob into her chest. We stand there for ages, Mum just patting my back as I cry. I hear the kettle boil and switch itself off.

'What's the matter, Summer?' Mum says eventually.

I shrug. 'I don't know. I just feel weird. I thought Nan would be like her old self.'

Mum makes a sympathetic face at me. 'Give her time, Summer,' she says. 'Give her time.'

'She looks like a ghost though,' I say, my voice cracking as I talk. 'She looks so ill.'

Mum doesn't say anything. She just makes a face that I think is meant to be a smile, but looks more like a grimace. I wipe my eyes and then go over and make the teas and coffee. Mum doesn't say anything.

'Thanks, Summer,' Grandad says, coming in and picking up the mugs. 'You're a good girl. I'll take these through.'

Then he sees my face and he kind of freezes. He

doesn't say anything for ages. When he finally does, he says, 'Everything all right, Summer?'

I nod my head. And then I pretend to busy myself at the dishwasher.

Johnny

It's Saturday morning – nearly Saturday afternoon, to
be accurate – and I'm still in bed. I can't be bothered
to get out of bed. I've been awake for a while and all
the time I've been thinking and staring up at the ceiling. I've been worrying about the Poisoned Dwarf
and trying to work out what to make of what I saw.
Her being let out of hospital has to be a good thing,
doesn't it? If she's been allowed out, she must be
better.

The thing is, she looked bad. She was kind of
hobbling. Her skin was the wrong colour. She looked
like a corpse. A zombie. A dead person walking. A
living person trapped inside a dying body. And I know

that it's all down to us, to what we did that afternoon.

Surely that's not it for her though. She'll get better than that. It's still only a week or so since it happened, isn't it? It must take a while for the body to recover. She'll get back to how she was before it happened. I hope.

My phone beeps to say I have a message. I roll over and grab it from my bedside table. It's from Jake.

Just had a call from Coach — we have next Weds off! Wanna go to the theme park then instead?

I text him straight back and say yes. What Jake said the other day is right. I need to relax about this. I need to act normal. I need to start having some fun. I need to get on with the rest of my life.

Summer

We hardly ever talk about Dad. I don't know why. We just don't. But sometimes, if you get Mum in the right mood – usually after she's had a couple of glasses of wine – she'll talk. Once she told me all about her and Dad's plans.

Right from when they first met, they decided that they wanted to have lots of kids. Mum reckons that Dad wanted enough to play five-a-side football in the garden. Their plan was that after I was born, they were gonna find a house in the countryside, one where they'd have some land, so they could grow their own vegetables and keep chickens and all that kind of stuff. They'd planned to buy an old house that needed loads of work done on it, but with tons of rooms so there'd be space to fit all their kids. There was gonna be an open fire in the living room. Maybe even some woodland around the house. Dad wanted a workshop as well, so Mum could do her painting and he could fix bikes to earn some money. That was their dream. They were gonna try and work part-time and start their own businesses in their spare time, just earn enough to pay the bills. Apparently Nan used to laugh whenever they talked about it in front of her. She called it their 'pipe dream'.

They even knew what the kids were gonna be called. Being kind of hippyish, they wanted all their kids to have natural kind of names. Which is why we're Sky and Summer. Obviously they didn't know if they'd have boys or girls, so they had a whole list of names they might use. Some of them were pretty cool, like River and Amber. Some were OK, like Leaf and Rainbow. And some were just outright lame, like Breeze and Jasper. Imagine going through high school with a name like Breeze. You'd be asking for trouble.

As it happened, they never had their five-a-side football team. Just me and Sky. And they never moved out of London into the countryside. Dad died before I was even born. And that was that.

I sometimes imagine it though, what it would have been like if it had all happened like Mum and Dad dreamed it. What if I had loads of brothers and sisters and we lived in this mad, rambling house in the country with lots of animals. I think it would have been amazing. I'd love to have younger brothers and sisters. Me and Sky have always got on really well, but she's been away at uni for the last couple of years and this summer it doesn't seem like she's gonna come home at all. I miss her. I feel kind of lonely in the flat every day on my own. I'd love it if there were more of us here. I don't know what living in the country would be like, seeing as I've lived my whole life in Tooting, but I like the idea of it. I'd love to be able to just walk out of the front door and be in the woods.

But it's never gonna happen. Mum had another boyfriend for a little while, years after Dad died. I didn't feel right about it. Neither did Nan. It didn't last very long. And Mum's never had another boyfriend since. I don't think I'd want her to either. It would be weird.

Johnny

I wake with a start. I sit up in bed and look at the clock. The red digits glow 2.43 a.m. I rub my head. My hair feels sweaty. I feel disorientated, not sure what on earth is going on. My heart's beating at a million miles an hour. I take a couple of deep breaths and try and get my thoughts together.

I look around the room. My window's wide open. The curtains are blowing in the wind and it's freezing cold. Moonlight pours in where the curtains blow open. I hear a train rumble along the railway line in the distance and cars on the main road. I get up and go over to the window, close it and lock it.

I sit on the edge of my bed. My bed feels kind of

damp from where I've been sweating. I run my hands through my wet hair. I feel on edge and I don't know why. I try and work out what made me wake up. I think about what I was dreaming about just before I woke up. It was the Poisoned Dwarf, the drive-by and then I saw her, lying in bed as her heart stopped beating. It must have been the bad dream that woke me up.

One thing's for sure – I'm wide awake now. But I'm struggling to work out what's real and what was the dream. I have this image in my head of the Poisoned Dwarf in bed, pale and grey and lifeless. No matter how hard I try, I can't shift it. It feels too real to be a dream, which sounds mad, I know. But it feels like it's something I've actually seen, something that's actually happened. I shiver.

I lie back down on my bed and pull the duvet over me. I close my eyes and move my legs and arms into the position I like them to be in to sleep. I try to go to sleep again.

I don't drift off though. I don't feel right. My head's buzzing, my heart's beating too fast. I can still see the Poisoned Dwarf every time I close my eyes and I can't get comfortable. I shift around my bed, trying to find a good position, trying to block the image from my mind, but it doesn't work.

I sit up, grab my pillow and try to puff it up. I lie down on my back, close my eyes and try again to sleep.

But when I close my eyes she's there – the Poisoned Dwarf, at death's door. Her eyes are open. She fixes me with a look that says, '*I know what you did*'.

I sit up again and look at the clock. It's after three now and I'm wide awake. There's no chance I'm going back to sleep at the moment. So I get out of bed, pull a T-shirt on and go downstairs. Everything's still and silent, illuminated in a kind of bluey grey colour by the moonlight coming through the back door and the kitchen windows. I go straight into the kitchen, open a cupboard and take out a glass. I open the fridge and take out the milk and pour myself a glass. It's supposed to make you sleepy, isn't it? At least, it works for babies.

I walk over to the back door and, as I sip the milk, I stare out at the garden. It looks unreal out there, bathed in the moonlight, everything completely still. I finish my milk and walk over to the sink, place the glass in there and put the tap on just long enough to fill the glass with water.

I walk back up the stairs to my bedroom. As soon as I open the door, I realise something isn't right. My room is seriously cold, like a freezer. I look over at the window. It's open again. The curtains are billowing wildly. I stand and stare for a second, my brow furrowed. I'm sure I shut the window. I locked it. For definite. How the hell did it come open again? I look around my room, kind of expecting to see Mikey lurking, smirking. But there's no one here except me.

I sigh, walk over to the window, close it and lock it. I take the key out of the lock and put it in the drawer of my bedside table. I climb back into bed and pull the covers back over me and try and get some sleep.

Summer

The first thing I hear is the telephone. I don't wake up properly to begin with, but it keeps on ringing. Just as I'm thinking that maybe I should get up and answer it, it stops and I can faintly hear Mum talking. I look at the clock. It's 6.38 a.m. I sigh, roll over and go back to sleep.

A little while later, I hear a gentle knock on my door and I look at the clock again. It's nearly seven o'clock. I think about closing my eyes and going back to sleep, pretending I didn't hear Mum knock. I'm tired. I didn't go to bed till after midnight because I was reading. But there's another gentle knock and Mum's voice.

'Summer, are you awake?'

I rub my eyes and sit up in bed. 'Yeah,' I say sleepily.

Mum comes into the room quietly. She perches on the end of my bed like she's nervous.

'Your grandad just phoned,' she says. And even before she says any more, I can tell from the tone of her voice and the look on her face that it's not good news. 'It's your nan.'

I look straight back at her. I get a sudden sinking feeling, even though I kind of knew she was gonna say that.

'She passed away in her sleep last night,' Mum says. She's not crying, but she looks sorrowful, like she's sorry for how I'm gonna feel about it.

I brush my hair back away from my face.

'Grandad tried to wake her this morning, but . . .' She trails off. She touches my face and gives me a sad, sympathetic smile. 'It would have been painless. She wouldn't have felt a thing.'

I don't know what to say.

'Is Grandad all right?' I ask.

Mum screws her face up, like she doesn't know what to think either. 'It's difficult to tell, Summer. I think he was still a bit shocked, to tell you the truth. He'd only just found her. I'm going to take the day off work today. I said I'd go over there and help him out.'

'Can I come too?'

116

'Of course, if you want to.'

'Yeah. I do.'

Mum touches my face again.

'Have you told Sky?'

Mum shakes her head. 'I'll give her a call later on.'

Johnny

I wake up late. My eyes struggle to focus on the digits on my clock as I open them. I feel rubbish. I haven't had enough sleep.

But that's not what's bothering me. It's the fact that I feel anxious, like something isn't right. I can't put my finger on it. Oh God, what am I on about? I must be tired.

Last night was weird, waking up in the middle of the night. It felt strange, as though someone was there, in my room. And so was the dream that I had before I woke up. The Poisoned Dwarf dying. Dead. It makes me feel ill with nerves. So I try and think about something else. I sit up in bed. I look over at the window.

It's closed, like I left it at three in the morning. I get up out of bed and go and take a look at it. I try the handle, but it's locked. I study the window frame and the sill. I haven't the faintest idea what I'm looking for, but I guess if someone had been messing with it, they might have left some sign. I know for sure that I shut the window before I went to bed and I also locked it before I went downstairs and got a drink. Somebody messed with it. Someone *must* have.

I can't see anything strange on the window though. It's just like it always is: a cheap white plastic frame. No odd marks on it. No sign of it being forced. I rub my face with my hands. Maybe I was wrong last night. Maybe I dreamed shutting the window. Maybe I even dreamed waking up and going downstairs. Who knows?

I go over to my bedside table and open the drawer. The window key's still in there. I take it out and walk over to the window. I unlock the window and open it, lean out a little and look on the outside. There's nothing strange there. I shut the window, lock it and put the key back in my bedside drawer. I go and have a shower to try and wash it all out of my system.

When I get downstairs, Mikey's already there, eating his breakfast like a wild animal – mouth wide open, gulping and gnawing and chomping. I see the free newspaper next to him on the table. I grab it to take through to the bin.

'Hey,' Mikey says. 'What are you doing?'

'What?' I say.

'The newspaper.'

'What about it?'

'I was reading that –'

I raise my eyebrow. 'Since when have you started reading the local paper?'

Mikey smiles. 'Since they started having cool stories about drive-by shootings on the cover.'

I shake my head. 'Idiot,' I say.

I drop the paper back on the table and then go through and make myself some breakfast. I bring my bowl through and sit at the table with Mikey, but I look out of the window as I eat so I don't have to look at or talk to him.

As I'm eating, I can tell Mikey's staring at me. Eventually, I decide to look back at him. I slowly and really deliberately switch my gaze from the window to Mikey, raising an eyebrow as I do it.

'What are you looking at?'

Mikey shrugs. He shakes his head. 'Dunno, it hasn't got a label,' he says through a mouthful of chewed chocolate flakes.

I stare at him. I roll my eyes. He continues staring at me and a strange look comes over his face, like he's trying to figure something out. It makes me feel paranoid.

'What?'

'You look rough,' he says.

'Thanks.'

I get an urge to give him a dead leg or something, but I resist; he'd just get me in trouble for it. So I look away from him and spoon cereal into my mouth.

There's no sound for a moment or two, apart from the sound of me eating and scraping my bowl. The whole time I'm eating, I can sense Mikey looking at me.

'What is it now?'

'You look tired,' Mikey says with a smirk. 'Did you sleep OK?'

'What's it to you whether I'm tired or not?'

He shrugs again. 'Just making an observation.' He picks up his bowl and the local paper and gets up from the table. 'Dunno why you're so twitchy about it though.'

Summer

I hate today. It's weird and horrible. The flat seems quiet and sad. I don't know what to say to Mum. I don't know what to do with myself. I tried watching TV for a bit. And then I tried to read. But it felt wrong. I feel like I shouldn't be doing anything that I like doing, that I enjoy doing. It feels disrespectful. I keep imagining what Nan would think if she looked down on me from heaven or wherever she is and saw me smile or laugh or something.

I always used to feel the same about Dad. Mum once told me he could see me from wherever he was. She was trying to be nice, I know she was. She said it once when I came home from school upset. It was just one of those things where someone talks about their dad and then looks at you and remembers that you don't have a dad and mumbles, 'Sorry. I didn't think.' Which always makes it much worse. I probably wouldn't even have noticed they were talking about dads till they pointed it out. And it upset me even though it was stupid. So Mum said her thing about Dad always being there, seeing me. And it made me feel better. It really did. It made me feel warm and special and normal. But the more I thought about it, the more I got freaked out. Because nobody wants their parents to know everything about them, to see everything they get up to, do they? How embarrassing would that be! There are some things which shouldn't be seen by anyone else, especially not your family.

So today I've been hanging around doing nothing, just stroking Petal and thinking. I haven't even cried. Which is strange because I am upset and I usually cry at the drop of a hat. I cry when I watch films or listen to music or read a book. I even cry when someone gives me good news. And even though I feel awful, and I feel sorry for Nan and for Grandad too, the tears haven't come. I can't explain it. Maybe I'm in shock.

'You should go and do something,' Mum says to me as she comes and sits next to me on the sofa.

I shake my head.

'You should,' Mum says. 'It'll make you feel better to be doing something rather than just moping around.'

I shake my head. 'I don't want to. Nan's dead. I don't want to do anything.'

Mum puts her arm round me. 'She wouldn't want to think of you just sitting around being unhappy, Summer. Would she now?'

I shake my head. Mum pulls me in towards her. And for the first time, tears form and start to fall.

Johnny

There was a list on the side in the kitchen this morning and with the list was a twenty-pound note. Whatever change is left from the twenty, Mum had written in the note, is for me. To be honest, I don't think the twenty will even cover all the stuff on the list. Why Mum can't go to the supermarket after work like any normal person, I don't know.

So here I am, on my afternoon off, in the supermarket again, scanning through the list, mentally checking everything off it. I realise I've forgotten potatoes, which are right back at the other end of the store, near the entrance. I think for a second that maybe I just won't go and get them. It would serve Mum right for treating me like a slave. But then I realise that it'll probably mean I won't get fed tonight.

I sigh, turn the trolley around and push it back along the central aisle towards the fruit and veg section, which is like trying to swim against the tide. For every five steps I take, I have to stop and make way for someone else. I lose count of the number of people that roll their eyes or tut at me for having the nerve to walk in the opposite direction to them.

As I'm standing in the fruit and veg aisles, searching for the potatoes, I catch sight of someone I recognise. Summer. My stomach does a somersault. I stare at her for a second. She's got a shopping basket in her right hand and she's inspecting a bag of carrots as though she's never seen anything like them before in her life.

I wonder what she's doing here. Maybe she has evil parents like mine who make her do all their chores while they're at work. If that's true then that's something else we have in common.

Just as I realise I've been staring at her for ages and I should be searching for potatoes, Summer glances up at me. Before I even think about what I'm doing, I look away, as though I've been caught doing something I shouldn't have. And when I look up again to see if she's still looking at me, she's vanished.

I hear a voice over my shoulder.

'Hello again, Johnny.'

I turn. It's her. My heart starts racing. My brain goes into overdrive, trying to think of something to say that isn't complete gibberish.

'Um. Hi,' I say. 'Summer.' Immediately I realise how stupid I sound. I wish I knew how to talk to girls. I haven't got a scooby what to say to her, but I know that I want to talk to her. I want her to talk to me. I want her to like me.

Summer looks at my trolley. 'You doing the family shop?' she says.

I feel myself blush. I suddenly become very aware of all the embarrassing things in the trolley, like cheap toilet roll and budget baked beans. 'Yeah. Something like that. My parents are slave-drivers.' I look at her basket. Her shopping is as dull as mine. 'How about you?' I say. 'Your parents slave-drivers as well?'

Summer smiles and then screws her face up. She nods. 'Pretty much, yeah. My mum made me go and shop for my grandad, which explains all the boring stuff in the basket.' She flourishes a hand towards the goods in her basket – mainly frozen meat pies and tinned vegetables – and screws her face up again.

I smile at her and try and think of something else to say.

'So, Johnny, what do you do when you're not running errands for your mum or riding buses?'

I shrug. 'Sleep?'

Summer laughs. 'Your life sounds about as rock and roll as mine.'

'Rock and Roll are my middle names,' I say.

She smiles. She looks down at the floor for a second and then bites her lip. It makes her look amazing.

'Well, Johnny,' she says, looking up at me, 'maybe we should meet up some time and be rock and roll together. What do you think?'

I'm silent. Shocked. Did she really just say that? 'Um. Yeah. Totally.'

She smiles.

And reality seems to distort. Before my very eyes, an amazing-looking, cool, interesting girl gives me her phone number and takes mine. This has never happened before. This is unprecedented. I have to pinch myself to make sure I'm not imagining it.

'You'll call me, right?' Summer says.

I nod my head.

Summer smiles. 'Brilliant.' And then she goes.

I stand and watch her for a second, still in shock. Then I take my stuff to the till and pay. God knows how I actually manage to do that though cos my head feels like someone's sucked my brain out and replaced it with candyfloss or something. I grin like an idiot all the way home.

Summer

I can't sleep. I've been in bed for ages. My brain won't switch off. I've been thinking about how weird it was at Nan and Grandad's house without Nan. I started imagining Grandad, sitting there in the evening on his own. I imagined him sitting there quietly, just the sound of all the clocks in the house ticking loudly for company, chiming every quarter of an hour.

And I wondered whether Nan has a spirit. I wondered whether she was just dead and gone and that was it, or whether she could see us from wherever she was now. I imagined her looking down at Grandad. I wondered what she'd be thinking as she watched him. Probably something like, '*It's about time you had a haircut, Harry*', knowing Nan.

And then I started thinking about Johnny. I can't believe that I was so brazen! I'm not usually like that. But I figured, life's too short to wonder what might have been. And it felt good. It felt right. I wondered whether it was fate that kept bringing us together or whether it was just coincidence. Maybe it was like some weird telepathy thing between us. Maybe we keep searching each other out, maybe we keep being in the same places as each other because we want to be.

I sat for ages and tried to work out whether I should text him. My heart told me to do it. I want to see him again soon. But my head told me not to. I should wait for him to get in touch with me. I was the one that took the initiative and suggested we swap numbers. It's his turn now. He promised he'd call. So it's his turn to show that he likes me by getting in touch.

But he hasn't been in touch. He hasn't texted, despite the fact that I've spent ages staring at my mobile, willing a message to come through. I even did what I said to myself I wouldn't do – I wrote a text message to him. But when I'd finished it, I couldn't send it. I'd look desperate – and that's not a good look for anyone. I saved it in my drafts folder instead. I'll wait for him. I'll give him till the weekend to phone me or text me. And if he hasn't by then, I'll do it. He does seem kind of shy after all.

I lean over and put my mobile down on my bedside table, switch the light off and, eventually, go to sleep.

Johnny

A jolt surges through my body. I see the Poisoned Dwarf in her car, slumped back in her seat. Unconscious? Dead? My heart thumps in my chest. I feel confused. I don't know where I am or what's going on. I feel panicked. I sit up and open my eyes. My heart pounds. I feel breathless.

Gradually, my heart slows a little and I realise I've been dreaming. I'm in bed, at home, freezing cold but drenched in sweat. My covers are off – half off the bed, in fact. I look over at the window. It's wide open. The curtains billow in the breeze. I look at the clock. 2.43 a.m. I sigh. Again. This is the second night in a row, same time both nights. How can that be?

I sit and stare for a while, trying to work out what's going on, how my window could possibly be open when I know for certain I shut and locked it before I went to bed.

I have a strange feeling, like I'm not alone. There's no sign of anyone else in the room with me, not that I can see. It *feels* like someone else is here though. Someone I can't see. I can't explain what it is. I just have the feeling. I know someone is here other than me. It makes me uncomfortable. I shiver. I feel vulnerable.

I open the drawer of my bedside table. The window key's still there in exactly the same position I put it earlier. I made sure I locked the window before I went to bed, I'm sure I did, though now I'm beginning to doubt myself. I don't like this one bit. This is freaking me out a little.

I take the key and go over to the window. I look at the frame, but I can't see anything strange. I look down at the moonlit garden. Everything seems completely still. I close the window and lock it again. I try the window, just to make sure it's properly locked. Just as I'm about to put the key back in the bedside drawer, I think again and change my mind. I'm gonna keep hold of the key, just in case. I close my fingers tightly around it.

I sit down on my bed feeling stupid, feeling like someone's watching me, laughing at me. Someone must be trying to wind me up, watching how I'm reacting. It must be Mikey. It's exactly the kind of lame thing he'd do to get a laugh.

I decide to investigate. I pull a T-shirt and some boxers on and open my bedroom door. Out on the landing I can hear snoring coming from Mum and Dad's room. I go straight past their door and put my hand on Mikey's door handle. I open the door silently and take a step forward into his room. It's dark. My eyes take a few seconds to adjust. The smell of Mikey's room assaults my nostrils – socks and body odour. He could do with opening *his* window more often.

I take another step inside and look at Mikey's bed. He's lying there asleep. I bend down next to him, check he's not just pretending. I hear him murmur something in his sleep, but I can't work out what he's saying. He seems fast asleep though. It can't have been him that was in my room – he's not that good an actor.

I back out of his room and shut the door behind me. I stand on the landing for a minute, collecting my thoughts. I feel strange. I almost wish Mikey had been sitting up in his bed, laughing at me. At least that way I'd know why my window was open. Because, if it wasn't him, then who was it? There has to be someone else in the house, hasn't there? The thought terrifies me. I look nervously at the dark corners around me, wondering if one of them is concealing someone, something.

I take a deep breath and think. Maybe I should wake Dad up, tell him someone's in the house. But I decide not to. What if there is no one? Dad will think I'm mad. No. I'll check the rest of the house myself. I go back to my room and grab my cricket bat for protection. The slightest movement and whoever it is, they're getting hit for six. No messing around.

I go into the bathroom first, cricket bat raised, ready to strike. I kick the door open with my foot, like they always do in films, and then wait for a second. I move quickly into the room, but it's empty except for me and the shadows cast by the moonlight streaming in through the window.

So I head downstairs, taking the steps slowly, my ears and eyes on stalks. I reach the last step and turn. And I stop still for a second, listen out for any noise. Absolute silence. I start creeping forward again, through to the kitchen. The door's already open. I check behind the door, in the boiler cupboard, by the back door. No one's there. I move back out of the kitchen. I put my hand on the dining-room door handle. I push the door open and stay where I am, just in case there's anyone in there. I want them to show themselves before I do. Nothing happens. Next I step into the dining room. I check behind the door, under the dining table. Again there's no sign of anyone.

There's only one room left. The front room. If anyone is in the house, they must be in there. My heart thumps even harder in my chest, so loud that I'm sure if there *is* anyone else down here, they'll hear it. I close the dining-room door as quietly as I can and creep a couple of steps along the hallway. I stretch my arms before I get to the door, make sure I'm ready to strike if I need to. I let the door swing open and then step inside. My eyes quickly scan the room and it's clear that no one else is here.

I lower the cricket bat and slouch into a chair. I close my eyes and think. What is going on? Am I losing it? I could swear someone else was in the house, that someone was watching me, that someone had opened my window. But my mind must be playing tricks on me cos there sure as hell isn't anyone awake here apart from me.

'Who are you?' I say aloud to the room, to the house, to whoever opened my bedroom window. 'What are you? Where are you?'

There's no answer. I realise how ridiculous I must sound, how useless I must look. And I feel embarrassed. I'm being totally paranoid. After a few minutes, I get up from the chair and head back upstairs. As I get to the top of the stairs, I hear footsteps. I freeze. I get ready with the cricket bat. And then I see him. Walking out of the toilet. Dad. He looks blearily up at me.

'Johnny? What on earth are you doing?'

I must look utterly stupid to him. I lower the cricket bat. 'I thought I heard someone downstairs.'

'Really? Was there anyone there?'

I shake my head.

'Are you OK?'

I nod. For a second I consider telling him, but I know that I won't. I sigh. 'Yeah, I'm all right.'

'Good,' Dad says. 'Go and get some sleep, Johnny. Next time tell me if you hear anything. I don't want you being a hero.'

I go back to my room.

Summer

I see Sky struggling with her bag and her ticket at the barriers before she sees me. When she walks out on to the station concourse I run over towards her.

'Sky! Over here!'

She stops where she is, drops her bags down and opens her arms wide. I throw my arms open and hug her.

'Wow, Summer,' she says. 'You pleased to see me or something?'

I smile. 'You could say that.' I grab one of her bags. 'Shall we go home, then?'

Sky scrunches her nose up. 'No,' she says. 'Let's go and get something to eat first. My treat.'

Sky leads us out of the station and along the high street. We walk along the street till Sky finds a café she likes the look of. She opens the door and holds it for me.

It's a trendy place – loads of recycled furniture and that kind of stuff. There are important-looking people tapping away at their laptops at most of the tables. We go over to the counter and order and then head upstairs, where it's much quieter. On the table there are plastic flowers made from cut-up bottles and drinking straws standing in old milk bottles. I look at Sky and smile.

'I like this place. It's cool.'

Sky smiles. 'Yeah. It'll do, won't it?'

I smile and look around the café. And I realise that it feels strange being with Sky, like she's a different person from the one that used to live with us. I've hardly seen her for ages and it feels like she's grown up loads. She's an adult now, not a kid.

'So what's been going on with you, then, Summer?' she says.

I shrug. 'Not much,' I say. 'Everything's been a bit rubbish really. Mum's been working all summer. Jodie moved up to Manchester with her family. Lauren's been away in France for the entire summer. And I've been sitting at home.'

Sky makes a face, like, that sucks.

'Oh, and then Nan had a heart attack and died, as you know.'

'Hmmm,' Sky says. 'That's rough, sis.'

'Tell me about it.'

A waitress brings us our drinks. Sky's is some frothy iced coffee thing. My lemonade comes in a foreign-looking can with a neon pink straw sticking out of the top. It looks way more glamorous than a can of lemonade has any right to look.

'So what have you been doing?' Sky says, stirring the froth on top of her coffee.

I shrug. 'Nothing much really. Hanging around the flat mainly. Reading. Helping Grandad.'

Sky takes a sip of her drink. 'Sounds like you need some fun.'

'If only,' I say. 'There's the funeral this week.'

Sky sips from her coffee again.

'So what about you?' I say. 'How's Edinburgh?'

Sky shrugs. 'OK. I've been working most of the time.'

'Are you still seeing Dougie?'

Sky looks down at her coffee and gives it a stir. And for a second she doesn't look quite so grown up. She looks more like the Sky that lived at home. 'Kind of,' she says. 'It's a bit complicated at the moment.'

She looks up at me and smiles, but it's a forced smile. I want to ask her how it's complicated, but I can't read in her face whether she'd be happy if I asked or not. So I don't. I slurp some of my drink and look around the café instead, people watching. I try to imagine who everyone is, why they're here, what they're talking about.

The waitress arrives and puts our food on the table. My sandwich hardly looks like a sandwich at all, more like a work of art. I pick it up awkwardly and take a bite. Sky and I are quiet for a little while as we eat. But then Sky puts her sandwich down and wipes her hands on her napkin. She looks at me.

'So is there anything going on in your love life, Summer?'

I smile. 'Not sure,' I say. 'Maybe . . .'

Sky's face lights up. 'Ooh, intriguing,' she says. 'Tell me more.'

'I met this boy on the bus the other day.'

Sky raises her eyebrows. 'On the bus?'

I nod. 'Yeah. I was forced to sit next to him on the bus. But then we got talking and it just felt like something clicked.'

'Wow. Exciting.'

I nod. 'I bumped into him again in the supermarket the other day –'

'The supermarket? Summer, you seriously have to hang out in some more exciting places.'

I give her a sarcastic smile. 'You would have been proud of me, Sky. I went straight over to him and within thirty seconds we'd swapped phone numbers!'

'Summer Hornby!' Sky says in fake admonishment. 'You are a brazen hussy!'

I look down at my food and smile. 'I know. Thank you.'

Sky takes a sip of her drink. 'So? Has he been in touch?'

I shake my head. 'Not yet. It was only the other day.'

Sky nods. She takes a bite of her sandwich.

'Do you think I should text him?'

She thinks for a second and then shakes her head. 'No. He'll call. Just wait.'

Johnny

I feel rubbish. Again. I haven't had enough sleep. But more than that, I feel strange about what happened last night. In the cold light of day it seems stupid, like it can't possibly have happened, like it was all a trick of the mind. There was nothing spooky about my room when I woke up this morning. It was just my room, plain and simple. How stupid was I for being spooked out last night?

Dad must think I've lost it, wandering around the house with a cricket bat in my hands. He was already at work by the time I got downstairs for breakfast, so at least there was no need to face him this morning.

Right now it's nearly lunchtime and Jake and I are on the football field, collecting up bibs and cones in silence. As we're carrying everything back towards Terry's car, he comes staggering over towards us.

'All right, lads?'

Jake and I nod.

'No coaching Wednesday, boys, don't forget,' he says. He looks vacantly into space for a second, like he's thinking about something else.

I nod again. Jake and me take the footballs and bibs and cones and put them in the boot of Terry's car.

'You got any plans for your day off?' Terry asks us.

Jake looks at me and smiles. He looks back at Terry. 'Fast rides and loose women.'

Terry laughs. 'Be careful you don't get 'em muddled. Fast women and loose rides are a recipe for disaster, believe me,' he says and then he wheezes out a laugh at his own joke.

He gets in his car and starts the engine. He winds down his window and lights a cigarette. In another second, he's started his car with a squeal and a cough and then turned and driven off.

Me and Jake amble out on to the road and start walking home. And as I walk, I try and work out whether or not to ask the question that's been floating around my brain all morning, or whether Jake will just think I'm a weirdo.

'Do you believe in ghosts?'

Jake turns and looks at me like I'm a weirdo. I knew he would. He breaks into a smile and shakes his head. 'No way.'

'What? Not at all?'

He shakes his head. He kicks at a squashed cola can on the road and sends it skidding to the grass at the kerb. 'It's all mumbo-jumbo,' he says. 'Don't you think?'

I shrug. 'I s'pose,' I say. Then I think again. 'Don't you ever get the feeling there's more out there than just humans though? That there are other forces? Spirits and stuff like that . . .'

Jake shakes his head again. He's caught up with the can now. He goes over to the side of the road and kicks the can. 'Sorry,' he says. 'I don't buy it. It's all just stories made up to scare people. Haven't you ever seen *Scooby-Doo*?'

I give him a look. 'What are you on about?'

'*Scooby-Doo*. They always think there's a ghost. Only when they catch up with them at the end, they rip the mask off and find out it was the mild-mannered janitor all along.'

I shake my head. 'You idiot,' I say. 'So do you base all your opinions on what you see in cartoons?'

Jake laughs. 'Most of them, yeah,' he says. 'Seriously though, there's no evidence, is there? Show me the evidence that there's such a thing as ghosts and then I'll start believing in them.'

'There is evidence though,' I say. 'People have seen ghosts before. And there are loads of ghost stories. Why would there be so many stories if they didn't exist?'

Jake gives me a raised eyebrow. 'There are loads of stories about dragons, but it doesn't mean they exist in real life.'

I sigh. 'Yeah, but people don't go round saying they've seen dragons, do they? They do about ghosts. There must be some truth in them.'

Jake shakes his head. 'All right then, who do you know that's seen a ghost?'

I feel my cheeks start to redden. I could say that I think I have. But I get the feeling I'd never live it down. So I try and think of someone I know that says they've seen a ghost. Only I can't think of anyone.

'No one I know,' I say. 'But –'

'Exactly my point,' Jake says. 'There's no proof that they exist. There are no photos, no film evidence.'

'Yeah, well, that's cos ghosts can't be caught on camera,' I say. 'They don't have a physical form – they're spirits.'

Jake looks across at me. He looks like he thinks I've gone mad. He stops walking. 'J, man. What's with all this ghost stuff? What's got into you?'

I stop walking too. I look at Jake and shrug. I wish I hadn't said anything. He'd think I'd lost the plot if I told him what's happened, or at least what I think has happened. He'd take the mickey mercilessly. So I say nothing about it and start walking again, trying to appear as normal and innocent as I can.

'You must believe there's some kind of afterlife though, Jake . . .'

'Nope,' he says.

'What happens to our souls, then, after we die?'

We've reached the junction that leads to my road in one direction and up towards Jake's in the other.

'Nothing,' he says. 'You die and then you're gone. That's it.'

I sigh. 'That's a bit depressing, isn't it?'

Jake smiles and shakes his head. 'Not unless you want it to be. It's just life,' he says. He starts walking off towards his house, then turns back and says, 'Think about it this way, right. If everyone that had ever lived – all the cavemen and everyone from history – if all their spirits were floating around the world, you wouldn't be able to move for ghosts. And seeing as no one I've ever met or anyone you've ever met has seen one, that leads me to think that ghosts don't exist. It's all make-believe.'

I don't really know how to answer that, so I don't. We say goodbye and then walk home.

Summer

There's a gentle knock on my door and then it opens. Sky comes in, dressed in the baggy old T-shirt she sleeps in and a pair of socks.

'Morning, Summer. I made you a cup of tea.'

I sit up in bed. Petal jumps down off the end of my bed. I look at the clock. It's already after eleven. I didn't turn out my light till late last night – Sky and me sat up chatting for ages.

'Thanks,' I say, taking the mug from her. I cradle it in my hands and take a sip.

Sky sits down on the end of my bed where Petal has just got up from. 'You sleep OK?'

I nod. I sip my tea.

Sky smiles. 'So, then, little sis. What are we gonna do today?'

I shrug. 'Dunno.'

Sky rolls her eyes. 'We can do whatever you want, Summer,' she says. 'Theme park? Shopping? We could spend the day pampering ourselves.'

'What, just you and me?'

Sky smiles. 'Yep.'

'Where's Mum?'

Sky shrugs. 'Dunno. Out,' she says. 'So what do you fancy doing?'

I sit and think for a second. 'The boating lake in the park.'

Sky smiles and nods, but raises an eyebrow as well. 'OK,' she says. 'If you want . . .' She pauses. I can tell from the look on her face that she thinks it's a lame idea. 'Are you sure I can't tempt you with a day of indulgence and luxury instead?'

I shake my head. 'No. D'you remember when we used to go out on the boats with Nan and Grandad when we were little? That's what I really want to do.'

'Can you remember Dad?' I ask as we drift around on the middle of the boating lake.

Sky sits up in her seat a bit. She looks at me for a split second and then gazes out across the lake. She takes ages before she answers. 'Yeah,' she says. 'Kind of.'

'Can you remember what he was like?'

Sky smiles a bit. 'Think so.' But then she shrugs.

'What was he like?'

Sky picks up one of the oars and idly moves it through the water, barely moving the boat at all. 'Dad was great,' she says. 'He was lovely. He . . .' She falls quiet. She smiles faintly, but she doesn't say anything more.

I will her to keep speaking. I want to know exactly what he was like. I want her to tell me everything for a change. But I get the feeling she's not going to. So I ask her again.

'What was he actually like though, Sky? What kind of things did he do?'

'You know,' she says, 'dad kind of things.'

I feel like saying that I don't really know what *dad kind of things* are. I've never had a dad to do *dad things* with. I want to say that it isn't fair, that she should share it all with me so I know.

'Like what?'

'I don't know, Summer. I can remember sitting on his knee while he read me stories. And he always played stupid games with me. You know, like bouncing me up and down on his knee.'

'What kind of things did he used to say?'

Sky stares into space, the oar resting across her lap. Then she looks back at me and smiles. 'What is this, Summer?' she says. 'Twenty questions? Haven't we been through all this before?'

I shrug. I look across the water. 'I just want to know everything about him, that's all. He was my dad as well.'

Sky nods. 'OK. Sorry.' She looks out at the water again and thinks. 'I remember he always used to look at my eyes and say that they were as blue as the sky. I always used to think it was a stupid thing to say just because of my name. It always made me laugh. He used to call me his "little piggy princess". He used to say loads of stupid little things like that. But, you know, I was only four when he died so it's all a bit hazy. I bet you can't remember much from when you were younger than four.'

I think about it. She's right. I can't remember things from when I was that young, or at least not clearly. 'Doesn't it make you sad though?'

'What?'

'That you can't remember the things he used to say.'

Sky thinks for a second and then nods. 'Yeah, it does. But I guess there's nothing I can do about it, is there?'

'At least you've got some memories, Sky,' I say. 'I've got nothing. All I have is a box of his things and other people's memories.'

Sky looks at me, a sympathetic smile on her face. And I have to look away. I look down at the bottom of the boat. I feel Sky move over towards me and put her arms around me. We sit like that in the boat for what feels like ages, till Sky sniffs and sits up straight. I look at her. She forces a smile.

'Right,' she says, making herself sound jolly. 'We're meant to be enjoying ourselves here. Let's have some fun.'

Johnny

I keep looking at my phone, opening up my messages and thinking about writing one to Summer. But I'm a total coward – I keep chickening out. I can't work out what to write. And besides I don't want to look desperate. For all I know, she just wants to meet up as friends.

One thing is for certain though – I won't find out unless one of us does something. So I bite the bullet. I've waited long enough. What's the worst that can happen?

Hi, Summer. Good 2 c u the other day. Still want to meet up? Johnny.

I don't send it right away. I sit and stare at the message thinking about how lame it sounds. But I can't think of anything better to write so I put my thumb on the button and send it. I feel nervous for a second. I wonder if she'll roll her eyes when she sees she has a text from me. But then I remember that it was her who came up to me in the supermarket. She must like me.

I stay on my bed, staring at my phone for a minute or so longer, waiting for my phone to glow and the message tone to tell me that Summer's replied. Nothing happens. And I realise that I'm wasting my weekend staring at my phone. So I go downstairs.

Mikey is lying on the sofa in the lounge like the lazy numbskull he is. For a change he's not staring at some rubbish on TV though – he's doing something on his mobile.

I sit down on a chair.

Mikey's mobile does a *bing* as he gets a message. He reads it and laughs.

'Who sends *you* messages?' I say.

'None of your business, ginger nuts,' Mikey says as his thumb goes into overdrive sending a message back.

'I bet you're sending them to yourself, aren't you?' I say. 'To make yourself look popular.'

Mikey stops texting for a second to give me the middle finger. 'No, Johnny. That's what *you* do.'

I sigh. I think about taking the mickey out of Mikey some more. But I'm hungry, and as Mum and Dad are out in the garden, I sense a chance to go and sneak a bag of crisps. I get up from my chair and go through to the kitchen and look out through the back window at the garden, at Dad mowing the lawn and Mum sitting on the patio with the newspaper and a cup of coffee. I open the kitchen cupboard and rummage around for some salt and vinegar crisps. As I do, I hear my mobile's message tone come from the lounge. I grab a pack of crisps and go back through.

When I get into the lounge, I see Mikey throw something towards the chair that I was sitting in before. I look down at the chair and see my phone.

'What have you done?' I say. 'Have you been reading my messages?'

'No!'

'You had my phone,' I say.

Mikey shakes his head and makes an innocent face. He can't help but smirk though.

I pick my phone up from the chair and look at it.

'What kind of a name is Summer anyway?' Mikey says.

I open up the message just as he says it. Sure enough it's from Summer.

Definitely. I thought you'd never ask. When is gd 4 u? Tuesday? x

I look up at Mikey, who's grinning back at me.

'You read my message?'

He shrugs his shoulders. 'Might have,' he says. 'Can't remember. I'm not sure if it was meant for you though cos it's from a girl and I thought you were gay.'

I roll my eyes. 'You're so immature.' I move over towards him and give him a punch on the arm.

Mikey rubs his arm but then smiles. 'I know. Good, isn't it?' He gives me the middle finger and then starts texting again. 'So is Summer your girlfriend, then, Johnny?'

'What is it to you?' I say.

'No reason,' Mikey says. 'It's just I think I might have sent a text back to her by mistake.'

'You what?' I say. I immediately go to the sent messages folder on my phone.

Sorry. Changed my mind. I'm gay. Xxx

I feel my cheeks start to flush. I see red. I can't believe Mikey did that. I want to smack him in the face. But before I do that, I have to text Summer back.

Sorry — my immature little brother sent that text. He's an idiot. Cld we meet Fri? J

I press send and then look up at Mikey. He laughs again. I lunge towards him just at the moment that his phone *bings* and a message comes through. I wrap my arm around his neck and then reach down to try and grab his phone from his hand. He tightens his grip on it, but my hands are bigger than his and after a few seconds I have his phone. I keep my arm around his neck and open the message. It's from his friend Asif. I don't bother to read it, but press reply instead.

There's something I've been meaning to tell u. I'm gay 4 u. I love u. Xxxxxx

I press send and then throw Mikey's mobile across the room. The back of the phone comes off and the battery spills out. As Mikey scrabbles around after it, I go upstairs with my phone and my crisps.

Summer

There's an odd atmosphere in Nan and Grandad's house today. Everyone's been rushing around most of the morning, getting food ready, making sure the house is clean and there are enough chairs and all that stuff. But it's also been really quiet and there hasn't been a cross word exchanged, even though I can tell from people's faces that on any other day there would have been.

Now we're all sitting stiffly in the front room. Everyone except Sky, who's still in the kitchen. Everyone looks smart in black. And whenever anyone catches anyone else's eye, they force a half-smile and don't say anything much. The house is full of the smell of all the flowers people have sent. They're mainly from Nan's relatives in Canada and Australia who couldn't make the funeral, but also from some of her neighbours.

As Sky is busy in the kitchen and Mum and Grandad talk quietly about who's coming to the funeral and who'll be travelling in which car, I think about whether Nan's spirit is watching us. I wonder what she'd make of us all, nervous, not really acting like ourselves, waiting to give her a good send-off. If she was here, she'd probably be telling Grandad that his shoes aren't clean enough or his hair needs cutting, or fussing about whether there are enough sandwiches.

Sky comes through from the kitchen with a tray and puts it down on the coffee table.

'Oh, Sky,' Mum says. 'You've used the good cups and saucers.'

Sky looks at Mum. 'Yeah. Why?'

Mum tuts. 'You should have used the ordinary mugs, Sky. These are for the wake. Now we'll have to wash them.'

Sky sighs and shakes her head. 'Yes, Mother,' she says. 'So I'll wash them. It's not a big deal.'

Sky pours the tea and hands the cups around to everyone. It feels surreal, sitting in Nan and Grandad's front room, feeling so on edge, drinking from the best china that never gets used. It feels horrible. I can't wait for it to be over and done with. I can't wait for things to be back to normal.

Johnny

As I step on to Exminster Avenue I see a hearse waiting in the road. My heart skips a beat. I stop still. Beside me I sense Mikey looking at me impatiently, wondering why on earth I've stopped. But I don't move. I can't say for sure, but from where I'm standing it looks like it's waiting outside the Poisoned Dwarf's house. I could be wrong, but I have a horrible, gnawing feeling in my guts.

'What are you doing?' Mikey says.

I don't answer. Instead I shrug and hurry along the road, sneaking looks at the hearse, trying not to make it obvious to Mikey that I'm freaked out, that I'm scared. As we get closer, I see that the hearse *is* sitting outside number fifteen. An undertaker stands by it, looking solemn, hands behind his back. There's another undertaker in the driver's seat. The porch and front door of the Poisoned Dwarf's house are both open. Inside the house I can see people in black moving around.

No.

Please.

No.

Oh my God.

This can't be happening.

But this *is* happening.

It must be the Poisoned Dwarf. She must have died. That must be her, right there in the back of the hearse, inside her coffin. I stare at it. There are flowers propped up against the side of the casket, spelling out the name Jean in capital letters. It is her. Jean Hornby.

And I know exactly why she's dead.

Because of us. Me, Jake, Drac and Badger.

A moment of madness.

And now this . . .

My heart is racing. Mikey must have noticed the way I'm reacting and will be wondering why I'm so freaked out about seeing a hearse. So I keep moving, trying not to draw attention to myself, trying not to look at the hearse or the house.

I keep my head down and reach the end of the road

and the turning on to our road. I look back quickly. I see the Poisoned Dwarf's husband come out of the house. He's wearing a black suit. He brushes his comb-over with his hand and then goes to speak to one of the undertakers.

I turn away and keep walking home.

'Are you all right?' Mikey says. But he doesn't say it like he's concerned for me – it's more like he's mocking me. 'You're acting even more strangely than normal.'

I give him a look – raised eyebrows, confused expression – as if I have no idea what he's on about. Then I try and get home as quick as I can.

Summer

What is there to say about a funeral? I don't think there are words to describe it. Nan's funeral was nice – for a funeral – but nice isn't exactly what I mean. There were loads of people there – more than I thought there'd be. There were relatives I haven't seen for years, like Great-aunt June. Lots of Nan and Grandad's neighbours were there too. I've known some of them since I was tiny. There were also loads of people I don't know, but Grandad knew them all and in a weird sort of way he seemed to enjoy seeing everyone. The main thing is, I think Nan would have been happy with the turnout, to see that she meant something to so many people. And *that* makes the funeral nice.

Almost everyone that was at the funeral has come back to Nan and Grandad's house for the wake. Right now, they're all standing around, wearing black, drinking tea, nibbling at sandwiches, making small talk. As for me, I'm trying my hardest to stay out of the way. I don't want to eat sandwiches or drink tea and, most of all, I don't want to make small talk. So as soon as we got here, I volunteered to help Sky and Mum sort out all the food and the drinks so I could hide myself away. And now that everyone has their tea and sandwiches, I'm tidying up in the kitchen, as slowly and as carefully as I can, waiting for people to finish and go home. Maybe when they do, things can start to get back to normal.

Johnny

I wake up, soaked with sweat again, my heart racing. I look at the clock. 2.43 a.m. Again. What is it with that time of night? I rub my face. I look around the room, on edge. I *know* there's someone else here. I can feel it. I look in the corners of my room, peer among the shadows. Everything is absolutely still though. If there is anyone else here, I can't see them.

I look over at the window. It's closed. My bedroom door is closed as well. In fact, everything is as it was when I went to bed. I rub my hands over my face again. I still have a nagging feeling, like I'm not alone. This has happened at exactly the same time for a week now. Something is happening. It can't be coincidence.

'I know you're there,' I say quietly. My voice is croaky.

I look around the room, expecting to see something, for something to happen. But nothing does. Everything is still and silent apart from the sound of some cars out on the main road.

'Who are you?'

There's a rustling sound. My heart starts pounding even more. I turn and look at my desk just in time to see a pen roll off and fall to the floor. I stare at it for a second. The room is silent and still again. I try to think of a rational explanation for what just happened. The pen could have just slipped off the desk. It might have been resting on something and then overbalanced. Nobody moved it, that's for sure. If they had done, I'd have seen them. I'd be able to see them now.

I switch on my bedside light. I get out of my bed, go over to the pen and pick it up. I hold it up with sweaty hands. It's just a pen.

I put the pen back on the desk and go back to bed. The sheets feel cold and damp. I sigh, sit up in bed and put my head in my hands. I must have been asleep for only an hour or so. I went to bed early enough, but I couldn't sleep. Whenever I closed my eyes and put my head on the pillow I started thinking about the hearse that I saw outside the Poisoned Dwarf's house and that led me to thinking about the drive-by soaking and the newspaper article.

However I look at it, the four of us are to blame. If we hadn't decided to get our own back, if we hadn't shot at her with water pistols, she would still be alive right now, scowling at the world from her porch. Which makes us murderers. If your actions cause someone else to die, that's murder, right? Or manslaughter.

I take my phone off the bedside table. I stare into space, turning my phone round and round in my hands, thinking. I kept this to myself. When I got home yesterday after seeing the funeral procession, I tried to pretend that it had never happened. Not that it worked because I couldn't stop thinking about it. But I didn't let the others know what I saw. I thought about it. I picked up my phone plenty of times and started writing a text to them, but something stopped me each time. I felt like I should tell them in person and yesterday afternoon I didn't feel like seeing anyone.

I look around the room again. I look at the pen sitting on my desk. It must have just fallen off on its own. There's no other logical explanation. No one is in the room with me. It's only my mind playing tricks. I sigh. I put my phone back on my bedside table and switch the light off. I lie down, close my eyes and try to get comfortable. I need sleep.

My phone alarm goes off. I open my eyes. I roll over, pick my phone up off the bedside table and switch the alarm off. I feel tired.

Today is a day off. Chessington day. I've been looking forward to it for ages, but now I don't feel like it. All I can think of at this moment is going back to sleep and blocking out the world. I consider sending Jake a text saying I'm sick and I'm just about to start writing it when I get a message. It's from Jake.

Meet me @ mine @ 10.

I put my phone back on the table and lie on my bed, staring at the ceiling. I make a decision. I'm gonna tell them what I saw yesterday. They have to know.

I have to walk past the Poisoned Dwarf's house on my way to knock for Jake. There's no other way to get there. Passing the house fills me with a mix of different emotions, all horrible, but mainly of guilt and fear. I keep my head down as I walk past. I don't want to look at the house. Though I don't know what I expect to see if I do look at it – the Poisoned Dwarf's ghost glaring at me; a poster of us four with the word *MURDERERS* emblazoned on it; or maybe just her husband, a broken old man. When the temptation to look becomes too great and I raise my eyes towards 15 Exminster Avenue, all I see is a house, like all the other houses on the street. The car is parked in the space out at the front of the house. The blinds in the house are all drawn. The front door and the porch are shut. I look away and reach the end of Exminster Avenue as quickly as I can.

I hear the latch on Jake's front door.

'Morning!' Jake says, cheery as anything. He looks like he's dressed up for a date. The smells of Jake's shower gel and aftershave fill the air. As he looks at me, his brow furrows. 'You OK?'

I nod. 'Yeah.'

'You look like death warmed up, J,' he says. 'You look knackered. You stay up all night playing with yourself or something?' He laughs.

I force a smile. 'Something like that, yeah.'

A little later, with Drac and Badger in tow as well, we get the train to Chessington. Most of the passengers on the train are going there for a day out. The whole carriage is filled with a kind of buoyant feeling. Everyone's looking forward to all the rides. Except me. I don't feel cheery. I don't feel excited. In fact, I feel like rubbish. I feel tired, guilty, confused and muddy-headed. I'd rather not be here. I'm not quite sure where I *would* like to be right now.

As soon as the train starts moving, the joking around starts. Jake kicks off by making fun of Badger for the white streak that he has in his otherwise dark bush of hair – the reason he's always had the nickname Badger. And then the same jokes and mickey-taking that we always go through. It's almost like a script now, we've been through the jokes so many times. But today I don't smile and I don't join in with my parts. I look out of the window as the train flashes through New Malden station and I think about when I tell them what I saw yesterday. I promised myself I'd do it. Is this the right time? It's gonna spoil their day, just like it's spoiling mine. But they have to know. Someone's dead for God's sake. We don't deserve to be having fun.

My lips stay sealed though. I don't say a word on the train journey or on the walk to the theme park. In the queue, as Drac and Jake are looking around, checking out girls in the line and making jokes, Badger turns to me.

'You feeling all right, J?'

'Yeah. Fine,' I lie. 'Why?'

Badger shrugs. 'No reason. You seem quiet, that's all.'

I think that maybe I should tell him – for his good and mine. A problem shared and all that. But I say nothing. I can't tell him here, not in this queue, not with all these people around.

The queue starts moving forward more quickly and in no time we're through the gates. Jake and Drac, who are leading the way, stop by the site map.

'Don't know about you, but I wanna go on Dracula's Revenge first,' Jake says.

A group of girls strut past us. Drac watches them like a big cat sizing up his prey. One of the girls looks back over her shoulder at him. Drac smiles at her and then looks at the rest of us.

'I think we should go wherever they're going,' he says.

'What do you reckon, Badger? J?' Jake says.

I shrug my shoulders. 'I don't mind. Whatever you want to do.'

Badger smiles. 'I wanna hang upside down like a vampire,' he says, slapping Drac and Jake on the back. 'There'll be plenty more girls in the park.'

Summer

We're walking along the pavement towards the high street. Sky has her backpack on even though I offered to carry it for her.

'Do you have to go back?' I say. 'It's nice when you're home.'

Sky puts her arm on my shoulder. 'I'd love to stay,' she says, 'but I have to work.'

I sigh. I'm gonna be bored without her. I'll be on my own again.

'You know you're always welcome to come and stay with me in Edinburgh,' Sky says.

'I asked Mum already,' I say. 'She won't let me.'

Sky shrugs. 'Just keep pestering her. She'll give in eventually.'

'Thanks for the advice,' I say. 'I'll start nagging her later.'

'Anyway,' Sky says, 'you've got a hot date coming up. I bet you'll forget that I even exist by tomorrow evening.'

I smile. I think of Johnny. I wonder what he's doing right now and I get a little nervous feeling inside.

We walk on in silence for a while, out on to the high street and left towards the station. It's busy on the high street, like always. There are people clustering around the grocers' shops. Cars are queuing on the road. Sky's phone starts ringing. She takes it out of her handbag and looks at it. She makes a face at me, like she's sorry.

'Do you mind if I take this?' she says.

I shake my head. And then for the next minute or so I listen as she argues with her boyfriend over the phone. Every now and then she stops and gestures with her hands or rolls her eyes. We get to the tube station and stand outside and I feel like a gooseberry even though it's only her and me here. She stands there, continuing some argument that I can't quite understand just from hearing one side of it.

'Look, I'll see you later,' she says eventually, sounding cross and kind of like she's softening at the same time. 'Bye. Love you.' And then she puts her phone away and makes an angry sort of growling sound.

'Are you OK?'

She looks up at me and rolls her eyes. 'I would be if he'd trust me a bit more!'

'Oh.'

'Sorry. You didn't need to hear all that.'

'It's OK.'

'I love you, Summer,' she says, putting her arms around me.

'I love you too,' I say, but the words get smothered by Sky's shoulder as I say them.

Sky stands back and looks at me. 'Don't forget to nag Mum to let you come and stay with me.'

'Believe me, it'll be the first thing I say when I see her tonight!'

'And good luck with the big date tomorrow,' she says.

'It's not a big date,' I say, laughing. 'We're just meeting up. He's a friend.' But inside I hope that it does turn out to be more of a date.

Sky gives me a kiss on the top of my head and then she goes into the tube station.

I stand there for a while. I get my earphones out of my bag and put them in. I put some gum in my mouth and then I look at the time.

Johnny

Jake rubs his belly. 'I'm starving. Let's go get a burger or something.'

Everyone agrees so we follow Jake in the direction of the burger bar. As we pass underneath Dracula's Revenge, I hear the rumbling of a rollercoaster car racing along the tracks towards us. I look up as it passes right overhead. The passengers scream as they twist upside down and then the right way round again, their legs flailing as the ride spins them through the air.

Drac turns to us with a grin on his face. 'Do you reckon you could grab someone's leg as they went past on Dracula's Revenge?'

Badger shakes his head. 'Not a chance. It's way too high.'

Drac stops walking. He looks up at the tracks above our heads. 'I reckon you could. Watch . . .' To try and prove his point, he jumps up and swipes an arm out towards the rails. He misses by about two metres.

'You're miles off,' Jake says, laughing. 'Idiot.'

Drac smiles. 'That's cos no one's going past at the moment. Imagine if someone was hanging down from the ride – I'd reach them, definitely.'

Jake shakes his head. 'And what would you want to do that for anyway?'

Drac shrugs and then carries on walking. 'Dunno. I was just wondering, that's all.'

We walk on, everyone but me laughing at Drac. A few minutes later we're all sitting on a wall outside the burger bar stuffing our faces in silence. The burger and chips, washed down with some cola, makes the weird nervous feeling in my stomach go away for a while. As soon as I start thinking about it though, the feeling returns. And I decide that I have to say something soon. The longer I go on not telling them, the harder it's gonna be to tell them. And they're gonna wonder why I didn't tell them straight away. I don't know how to start, so I just open my mouth before I can chicken out again.

'I saw a funeral car yesterday,' I say.

The others don't bat an eyelid. They just chew on their burgers.

'On Exminster Avenue,' I say.

Drac and Badger still look blank. But I see the expression on Jake's face turn from blankness to a furrowed brow as he realises what that could mean. He looks at me for a second and then looks away almost immediately, down at his drink. He takes the lid off and starts stirring it with his straw.

'Why are you telling us this exactly?' Drac says.

'It was outside the Poisoned Dwarf's house,' I say.

Badger and Drac both stare at me, confused.

'The old lady we soaked in her car,' Jake says without looking up from his drink. 'The witch that slashed your football, Drac.'

Drac and Badger stare in disbelief, first at Jake, then, when he doesn't look up, at me.

'Jesus,' Badger says. 'Are you serious? Please say you're winding me up.'

'No. It's true.'

'You don't know it was for her though,' Drac says. 'Loads of old people live on those roads near you. It could have been for anyone.'

'The front door of her house was open,' I say. 'There were loads of people inside, wearing black. There were flowers around the coffin that spelled out her name, Jean. It was her, Drac. No question.'

No one says anything. Badger looks down at his shoes. Drac closes his eyes for a second and breathes in and out really slowly. Jake keeps staring at his drink.

I can't take back what I've said.

'What did she die of?' Badger says quietly. He doesn't look up as he speaks.

'Dunno, I only saw the coffin.'

'Do you think it was because of what we did?' Badger says even quieter. This time he looks up, making sure no one's listening in.

I shake my head. 'I don't know. Not for sure. But . . .'

No one speaks. We all look at each other, all thinking the same thing. It must have been because of us. The silence extends to a minute or so. There's a horrible, tense atmosphere. Then Jake looks up and takes a deep breath. We all look at him expectantly. He holds up his drink.

'This is wrong, man. I just counted forty-two ice cubes in my drink. Can you believe that rubbish? That shouldn't be allowed,' he says, like nothing just happened, like we've been talking about nothing important. 'How is there any room for drink when there are that many ice cubes in there?'

We all just stare back at him, silent.

'What? Don't you think that's a liberty? Forty-two ice cubes in one drink!'

No one answers him.

Jake looks at his drink again and then he stands up. 'I'm gonna go and complain,' he says. 'It's a total rip-off, man.' With that, he walks back into the burger bar with his drink.

The rest of us stare at each other. I have no idea what to say or think or do. I look in through the door of the burger bar, watch Jake go up to the counter and talk to the person behind it. I can't make out what he's saying, but I can see him waving his arms about and shoving the drink under some spotty cashier's nose. I look back at Badger and Drac.

'This is messed up, man,' Drac says as I catch his eye. 'I feel bad.'

'I know,' I say in a low voice. I sigh. 'I wasn't sure whether to tell you or not, but . . .'

He nods his head.

Jake walks out of the burger bar, shaking his head. He throws his cup at the bin, but it misses and showers ice cubes all over the ground. 'What an idiot,' he says. 'The manager was about twelve years old! I told him I'd call the customer service line and he'd have all the stars on his stupid name badge taken away. He just gave me this really sarcastic smile, handed over the customer service number and said it was company policy and good luck with making a complaint. Loser.'

The rest of us don't say a word. How can that be the most important thing on Jake's mind at a time like this? He comes and sits back on the wall with us, but doesn't look at anyone. Instead he stares into the distance, furious.

The weird atmosphere lasts the whole afternoon. Badger and Drac are as quiet as I was this morning. It's difficult to get excited about rides and candyfloss and stuff when you have someone's death on your conscience – at least, it is for everyone except Jake. I honestly have no idea what's going through his mind. I start to wonder whether he's understood what I told him earlier, because he spends the whole afternoon throwing himself into all the rides and then wastes his money on sweets and drinks and all sorts of rubbish, like he hasn't a care in the world.

By the time we get off the train in Raynes Park, I feel relieved. I need to get away from them all. I need to be on my own.

I've been lying on my bed pretty much since I got home. I have no idea how long I've been here. I haven't looked at the time. All I know is that when I first sat down here, the sun was still streaming in through the window and I'd put some music on, but the music stopped ages ago and now there's barely any light left in the sky. I can't even make out the skull and crossbones on the stupid helium balloon Jake bought for me earlier. The balloon's only a dark shape now, drifting around just below the ceiling.

I've been thinking about the funeral car. I mean, first of all, it makes me feel guilty. The old lady may not have died when we gave her the shock – she may have had heart disease already anyway – but what we did must have contributed to her death. It must have. Even though I'd like to think the two things were completely unrelated, I know they're not. And that makes me feel like dirt.

I also know I'm gonna have to keep this thing a secret for the rest of my life, like a coward, because I know that if I tell anyone, I could get into trouble. I'm way too scared of the consequences, of what will happen to me, of what people will think of me, to confess.

And lurking somewhere in the back of my mind, there's a question. A shameful, self-centred question. Am I a murderer? Every time I think it, I realise that I'm more concerned about what might happen to me than what happened to the Poisoned Dwarf. But I can't help it. We did something stupid and someone died. The consequence of our actions was someone's death, even if it happened after the event. But is that murder? Is it even a crime?

I listen to the distant rumble of trains on the tracks and the buzz of traffic. I close my eyes and let my head fall back against the pillow. I sigh. And as I'm lying there, I realise how tightly my teeth are clenched. I feel so unbelievably tense. This is the complete opposite of what this summer was supposed to be. This was supposed to be the best laugh. It was meant to be relaxing – some free time and a chance to unwind after finishing my exams. How did it come to this? One moment of idiocy. One stupid mistake.

The message tone on my mobile shatters the quiet in my room. I sit up and look over at the bedside table, where the screen of my phone is glowing. I pick my phone up and read the message. It's from Badger.

I've been thinking about what u said. Can we meet 2moro?

I text him straight back. **Course. How about after football?**

Then I go through to the bathroom, brush my teeth and get ready for bed. Maybe I'll feel better if I can get some sleep.

She's there in front of me. Jean Hornby. Standing in her porch looking unsteady. Her face is grey and drawn and even more creased and wrinkled than I remember it. She scowls out, then, as she notices me, her eyebrows furrow. I can't help but stare back at her. Her eyes follow me as I walk along the pavement towards her house. As I get close, she shuffles forward and opens the porch door.

'Murderer!' She spits the word out at me in her cracked voice. 'Murderer!'

I look away from her and quicken my pace. I have my head down. I can feel my heart thumping. I'm sweating. I don't want to be here.

'Murderer!' she calls again, louder. 'Murderer!'

I glance behind me and I see her, following me along the pavement, hobbling along in a hospital gown.

'MURDERER!' comes her blood-curdling shriek. 'MURDERER!'

I look round again. She's running after me, hobbling, tubes trailing out of her nose and hands and arms.

I quicken my pace to a fast walk and then to a run. I look up ahead of me. At the end of the road are Mum and Dad with Mikey beside them. They're shaking their heads at me, disappointed. Disgusted.

'MURDERER!' the Poisoned Dwarf shouts again.

I don't look around. I don't look at my family. Instead I look at my feet and run as fast as I can. I have to escape. I have to get away. But after a couple of strides something hits my back and nearly knocks me over. I feel something heavy on my back. I glance up to see the Poisoned Dwarf staring straight at me, her ice-blue eyes boring into mine. She clings desperately on to my back, digging her nails into my flesh.

'Murderer,' she whispers in my ear. 'I know it was you.' She sounds angry, mad, broken.

I run on. I look at my parents again. They shake their heads one last time and then turn away. Mikey smirks. The Poisoned Dwarf clings to my back and as I run she wriggles and pulls at my hair and kicks at my sides till I fall to the ground. We land in a heap on the floor, the Poisoned Dwarf lying on top of me, cold and stiff. Her eyes roll in her head. Her tongue lolls out of her mouth. She's dead.

I wake with a start. Heart pounding. Soaked to the skin with sweat. I look around the room. Over in the corner, I see a strange shape floating around up by the ceiling. As I watch, it floats closer towards me. My heart beats even faster. I reach straight for the bedside lamp and switch it on. The light hurts my eyes as it floods the room. I narrow my eyes for a second till they adjust to the light. Then I see that the shape in the corner of the room is the stupid balloon that Jake bought from the theme park. I stand up on my bed and throw a punch at it. The balloon bobs away across the room, dips down and then floats back up to the ceiling.

I sit on my bed and look at the time. I could have

guessed though. 2.43 a.m. The same time as always. This is getting stupid.

I sigh and bury my head in my hands. It's her. It's the Poisoned Dwarf. It has to be. She's the reason I'm waking up every night at the same time. None of this happened before. I used to sleep like a baby.

I take my head out of my hands and look around the room. My *empty* room.

'I know you're there,' I say. 'I know you're watching me. I know who you are.'

There's no response. The balloon bobs about in the corner. The skull stares at me.

'What do you want with me?'

Again there's no answer. Not that I expected one.

'I wish you'd leave me alone,' I say. 'I've had enough of this. Go away!'

No answer. Nothing. I sigh. What the hell is happening to me? Am I losing the plot?

I lie back in bed and stare at the ceiling. I keep the light on and my eyes wide open. I can feel the thumping of my heart in my chest.

When is this going to stop? Is this ever going to stop?

My alarm goes off. I open my eyes and notice my bedside lamp is still on. I sigh. What I'd really like to do right now is go back to sleep. I feel wrecked. *So* tired. But I can't do that. I have football training. And I have to meet Badger.

I stare at the ceiling directly above my bed and I start counting to sixty in my head. When I get to sixty, I'll get up. Only, I don't stop when I get to sixty. I keep going. On past a hundred. And I decide that I'll get up when I get to two hundred instead.

I'm past four hundred when I finally get out of bed. I sit up and rub my face, rub the sleep out of my eyes. And I notice the balloon again. It's still hovering in the corner of my room, not floating right up against the ceiling any more, but hovering just underneath. Some of the helium must have escaped. I stretch and then get out of bed. I walk over to the balloon and take a swipe at it with my fist. It makes a *boof* sound as I hit it. The balloon smacks against the wall and then bobs across my room.

Mum and Dad have gone to work, but Mikey's already downstairs when I get down there, sitting on the sofa with a bowl of cereal resting on his lap, gawping at the TV. He holds his spoon halfway between his bowl and his face, his gob wide open, looking gormless as always. I go into the kitchen and get myself some cereal and then come back through to the lounge, sit next to Mikey on the sofa.

'Why do you have to watch such rubbish?' I say. 'Can't we watch something better?'

Mikey doesn't look at me. 'I was in the lounge first,' he says, 'so I get to choose what we watch. That's the rule.'

I shake my head. 'There's also a rule about eating in the lounge,' I say. 'If I remember correctly, since you stained the carpet by spilling tomato ketchup, no one's meant to eat in the lounge.'

Mikey turns to me and rolls his eyes. He looks down at my breakfast. 'Well, then, you shouldn't be eating in here either, smart arse.'

I smile. 'I'm not eating. I'm just holding my bowl,' I say.

Mikey turns back to the TV and shakes his head. 'You are a sad case, Johnny,' he says.

We both sit watching the box for a while, eating breakfast without saying a word. If I could be bothered I'd take the remote control from Mikey by force and switch over to something else. But I can't be bothered so I let him watch the lame sitcom instead. As the adverts come on, Mikey puts his empty bowl on the carpet and turns to me.

'Did you hear noises last night?' he says.

It takes a second for what he just said to sink in. What does he mean? I look at his face for a second, trying to work him out. I shake my head. 'No.'

Mikey smiles. 'It was about three in the morning, I think. You must have heard it. There was some nutter talking.'

'You what?'

He smirks. 'You mean you didn't hear it?'

I start to wonder what he knows, what he heard. I shake my head. 'Hear what?'

'It woke me up,' he says. And then he makes a pretend sorrowful, scared face and does an impression. '*What do you want with me?*' He creases up with laughter.

I try to ignore him. I concentrate on spooning some cereal into my mouth.

'It was a bloke talking,' Mikey says. 'He kept saying stuff like "I wish you'd leave me alone" and "I've had enough of this".'

I shake my head and swallow my mouthful of cereal. 'Didn't hear a thing. You must have imagined it.'

'Nah,' Mikey says. 'I definitely heard it. I'd say it came from your room. I thought you and your boyfriend were having an argument.'

For a split second I think about giving him a dead arm. 'Grow up, Mikey.'

He laughs. 'Don't act innocent. You know what I'm talking about. You must have heard it.'

I sigh. I restrain myself from inflicting physical pain on Mikey. 'I think you've gone mad,' I say.

Mikey shakes his head. 'No. I think you'll find it's *you* that's going mad,' he says. 'I know all about it. I heard Dad telling Mum that he caught you sleepwalking the other night – with a cricket bat.'

'Give it a rest,' I say, as though it's nothing. I look away from him.

'It's true though, isn't it, Johnny? Were you off for a quick game of night cricket?'

I don't answer that. I can feel my cheeks flushing. I feel like smashing Mikey in the face, but I don't want him to see that he's got to me.

'Are you going mad, Johnny?' Mikey says in a sing-song voice.

I ignore him. I turn to the TV and watch the adverts.

'You are though, aren't you? A little bit. Admit it.'

I close my eyes for a second, try and let the comment wash over me. But then I hear Mikey laughing to himself and before I can even think about it, I've punched him hard on the arm.

'Ah. Christ. What was that for?' he says, rubbing the spot on his arm where I hit him.

'For being an annoying little parasite,' I say, standing up and taking my breakfast stuff through to the kitchen.

'Yeah, well, at least I'm not going mad,' Mikey calls back.

I go upstairs to get ready. The pirate balloon has somehow floated out of my room and is hovering around the landing. I bat it out of the way and go into the bathroom to get washed. By the time I've showered and brushed my teeth and all the other stuff that you don't need to know about, the balloon has floated over towards my room and is floating back inside. I stand and watch it for a second and then go into my room. The balloon is waiting for me, hovering in the centre of the room, the hollow eyes of the skull boring into me. I get my clothes out, get dressed and head for the door. As I get to the door, I turn and look at the balloon again. It's floating towards the door, after me. I swear it's following me.

Maybe Mikey's right. Maybe I am losing it. Something's not right in my head.

Nothing was mentioned this morning at football. Nothing of what I told Jake yesterday. Jake just did the usual – looking at all the mums and the au pairs and the childminders who dropped the kids off, leering at them and rating them out of ten. I said nothing, not because I didn't want to say something – I was dying to – but cos it didn't seem like the right time.

We're on our way back from training now, about to walk past the row of shops where the drive-by took place and we're both quiet. We both have our heads down as we walk as though we're thinking about something deep. I wonder whether Jake's thinking the same as me.

'It gives me the creeps,' he says quietly as we get close.

'What does?'

'Going past here every day.'

I look up at Jake. He's not looking back at me. He's looking at the space on the road outside the shop where the car was parked that day.

'Me too.'

And that's it. Neither of us says any more and when we get to the top of his road, we go in our different directions.

I cross Exminster Avenue so I don't have to walk on the side where the Poisoned Dwarf lived, but I glance up at the house as I get close. The car's parked out front. The blinds are all pulled shut. I don't see anyone. Still, my heart thumps and I remember the dream from last night. I hurry along the road.

Badger's already sitting on the front step, reading a comic book, when I get home. He looks up as I walk up the drive.

'Wanna come in and get some lunch?' I say, putting my key in the lock.

Badger nods and gets up from the step. 'Yeah,' he says. 'Food would be good.'

Mikey's there as soon as we get in through the door. He's in the hallway with his friend Asif, as though they're just about to go upstairs. They stop and look at me and Badger. I think about stirring after the text I sent from Mikey's phone the other day. But before I can, Mikey speaks.

'Is that *your* stupid balloon in the lounge?' he says.

'Uh?'

'The lame pirate balloon. Is it yours?'

'Yeah,' I say. 'What's it to you?'

'Well, maybe you can put it in your room. It's been getting in my way all morning,' he says, and then he turns and walks up the stairs with his little friend.

I shrug my shoulders at Badger and go through to the kitchen to get us some sandwiches and crisps and stuff.

A few minutes later we're sitting upstairs in my room, eating.

'I couldn't sleep last night,' Badger says between bites of a sandwich. He looks at me.

I get a strange feeling – relief, I think. Someone else might actually be going through what I am. Maybe I'm not going loopy. Maybe this is normal. 'Yeah?'

'I was just thinking about . . .' He tails off.

'Me too.'

'So do you know any more about what happened?'

I shake my head. 'Only what I said yesterday. She had a heart attack after we did the drive-by. According to the newspaper she had a heart problem even before we did that. She went into hospital and came out a couple of days later.'

'Are you sure?'

I nod. 'I saw her getting back home. She looked awful. She looked like she was pretty much dead already.'

Badger lets out a long, slow breath.

'And then she died. I don't know exactly when, but I guess it must have been about a week ago cos the funeral was on Tuesday. That's it. I don't know for sure what she died of.'

Badger sighs. 'It doesn't take a genius to work it out though, does it?'

'I know.'

'I feel so bad,' Badger says.

Neither of us speaks. We've both stopped eating. We sit and stare into nothingness for ages.

'Is it murder?' Badger says eventually.

'I don't know,' I say. I pause. 'Feels like it though.'

'Jesus, man. Maybe we should tell someone.'

'Like who?'

Badger shrugs. 'I dunno. The police?'

I shake my head. 'Why would we do that?'

He shrugs again. 'I don't know. I just thought maybe we should. I mean, it's not like we meant to give her a heart attack, is it?'

I shake my head. 'No. I think we should stay quiet. The police haven't come knocking at our doors, have they? And they would have done if they'd known what we'd done. They know she got shot at on the parade of shops cos it was in the paper. If they knew it was us, they would have found us by now. Besides, the only witness is dead.'

I feel really awful for saying it. It seems like a sick thing to say, like I am a murderer. But it's true. She can't identify us if she's dead. And if she can't, then no one can.

Badger stands up. He walks over to the window and looks out. 'How do we know she *was* the only person that saw us? And how do we know that she didn't tell anyone?'

'We don't,' I say.

He nods. He comes and sits back down.

'I did think of one thing though,' I say.

Badger stares at me. 'What?'

'CCTV cameras. There might be some on the parade of shops. They might have recorded what happened.'

'Good point,' he says. 'We should go and check.'

Summer

The shopkeeper looks at me like he recognises my face but can't place it. He always does when I go in there. I know who he is though. Afsheen. When I was little and Nan or Grandad used to bring me and Sky in here, the shopkeeper would always reach under the counter and get us a lolly when we went up to the till. He'd always say, 'Sky and Summer. Such beautiful names for such beautiful girls.' After a couple of seconds Afsheen gives up trying to work out who I am though and looks at the newspaper and bread and milk on the counter. He scans them all through.

'Three pounds eighty-seven,' he says.

I hand him four quid, get my change and then leave the shop.

As soon as I'm outside, I see him. Johnny. He's standing around with another kid – a tall, black kid who has a white stripe in his bushy Afro. They're looking around at the front of the shops and at the parking spaces and stuff. God knows what they're doing. They turn in my direction. I smile at Johnny. He notices me and smiles back so I walk over to him.

'Hello, Johnny,' I say. 'We must stop meeting like this.'

He smiles, but then looks down at the pavement. 'Hi, Summer,' he says. He looks back up at me. 'Oh, sorry. Summer, this is my friend, Badger. Badger, this is Summer.'

'Badger,' I say. 'Cool name. Your parents must have been even bigger hippies than mine.'

He laughs and runs his hand through his hair, right across his white stripe. 'It's not my real name unfortunately,' he says. He's even shyer than Johnny – he barely even looks at my face as he talks. 'But you probably worked that out, didn't you?'

I smile. 'What are you two doing, then?'

They immediately look at each other and I get a weird vibe off them, like I've just walked in on something I shouldn't have. They exchange this strange, wordless look.

'Nothing,' Johnny says. 'Just hanging out really.'

I don't know whether he's telling me the truth or not. Somehow I get the feeling he's making something up. But what does it matter?

'How about you?' he says.

I hold up the blue carrier bag. 'Running errands again. I told you my life was rock and roll.'

No one says anything for a while. In the background I can hear clanking sounds from the building site across the road.

'You still up for meeting tomorrow?' Johnny asks.

'Course. You?'

He nods and smiles. 'Definitely.'

There's another silence for a couple of seconds and then he turns to look at Badger and back at me.

'Better get going,' he says. 'See you tomorrow.'

Johnny

We're back at my house, in my room, door closed. I'm sitting on the edge of my bed and Badger is on my desk chair.

'There weren't any cameras on the parade of shops as far as I could see,' I say.

Badger shakes his head. 'Nope.'

'But there's one in the newsagent's.'

Badger nods. 'The camera's inside the shop though. With all the stickers and posters and stuff on the newsagent's door, there's no way it's gonna pick up what's happening outside on the pavement. Besides, those places record over the CCTV tapes every couple of days.'

'So I s'pose we're in the clear, then,' I say. It doesn't come out sounding very triumphant. More apologetic. I feel rubbish for saying it, for even thinking it.

'Looks like it.' Badger pauses for ages. 'There is one thing though.'

I look at him. He puts his hand through his hair.

'The building site,' he says. 'There are people on it all the time, going in and out. There are builders working up on the scaffolding. There's a security guard on duty as well. And they're right across the street from where it happened.'

I take a deep breath and slowly blow it out. 'Jesus,' I say. 'You're right. I didn't even think of that.'

'I dunno if they'd have seen anything,' he says. 'It is a busy road . . .'

'Do you reckon anyone did?'

'I don't know. Probably not. There would have been so much noise and too much going on for anyone to have noticed a couple of kids on bikes.' Then he pauses. He looks down at the floor. 'We can't be sure though, can we?'

'If anyone saw anything they'd have told the police by now, wouldn't they?'

Badger shrugs. Then he nods his head. 'Yeah.'

We sit in silence again. I hear all the usual noises – the drone of the main road and the rumble of the trains, sirens in the background – but I hear something else too, coming from the other side of my bedroom door. It's quiet, but unless I really am going mad, I'm sure it's laughter. I get up from my bed and walk over to the door. I open it and there, crouching down with stupid grins on their ugly little faces, are Mikey and Asif.

'What the hell are you doing?' I shout. I stand over them and anger wells up inside me. I have to stop myself from hitting out at them. The implications of them sitting out there while me and Badger have been talking start to stack up in my mind. I feel my face start to flush. I try to work out what I'm gonna do, how to react.

Mikey and Asif look at each other as though they're not sure how to react either. They start off looking scared, but in a millisecond their expressions turn to amusement and they start laughing and run downstairs.

I turn back to Badger.

He shakes his head like he can't believe this is happening and then he closes his eyes. 'Jesus.'

'Do you think they heard anything?'

He opens his eyes. 'Who knows?'

Summer

I take the shopping straight to Grandad's house. When I get there, he's at the dining-room table, staring out of the back window. There are old photo albums spread across the table. I go and make him a coffee and sit down with him.

'You're a good girl, Summer,' he says.

Grandad looks at me for a few seconds and then looks back out into the garden. He doesn't say anything, but just sits and sips his coffee. I try and work out what he might be thinking. He's thinking about Nan, I bet. He must be. I don't know what to say to him. I don't know whether I should talk about Nan, say how amazing she was and how I miss her. Or maybe that would make him feel worse. Maybe he doesn't want to think about her right now. So I look at the sparrows flitting around the stale slices of bread I threw into the garden, watch as they fly off when the pigeons land and start pecking at the bread.

After a while, I look at the table and pull one of the photo albums over towards me. I start flicking through it. There are pictures of Dad in there from when he was just a kid. They look faded.

Looking at pictures of Dad always makes me feel weird. It makes me think about what he'd be like now. It makes me wonder whether things would have turned out differently if something could have stopped it happening, stopped Dad from dying. Like if he'd stayed in bed that day instead of going out. If he'd been delayed and been in the same places but at different times, he might be alive now. And that always makes me think about what my life would be like now, how it would be different. Would I be different if I had a dad? If I had *my* dad?

All the photos are of days out and things. Dad as a little kid on a beach, wearing some really disgusting swimming trunks, digging a moat around his sandcastles. Dad on a fairground ride. Everyone sitting around a table in the garden eating barbecued food. Nan stepping out of a caravan. She looks much younger in the picture. Which is obvious, I s'pose, as it was taken about forty years ago. But she almost looks like a different person. She looks pretty. I never really thought of Nan as being pretty. She's always been old to me. That sounds kind of mean, I know. But in the picture, her face looks different – I mean, aside from the fact that she's younger. I don't know how to describe it. She looks softer. Happier. She's smiling in the picture and not just with her eyes – with her whole face. I keep flicking through the photos, and as I'm doing that I realise Grandad's looking at them with me. I feel like I should say something.

'She was really pretty, wasn't she?'

Grandad smiles sadly and for a second I think he's gonna cry. He nods his head. 'She was,' he says. 'She was beautiful.'

He gazes at the pictures of Nan and Dad as I flick through the album. There aren't many of Grandad. Must be because he took the photos.

'Your dad would be in his forties now,' Grandad says after a while. He sounds matter of fact about it.

I look at him. He hardly ever talks about Dad.

'Do you miss him?'

Grandad straightens himself up in his chair. He takes another sip of his coffee, carefully places his mug on his coaster and looks at the photos and nods. 'Every day. Every single day, Summer.'

'Me too.'

We sit and look at the photos and we're silent for a while longer.

'Your nan missed him a lot,' Grandad says all of a sudden. He sighs. He sits up straight in his chair and looks into the garden.

I nod. It feels like Grandad's left a space for me to say something, but I don't know what to say.

He nods as if I have said something, still looking out of the window. 'They had a bit of a love/hate relationship most of the time,' he says. 'They always did, right from when he was a little lad. But the truth was, they had more in common than either of them would ever have admitted. They were both stubborn as mules for a start.' He laughs for a second.

I look at a picture of Dad in the album. He's standing outside Nan and Grandad's house, leaning on a car. He's smiling, laughing at a joke or something. He's got a really awful haircut – a totally wonky fringe.

'The thing is, because they were so similar, they always knew how to press each other's buttons,' Grandad goes on.

I kind of knew this much from Mum. She's told me before that Nan didn't really approve of the lifestyle she and Dad chose. She thought it wasn't right. Mum and Dad always thought they were 'alternative'. Hence my and Sky's hippy names. But Nan always wanted

Dad to get a good job and earn some money. Mum and Dad weren't interested in that stuff though.

'Problem is, because they were both stubborn, they both thought they were right and neither ever backed down,' Grandad says.

'Oh,' I say. I'm not sure this is what I want to hear about them right now even though I know it's true. Right now, I'd like to hear about how good they were as people, not hear about their shortcomings. 'They loved each other though, didn't they?'

Grandad gulps down some of his coffee and places his mug on the coaster. He looks at me and smiles. 'Of course,' he says. 'They were close. Your nan would have done anything for your dad. And he loved her. They just had a funny way of showing it sometimes.'

I smile back at Grandad, but I feel sad.

'It's a shame,' he says. 'The way it all worked out.'

I expect him to go on, to say more. I'm desperate for him to, but he doesn't. He gets up from the table and takes his mug through to the kitchen. I follow him through. He puts his mug in the sink and then just stands there looking out of the back door.

'That lawn needs cutting, Summer,' he says. 'I must do that this afternoon.'

I think about what to say next, whether I should ask him if he needs any help around the house. Or whether

I should just leave him to it and go home. And as I stand and look at him, I feel sorry for him. How must he be feeling? It must be awful to live with someone for most of your life, to build your whole life with them, and then one day they're gone. It feels so empty in the house without Nan. There are reminders of her everywhere.

Before I can say anything, Grandad turns to me and says, 'She was never the same after your dad died, you know.'

I'm taken aback. I get the same knot in my stomach that I had when I went to the hospital to see Nan after she had the heart attack.

'She wasn't happy. She went into herself,' he says.

'Really?' I say, because I don't know what else to say. 'Why?'

Grandad turns and looks at me. 'She took it really badly. We all did, I s'pose. You don't expect something like that to happen. It was so sudden, so unexpected. It felt like he'd been stolen away from us.'

I nod. I feel a bit uncomfortable listening to this. But at the same time I want to hear more.

'She even went to see spiritualists for a bit, you know,' Grandad says.

'Really? What's a spiritualist?' I say. 'Is that someone who contacts the spirit world?'

'Good question,' Grandad says, and he sort of laughs. 'They're frauds if you ask me. Charlatans. They say they can contact the dead. But I think they just make money out of vulnerable people. I told her not to go, but . . . I suppose she had to do it.'

'Oh,' I say. 'I didn't know Nan was into that kind of thing. Did she find anything out?'

Grandad sighs. 'Yes and no,' he says. 'Depends whether you believe that sort of nonsense or not. Your nan believed it. As far as she was concerned, they contacted James. All I know is, she didn't feel any better at the end of it.'

'Oh.'

'She had it all recorded. She has tapes of it somewhere. Up in the loft, I think.'

'Oh my God,' I say. I feel quite shocked. I never knew about this. I don't even know if Mum knows this. She's never mentioned it. 'Can I listen to them?'

Grandad looks at me. He looks so tired. He looks like he's kind of shrivelled, like a balloon deflating. I'm sure it's happened since Nan died. Or maybe he's been like that for a while and I just didn't notice it before.

'I don't think that's a good idea,' he says. And then he sighs again. 'I shouldn't have said anything, Summer.'

We're both silent. I hear the trains rumble along in the background.

After a while, Grandad very suddenly springs into action, like he's just woken from a dream. 'Right, then,' he says. 'I'm going to mow the lawn.'

Johnny

I'm in the lounge watching TV with the balloon. It followed me in here. It's bobbing around just behind the TV – the stupid skull is staring at me, like it's mocking me.

I hear the door open. Mikey walks into the room. I ignore him. He comes over and sits down next to me on the sofa. Out of the corner of my eye I can see he's staring at me, trying to get a reaction. But I don't give him the satisfaction. I look straight ahead at the music video on TV.

After a while he gives up and sits back on the sofa. He's silent for a while. But I can sense he's waiting for his chance. I know exactly what he's up to.

'I know your secret,' he says. And even without looking at him, I can tell that he's got a smirk on his face.

I don't say anything. I try not to react. And I wonder what he knows, what he overheard.

'So, what's it worth not to blab?' he says eventually.

I don't look at him. From his tone of voice, I can tell he's enjoying this, that he's got an expression on his face that I'd like to smack. But I don't. I ignore him. I'm pretty sure he doesn't know anything. Nothing concrete anyway.

'You'll be in trouble when they find out,' he says. 'You know that, don't you?'

I still don't react. I stare straight ahead at the TV, but I don't take in any of the music video. What if he does know something?

'Even if it's not on CCTV, *I* know about it,' he says. 'I know what you did. And I'll tell someone. Mum. Dad. The police.'

I turn and look at him even though I know I shouldn't. 'Shut up, Mikey.'

This makes him smile even more. 'Of course, we could come to some sort of agreement,' he says. 'Something along the lines of you paying me some money and me keeping your little secret. And then there's Asif too. He'll need paying off. He heard it all as well.'

I tut at him. 'You're so immature.'

He smirks. 'You'll be in so much trouble when I grass you up.'

'I haven't done anything.'

'Why were you and Badger whispering in your room, then? Why are you so worried about the CCTV cameras and whether anyone saw you?'

I don't answer his questions because I don't have any answers other than the truth. 'Here's a deal for you,' I say. 'If you can make it up to your room before I count to five, I won't kick your head in.'

The threat doesn't work. Mikey stays where he is, doesn't even shrink away from me. And the annoying grin on his face stays in place. He shakes his head.

'We still have business to deal with,' he says. 'Unless, of course, you want me to blab to Mum and Dad . . .'

I take a deep breath to stop me from doing or saying something that we'll both regret. 'Don't you think Mum and Dad would be interested to hear that you and your little friends have been spying on people, Mikey?'

'Maybe,' he says. 'But my guess is they'll be more interested in knowing what *you*'ve done.'

'Yeah?' I say. 'So come on, then. What do you know? What is it that's so bad? What happened that Mum and Dad are gonna be so outraged by?'

He stares at me for a second. The smug look on his face stays put. He pats his nose and winks. But he's bluffing, I think.

'Spit it out, then, Mikey. What are you gonna tell Mum and Dad?'

He gets up from the sofa and walks towards the door. 'If that's how you want to play it, fine,' he says. 'It's your funeral.'

Summer

As soon as I hear Mum's key in the door, I put my book down, move the cat off my legs and get up from my bed. I take the empty mug from my bedside table and go through. Mum's already in the kitchen by the time I get there, putting shopping away in the fridge. My mug clunks against the sink as I go to wash it. Mum looks up.

'Oh, hello, Summer,' she says. 'I didn't see you there.'

'Hi.'

I go and sit at the table and start fiddling with the candle that's sitting in the middle of the table, move it around across the checkered plastic tablecloth, like it's a chess table and the candle is a knight. One place to the side and two places forward over and over again till the candle gets right to the other side of the table. I can hear Mum going through the cupboards, getting out saucepans.

'Did you have a nice day?' Mum says.

I look up. I'm not sure if it was good or not. It was just weird. 'Yeah,' I say, because I don't feel like going into the details.

Mum doesn't say anything. I watch as she starts to chop an onion. It makes me cringe slightly. Mum's left-handed and it never looks safe when she chops. So instead I start moving the candle across the table like a bishop, diagonally, trying to cover every dark blue square in as few moves as possible. After a while I get bored and look up at Mum.

'I went to Grandad's today,' I say.

'Oh, you are good for doing that, Summer,' Mum says. 'How was he?'

I don't answer right away. I think about it. Grandad was kind of weird today, the way he was talking to me. I've never really heard him talk about that sort of stuff before. I always thought he didn't have any feelings, because he never shows them.

'OK,' I say. 'I think.'

Mum doesn't say anything. She's concentrating on cooking tea rather than the conversation. The onions start to hiss as they drop on to the hot oil. Mum stirs with a wooden spoon and then turns down the heat.

'I did his shopping for him, like you asked.'

Mum starts chopping some garlic. 'Thanks, love,' she says. 'I do worry about him eating well. Do you think he's looking thinner?'

'I dunno,' I say. 'Not that I've noticed.'

'I worry about him though,' she says. 'Your nan did all the cooking in that household. She wouldn't let anyone else into her kitchen, certainly not Harry. I doubt he even knows how to boil an egg.'

She doesn't need to tell me this. I know this much.

'I could make him some batches of food to put in the freezer,' she says. 'Lasagne and stews and things. You can help if you want.'

I don't answer her. I go over to the sink, get myself a drink of water and then go back to the table.

'Mum,' I say, 'do you ever wonder what happened to Dad when he died?'

Mum stops opening the can of tomatoes and looks at me. 'What do you mean?'

The way she looks at me makes me feel like I just brought something up that I shouldn't have. 'I mean, when he died, what do you think happened to him? Do you think he just stopped existing or did his spirit go somewhere?'

Mum keeps opening the tomato tin, then turns to me. 'I'd like to think so,' she says. 'Definitely. It would be sad if death were the end, wouldn't it?'

I honestly don't know what to think. 'S'pose,' I say.

Mum pours the tomatoes into the pan. I hear them bubble and spit as they meet the hot oil. 'I sometimes think that I can feel Dad's presence,' she says.

'Do you?'

'Not all the time,' she says. 'But sometimes I just know that he's there, watching what's going on, guiding us, helping us.'

'Like a ghost?'

Mum shakes her head. She stirs the pasta sauce and then lets the wooden spoon rest against the edge of the pan. She turns around, leans against the cooker. 'Not exactly,' she says. 'Not like he's haunting us. More like he's still sharing the special things that happen. Don't you think so too?'

I make a face like I don't know, because I seriously have no clue.

The room's silent for a while except for the sounds of the gas hob and the sauce in the pan bubbling away. Mum fills the kettle and puts it on. 'Do you want a drink, Summer?'

I shake my head.

Mum gets herself a mug and a herbal tea bag.

'Did you know Nan went to see spiritualists after Dad died?'

Mum immediately stops what she's doing and looks at me. 'Pardon?'

'She went to spiritualists. Grandad told me today.'

'*Did* he?'

I nod. 'Spiritualists are the people who do ouija boards and stuff, aren't they?'

'No. Not exactly,' Mum says. 'They believe they can communicate with spirits. I don't think they use ouija boards though.'

'Do you think they can, then? Communicate with spirits?'

'I doubt it,' Mum says. 'I've got an open mind to most things, but that sounds like a load of mumbo-jumbo to me.'

'But you said you believe in spirits.'

Mum shifts uncomfortably. She looks away from me and stirs the saucepan. 'That doesn't mean I believe people can speak to them though, Summer.'

Neither of us says anything for a while. As I'm sitting here, staring at the tablecloth, I can't help but think about the tapes in Grandad's loft. I try and imagine Nan sitting at a table with a medium, hands linked, eyes closed, hoping to get a message from Dad, feeling desperate, guilty, sad. And it makes me feel sad too.

'So, what did your grandad say about the spiritualists?'

I look up. Mum's trying not to look too interested, but I can tell she is.

'Not much,' I say. 'He said they were frauds and that he told Nan not to go. And when I asked him for more information, he said that he shouldn't have said anything in the first place.'

Mum leans against the cooker again and stares into space. She lets out a noise kind of like a sigh.

'He also said that Nan had recordings of the sessions.'

Mum looks at me again. 'Really?'

I nod. 'They're in the loft at his house.'

'Hmmm . . .'

Mum doesn't say anything else after that and I let the subject go. But Mum slips into a strange kind of mood, like she's not there at all, like she's thinking about something. About Dad, I s'pose. I feel bad for bringing it up. Maybe I shouldn't have said anything.

Johnny

It doesn't take long for me to come round. I've started to expect this to happen now – to wake up in the middle of the night. I look at the clock. 2.43 a.m. Again.

I put my head in my hands, squeeze my eyes closed and press on them with my fingers till I see swirly shapes swimming around in my head. I was dreaming about her again. The Poisoned Dwarf. I saw her staring at me. She shook her head sadly, like she was disgusted I could sleep after what I'd done.

I look around the room. I have that same feeling again. Like someone else is here. Like I'm being watched. I sigh. I put my head in my hands again and rub my face. This is beyond a joke. I'm waking up every single night like clockwork. I see things. I'm on edge all the time. Every time I see a shadow, I think something's there, lurking, watching me, waiting for me. And I really don't know what to do about it because I don't know if this is real or I'm imagining it or whether someone's winding me up or what. I want to tell someone else what's happening, but how can I? If I tell anyone, I'll have to tell the whole story. The only people I could tell are Jake or Badger or Drac – and I can't imagine they'd have any sympathy. They'd tell me to get a grip.

I look up again. There's no one else in the room, but the window is wide open again. And the stupid helium balloon that Jake bought is hovering around halfway between the floor and the ceiling, bobbing around in the breeze, now half-deflated.

I get out of bed. I shut the window and then go through to the bathroom to take a leak. When I turn to go back to my room, the balloon's waiting in the bathroom doorway. The skull is staring at me, mocking me, following me. I *am* going mad. Only mad people think they're being followed by balloons. I take a swing at it and punch it. There's a dull *boof* as the balloon moves away a bit. Then it bobs around so that the skull is facing me again.

'Leave me alone, you stupid balloon,' I say. 'I'm not scared of you.'

And at that very second, I see Mikey's bedroom door open. He comes out of his room, looking sleepy. He looks at me and the balloon and smirks.

'Jeez, J. You really are going mental,' he says. 'You do know it's not normal to talk to balloons, right?'

I take a deep breath and ignore the urge to punch Mikey. I walk back to my room and close the door before the balloon, or Mikey, can follow me.

Summer

The more I think about Nan's tapes, the more that I think it's my right to listen to them. From what I've been told, they're tapes that *my* nan made when she wanted to find out about *my* dad. And seeing as no one ever tells me anything about my dad, seeing as I never even got the chance to meet him, I think I should be allowed to listen to them.

I went round to Grandad's again earlier to check in on him and make sure he's all right. Which he was. Kind of. He's looking after himself OK, but something's different. I guess that's to be expected. To be honest, there's not that much I can do to help Grandad apart from making him the odd cup of coffee and popping to the shops. He's too proud to accept help. As far as he's concerned, he doesn't need it. So I spent a lot of the time there just milling around, looking at the pictures on the mantelpiece, sitting in Nan's chair, looking in the basket beside her chair where she kept her cross-stitch things, all the time wondering about the spiritualist tapes that Grandad mentioned, wondering where they are, whether I could have them and what's on them.

I asked him about them at one point. But he acted like they didn't exist, like I'd imagined the conversation we had the other day. I let the subject drop cos I didn't want to upset him.

When I got home from Grandad's, I searched the internet to find out exactly what spiritualists do, but I struggled to get my head around it all. What I did understand is that spiritualists believe people have spirits that still exist after they die and that they can communicate with the living. Kind of what I guessed anyway. I also found out that spiritualism is a religious movement and there are churches that have spiritualist services where they do the same thing – contact the dead. There's a church near here.

I'm not sure whether I believe in it all, but I definitely want to hear Nan's tapes. And I will. I have to find out what Nan found out. I have to find out about Dad. And I want to hear Nan's voice again. Short of sneaking up into the loft and finding them for myself though, I don't know how I'm gonna get the tapes.

Johnny

As soon as I get back from footy training, Mikey's there, coming out of the living room, smirking. I knew he wouldn't be able to resist.

'All right, Johnny, you big ginger weirdo,' he says to me.

I step inside the house and shut the front door behind me.

'Did ickle J-J have a nasty, horrid dream last night?' he says in a baby voice.

I ignore him. I walk straight past him to the kitchen and get myself a drink.

Mikey follows me. 'What's the matter? Don't want to talk about it?'

I finish my glass of water. 'Grow up.'

'I think it's you that needs to grow up,' he says. 'Talking to balloons is not normal.'

I shake my head. 'Shut up, Mikey.'

'Don't worry,' he says. 'It's probably just your guilty conscience sending you a little bit cuckoo. Guilt can really mess you up.'

I barge past Mikey into the hallway and then on to the stairs. He follows me and stands in the hall. I stop on the stairs.

'If you don't stop acting like an idiot, I'm gonna beat you to a pulp before long,' I say.

That doesn't wipe the smirk from Mikey's face. If anything, the smirk gets wider. 'Maybe you should tell someone what's on your mind. Confess,' he says. 'I'm sure the police would love to know your story.'

'You don't know what you're talking about,' I say. And then I go up to my room.

Summer

I'm feeling nervous. Why did I think it was a good idea to approach a stranger and ask him to go on a date? It *so* isn't the kind of thing that I normally do. We've barely even spoken thirty words to each other. He could turn out to be a total idiot for all I know. Or, more likely, he's wondering who the freak in black is who asked him on a date when she didn't even know him.

But I have a feeling, a hunch, a conviction deep down. I can't explain what it is because I don't know myself. There's just something about him that's right. He's normal. He's not putting on an act like most boys my age. I feel comfortable with him.

I guess I'll find out if I'm right soon enough because here I am, waiting outside the shopping centre in Wimbledon. It was the first place I thought of when I texted him back, but now I'm here it seems like a pretty lousy place to meet. People usually do stuff like this at the cinema or a restaurant or something, don't they? It's so like me to choose the lamest place on the planet to meet. I'm so rubbish at doing things like this. This is why I've never had a boyfriend.

I look at my watch. It's coming up to the time we're meant to meet. I start to wonder whether he's gonna turn up or not. I chew my gum, blow a bubble that pops in front of my face. I check my phone, see if he's called. I check my watch again, shuffle my feet nervously. He's gonna stand me up. I know it. He thinks I'm a freak. And he's probably right.

Then I see him crossing the road from the bus stop. He looks up, sees me and smiles nervously. My heart starts to beat faster.

I take my earphones out and put them in my bag. I take my gum out and put it in a tissue.

'Hi,' he says. 'I'm late, aren't I?'

I shake my head. I think about saying something, making a lame joke, but all of a sudden all my words have dried up.

'You look nice,' he says, sounding kind of nervous.

229

I look down at my clothes. Same old black clothes. To be fair though, this afternoon I spent ages choosing exactly which black clothes to put on. 'Thanks,' I say, realising I sound surprised as I say it.

There's a pause. Maybe I should be the one filling it.

'You look nice as well,' I say.

He smiles shyly. 'Do I? Thanks.'

And then there's another pause. We look at each other and smile awkwardly, nervously.

'We should go and get a drink or something . . .'

He nods. 'Definitely.'

So we go into the shopping centre, talking as we walk about stupid things, like how stinky the bus was that he travelled on, which makes me feel good. At least I'm not the only one who notices stupid stuff like that.

We go straight up to a café in the food court. Frothy, creamy, iced coffee for me and orange juice for Johnny. We sit at a table with a view out over the high street.

We sit in silence for a bit. I stir my coffee with a straw. And I start to wonder whether this is gonna be awkward. We know nothing about each other. Who knows if we have anything in common apart from being made to do all the errands and hating smelly buses? I take the straw out of my coffee and lick the cream off it. I stir it around again as I think about what

I'm gonna ask him. Then I take it back out again and lick the cream and coffee off it.

'You look like you're enjoying that!' Johnny says.

I immediately feel my cheeks flush. 'Sorry. Was I being gross?'

He laughs, then shakes his head. 'Not at all.'

I look down at my coffee and think of something to say. 'How old are you?' It sounds a bit rude and abrupt when it comes out. It sounds like a dumb question.

'Sixteen,' he says. 'You?'

I smile. 'Same. So do you go to school around here?'

'Yeah. Shannon Corner High. In Raynes Park. How about you?'

'Tooting. St Martin's,' I say.

He nods. He sips some of his juice and looks out of the window at the high street. He looks back at me and smiles.

'It's weird, don't you think?' I say.

'What?'

'The way we've never met and then all of a sudden we keep bumping into each other.'

He nods his head.

'Maybe it's fate or something.'

He nods again, gulps down some of his drink. 'Either that or one of us is a stalker!'

I smile. 'Oh, so you figured me out, then!' I sort of wish I hadn't said it as soon as it comes out of my mouth. If he didn't think I was a stalker beforehand, he does now. I slurp some of my coffee to try and hide my burning cheeks.

But Johnny just smiles. 'You're right. It must be fate.'

I nod. 'Totally. It has to be, doesn't it?'

Johnny looks at me, holds my gaze for ages. I look at his pupils. I watch them dilate. I heard that it's a way you can tell if someone likes you – if their pupils dilate when they look at you, they're attracted to you. I don't know whether that's true. His pupils dilate though. He likes me. But he looks away again.

'I checked out a couple of Cure albums online,' Johnny says. 'After I met you the other day.'

I nod and stir my coffee. 'Really? Cool.'

He smiles and nods. '*The Head on the Door*, is it called?'

I smile. I feel a sensation in my tummy, like butter-flies. 'That's my dad's favourite record ever.'

Johnny nods. 'Your dad has good taste.' He smiles.

'He's pretty cool.'

Johnny's smile gets wider. 'So have you got any more music tips? What else should I be listening to?'

I smile. We're away. The ice is broken. I tell him some more of my dad's favourite records and some of mine as well. After that we sit and chat for ages. The little silences between us get shorter and less awkward.

And I find out all kinds of stuff about him. Like he has a younger brother that annoys him like mad. He has a paper round. He wants to be a scriptwriter when he's older, writing films, which is very cool. In return, I give him a potted version of my life story, but heavily edited to leave out the stuff I don't want him knowing.

Our drinks are long finished when a cleaner comes over and takes the empty cups off the table and wipes it with a cloth and some spray. The conversation suddenly dries up as we watch the cleaner work. And then, as soon as he's gone, we look at each other and laugh.

'Do you think that was a hint?'

'I think so,' he says. 'Let's go somewhere else.'

We get up and start walking out of the food court, down the escalator and out of the shopping centre. Neither of us seems to be taking the lead in where we're going. We just kind of amble along, chatting and laughing, along the high street till the high street peters out into a load of newsagents and restaurants. We take a turning on the left on to a residential road of posh-looking houses.

'Is this where you live?' Johnny asks.

I laugh. 'God, no. I live in a seriously scuzzy little flat in Tooting. These places are palaces.'

'So do you know where we're going?' he asks.

I shrug. I stand and think for a second. 'Not really.'
And then I have an idea. 'Seeing as we both agree that
fate brought us here, maybe we should let fate decide
where we end up.'

'What do you mean?'

I open my bag and search for a coin. I flip it in the
air, trying to look cool, but only just manage to catch
it. 'We let the coin decide,' I say. I point up the road.
'See that turning up ahead? Heads, we go straight on.
Tails says we go right.'

Johnny smiles. He nods. 'Cool,' he says. 'All right,
then.'

I toss the coin in the air and then catch it. Slowly I
take away my top hand.

'Tails,' Johnny says. 'We go right.'

So we do. And for the next couple of minutes we
keep doing the same thing, letting the coin decide, till
we end up next to a church with a low wall and a
churchyard out front. I stop walking. I take the coin
out once more.

'Heads, we sit in the churchyard. Tails, we keep
walking.'

The coin arcs through the air and lands in my hands.
I look directly at Johnny as I take my top hand away.

'Heads,' Johnny says. 'We go into the churchyard.'

I look at him and smile, shrug my shoulders. And
then I unlatch the little gate into the churchyard and

hold it open for Johnny. We walk in along a path and sit on a bench outside the church.

Johnny looks kind of nervously around at the gravestones. 'So this is where fate brought us?' he says, still looking at the graves. 'Do you think that's a bad sign?'

I laugh. 'I hope not. Anyway, there's nothing wrong with graveyards,' I say. 'Though I have to admit that going to one on a first date is a bit . . . well, strange.'

Johnny looks at me. He smiles. He doesn't say anything. Our eyes lock in on each other. For a second I think he's gonna lean over and kiss me. And I sort of wish that he would. But then he looks away as though something just occurred to him. He stares at the graves.

I look at the rows and rows of gravestones as well. How rubbish am I? I decide to try and look cool and impulsive by letting the coin decide, to make Johnny think that's the kind of person I am, and we wind up sitting in a graveyard in silence. Talk about a mood killer.

Johnny stares at the headstones. He still looks nervous. I think maybe he'd rather be somewhere else.

After a while he clears his throat. 'Do you believe in ghosts, Summer?'

'Yeah, I think I do.' I turn to him. 'Do you?'

He shrugs. 'I don't really know,' he says. 'I think so.' Then he goes quiet, staring out across the graveyard. I wonder what he's thinking about.

'I don't believe in white sheets and howling and all that stuff though,' I say. 'I believe in spirits.'

Johnny nods. He doesn't say anything. He slowly turns and looks at me. Our eyes lock in on each other again. But then I start thinking about things. About Dad. About Nan. I look down at the ground and try to let it pass.

'Are you all right?' Johnny says. I can sense him sitting uncomfortably on the bench, thinking that he's done or said something that's upset me.

I nod my head. 'I was just thinking about my dad. Sorry.'

There's a pause. Johnny doesn't say anything. He looks awkward, confused. It's time to explain.

'He died before I was born,' I say, still looking down at the ground. 'A road accident.'

'Oh no. I'm sorry,' Johnny says.

I look up at him. 'It's OK,' I say. 'It was a long time ago.'

Johnny doesn't say anything.

'He was driving to work and got hit by a white van.'

'My God. That's awful.'

'I never even met him. He never even held me. When I asked about him Mum always told me that his spirit was watching over us. She said that he could see me, that I should sense him around me.'

Johnny nods.

'It made me totally paranoid,' I say. Then I laugh. 'Imagine your dad being able to see *everything* you do . . .'

Johnny looks horrified. 'Uh, no thanks.'

'But I think there was something in what my mum said. I think he is around still. His spirit.'

'I know what you mean,' Johnny says. 'I've had the feeling that there are spirits about.'

I look at him. He looks away immediately, like he wishes he hadn't said anything. 'Yeah?'

'I don't know what it is exactly, but sometimes I just get a feeling like I'm not alone.'

I nod. I wasn't expecting him to say anything like that.

'I never see anyone or hear anyone, but I just know there's someone there.'

'Do you know who it is?' I ask.

Johnny doesn't answer right away. He looks at his feet. 'I'm not sure,' he says eventually. Then he pauses. 'Did you ever try and speak to your dad's spirit?'

I nod my head even though I feel a bit stupid admitting to it. 'Of course. I used to all the time. Not so much now.'

'Did he ever answer?'

I smile. 'Kind of, I think. Sometimes he'd send a sign. He'd do something, like an object would move in the room. Or I'd feel a breeze. Or I'd just happen to see a word, like on a sign, that was to do with what I'd spoken to him about.'

'Really? You think it was him, then?'

'Yeah. I think so,' I say. 'You know, my nan went to a medium to try and get in touch with my dad after he died.'

'And what happened?'

I shrug. 'I don't know. I only found out recently, after she died. I asked my grandad about it and he said it didn't make it any easier for her. But he said that there were tape recordings of the sessions. He's still got them.'

Johnny sits staring at his trainers. He nods his head. 'Have you listened to them?'

I shake my head. 'I want to. I don't think my grandad wants me to though. I'd love to hear what she heard and even just hear her voice again.'

'You should borrow them,' Johnny says. 'Without your grandad knowing.'

I shake my head even though it's just what I'd like to do. I get up from the bench. Johnny gets up too.

'There's no way I'd be able to get them without him knowing,' I say as we walk back down the path. 'I don't even know exactly where they are.'

Johnny opens the gate and holds it for me. I put my arm through his as we start walking down the road.

'I've been thinking about it a lot,' I say. 'I'm gonna try and get in touch with my nan and my dad myself.'

Johnny looks at me. 'What? How? Like a ouija board or something?'

I shake my head. 'There's a spiritualist church nearby. They get in touch with the dead apparently. I'm going next Tuesday.'

'Seriously?'

I nod. 'Do you want to come with me?'

Johnny doesn't answer straight away. And I wonder whether I'm starting to freak him out. First a church-yard, now communicating with the dead. Maybe it wasn't the brightest thing to ask right now.

'Sure,' he says. 'I'm up for it.'

Johnny

I'm walking home from the bus stop, going over everything in my mind. It wasn't what I expected at all. It's not like I have a lot of experience in these matters, but I didn't think in a million years that we'd end up in a graveyard talking about ghosts.

Maybe I should've stayed quiet about what's been happening to me or changed the subject. But I like Summer. I feel like I can trust her – as long as I don't tell her too much. It's cool that she's happy to talk about things like that. It was good being able to say things without her thinking that I'm soft or weird.

I walk along Exminster Avenue with my head down. I glance up at number fifteen, which looks just the same as always. I turn on to my road and get my keys out of my pocket as I walk up to my house.

Inside, I go into the living room and flop down into the sofa. Mikey's already in there, lying on the floor flicking through a dumb sci-fi magazine. He looks up at me.

'Where have you been?'

I grab the remote control and switch the TV on. 'Nowhere,' I say. 'What's it to you?'

Mikey sits up and smirks. 'Nothing,' he says. 'It's just that the police were here earlier and they wanted to know where you were.'

I freeze. 'What?'

'The police,' he says, cool as you like. 'They wanted to talk to you.'

I don't say anything. A million thoughts flash through my mind at once. I wonder whether they've been to Jake or Badger or Drac's houses. Jesus. My heart thumps. I try and stay as calm as I can.

'What for?' I say. 'Did they say why?'

Mikey shakes his head. 'Not really. They just said you were in big trouble.'

I stare back at him. He holds my gaze. And then all of a sudden he smirks and has to look away. He starts laughing, rolling around on the floor.

'What are you doing?' I say.

Mikey stops for a second and looks at me. 'You

241

really are stupid,' he says. 'You must have one hell of a guilty conscience if you believed me.'

I feel confused. It takes a few seconds for it to sink in. He's lying. He made it up. There was no visit from the police. I don't know whether to feel embarrassed or relieved or what. I shake my head.

'You're a sad case, Mikey,' I say. I look away from him and stare at the TV.

'You're the sad case who fell for it,' Mikey says. 'You know, if you're feeling that guilty, maybe you should hand yourself into the police. Maybe they'll go easy on you if you fess up.'

Summer

I'm still in my dressing gown, drinking a glass of juice at the kitchen table, when the front door opens and a couple of seconds later Mum comes in. She puts her shopping down.

'Morning, Summer,' she says and plants a kiss on my cheek. She goes over to the sink and fills the kettle.

'You been to the shops?' I ask, just for something to say.

'Yes.' Mum switches the kettle on and then unpacks the shopping from the bags. 'I looked in on Harry as well.'

I nod. 'Was he OK?'

Mum opens the fridge and puts some food away. 'Yes. I think so,' she says. She turns and stares into space as though she's thinking about it. 'He's not quite himself though, is he?'

I shake my head. 'Not really.'

Neither of us speaks for a while as Mum finishes unpacking the shopping. The kettle boils and she makes a herbal tea. While she's doing that, I finish my juice and think about whether I should have breakfast or just go straight for lunch.

When she's finished, Mum sits at the table. She looks at the front page of the newspaper and snorts at the headline. 'Stupid politicians!' she says.

'Mum,' I say, 'did Grandad mention the tapes to you?'

Mum looks at me, an expression on her face that I can't quite read. 'Not exactly,' she says. 'I got the feeling he wished he'd never said anything about them.'

'Did you ask him about them, then?'

Mum nods. She takes a sip of her tea.

'And?'

She shrugs. 'Like I said, he didn't want to talk about them.'

'So that was it?'

'I asked him why they'd never told me about the tapes,' she says, cradling her cup. 'He said he didn't know, but that they were your nan's tapes anyway, not his, so it wasn't really up to him. I asked him if we could borrow them.'

'And?'

'He said no,' Mum says. She takes another sip of her tea. 'But I insisted. And he gave in eventually.'

'Really? How did you do that?'

Mum shrugs again. 'Well, I pointed out that if there was anything about your dad on there, then we had a right to hear it.'

'And he agreed?'

'Sort of,' Mum says.

'Where are they, then?' I ask.

Mum looks into one of the jute bags on the table. She brings out two dusty cassette tapes and places them on the table.

I pick one of them up and look at it. The tape is labelled with the date and the name of the spiritualist, *Mrs Pam Davies*, and underneath that, *New Malden*. All in green ink, in Nan's capital letters. She wrote everything in capital letters. I open the box and take the cassette out. Seeing Nan's handwriting makes me think of her. I get a slight pang as it dawns on me once more that I'll never see her again. I imagine her at her dining-room table, writing the labels.

I look at Mum. She's staring at the tapes, still cradling her cup of tea.

'Can we play them?'

She looks up at me. I can tell she's thinking about it. She sighs. 'I don't know about that, Summer.'

I sigh. 'Why not?'

Mum takes a sip of her tea. 'I don't know what's on them yet.'

I roll my eyes. 'Well, that's sort of the point of listening to them.'

'That's not what I meant.'

I raise an eyebrow at her. I'm being patronised and I don't like it.

'What I mean is, I don't know what's on the tapes yet. And like your grandad said, it didn't help your nan to deal with it any better.'

'But –'

'I think maybe I should listen to them first, at least one of them, before you do.'

I snort indignantly.

Mum puts her hand on mine. 'I just don't want you to hear something that's going to upset you.'

I pull my hand from underneath Mum's. 'You are joking, aren't you?' I say, my voice raised, just about managing to stop myself from shouting.

Mum looks back at me, saying nothing.

'Mum, I'm sixteen! I could move out of here if I wanted. I could go and get a job. I could get married. I could even have a baby!'

Mum sighs again. 'I know, Summer. That doesn't

stop me from wanting to protect you though, from not wanting you to hear things that are going to upset you.'

I feel like I'm gonna explode. I can't believe she's treating me like this. Like a kid. I tut. I try and think before I say something I'm gonna regret. 'So it's OK if you hear it and get upset? But not if I do?'

Mum shifts in her seat. She looks away from me for a second. 'No, I don't mean that. I'm just –'

'You're treating me like a baby, that's what you're doing,' I say. 'I have just as much right as you to listen to those tapes. He was *my* dad. The tapes belonged to *my* nan.'

'But, Summer –'

'You even said it yourself, when Grandad wouldn't let you have the tapes – Dad was related to us, so we should be able to hear them. You *and* me.'

Mum makes a face and sighs. She's thinking hard. But she doesn't say anything for ages.

'Please.'

Silence. It seems to go on for ever until, finally, she says, 'OK.'

I jump up from my seat and kiss her on the cheek.

'On the condition that we listen to one together and then I make the decision whether you should hear the other. OK?'

I smile at her. 'Deal.'

Johnny

I woke up this morning at exactly the same time as usual. I'd been dreaming about the Poisoned Dwarf again. We were in the graveyard. At least, I was. I was sitting on the bench, just about to kiss Summer, when the Poisoned Dwarf rose from a grave and went for me.

I had the same feeling as always, like I wasn't alone in my room, but there was no one around. I was covered in sweat, but my room was freezing cold and the window was wide open. I put the light on and when my heart had slowed down a little and I'd managed to get the image of the Poisoned Dwarf's corpse out of my mind, I just sat there for ages in my bed. To begin with, I stared into space as thoughts flew through my brain. Thoughts of the Poisoned Dwarf . . . Summer . . . Mikey and what he might know. But the thoughts flew so fast through my mind that I struggled to get a hold on any of them.

I was awake for hours. Gradually my thoughts stopped rushing and I could grab on to one thing and try and think it through. Not that I actually worked anything out. I mean, even when I managed to slow my thoughts, I was still confused.

I don't know what Mikey knows – whether he knows as much as he makes out, or if he's just trying to wind me up. And I don't know much about Summer. I know I like her and I think she likes me. As for the Poisoned Dwarf . . . Well, I know that I feel guilty as hell. I know that I wish I had a time machine so I could go back and make sure that none of it ever happened. But that doesn't help. There is no way to make it right. I doubt I'll ever stop feeling the way I do now. I can't imagine a time when I'll feel anything other than overwhelming guilt. And that scares me.

Eventually the thoughts left my brain. I sat in bed, eyes wide open. And I did nothing but look and listen. At first it seemed like the house was silent, but the more I listened, the more I could hear. A clock ticking from downstairs that seemed to be telling me with every tick and tock that another second had passed and I was still wide awake. Sleep sounds came from my parents' and Mikey's rooms. Snores. Groans. The whoosh of cars out on the main road. The creaks of the house. I listened right through till I heard the electric buzz of a milk float coming down the road. I looked at the clock then. It was after five o'clock. I put out my light and went to sleep.

And I've only just woken up. It's after midday. I can see from the way that the sun is pouring light upon the closed curtains that it's a hot, sunny day out there. But it's one that I'm not sure I want to be a part of. I feel like hiding away from the world.

Summer

'There,' Mum says as she finishes setting up her old cassette deck. She turns to me and smiles. 'Now, are you sure you want to listen to this? It might be upsetting . . .'

'Positive,' I say, even though I feel totally nervous about what I'm gonna hear.

Mum presses play and then comes and sits on the sofa beside me, pulling a cushion up from behind her back and putting it on her lap.

My heartbeat quickens as the tape starts running – silence for a few seconds till there's a loud clunking noise that makes me jump. Two voices start talking to each other, too muffled to work out what they're saying. I can't even work out whether the voices are male or female.

Then slowly the voices get clearer and I hear Nan. All she says is, 'Yes, that's right.' She says it in a nervous voice. She sounds like she's trying to sound posh – the same voice she always used for answering the phone. A shiver runs down my spine.

The tape goes quiet again. No voices. Just hissing and crackling.

'OK, Jean. Now I'm going to try and contact the spirit world,' says a voice. The medium, I s'pose. She has the kind of voice that should be working in customer service.

The noise of someone moving things around in the background fills the air. I try and work out what's going on – it sounds like things being arranged on a table.

'Jean, when I make contact with a spirit, I'll go into a trance to allow the spirit to talk through me.'

'OK.'

'You'll be perfectly safe.'

The tape hisses.

'Are you happy to start, Jean?'

'Yes,' Nan says. Her voice still sounds weird and nervous. She's lost the false poshness in her voice now.

There's more silence.

And then, in this spooky voice that I think is probably staged, the medium says, 'Spirit world, I have Jean Hornby here with me.'

Silence. I feel almost sick with nerves. Mum grabs hold of my hand.

'Is there anybody there that has a message for her?'

No one says anything for what seems like ages. The tape hisses and crackles.

'Hello? Is that you, Mum?' a voice says. It sounds weird, like the medium is putting on a voice.

'Yes,' Nan says. She sounds completely terrified. 'Who's there?'

'James,' the voice says. I look at Mum. She smiles at me, but I feel terrified. She squeezes my hand.

'Oh, James,' Nan says. She sounds like she's about to cry. 'We miss you. How are you?'

No one speaks. I hear a few clunks and I wonder what they are; whether things are moving around the table on their own like in a horror movie, or whether someone's just picking something up and putting it down.

'Tell everyone I miss them,' the voice says. Dad. The medium. A spirit. It's confusing.

'I will,' Nan says. And I'm sure that she's crying now. She sounds almost too upset, too scared to talk. She sounds small and meek and hesitant.

There's a silence. Just the tape noises.

But then the voice cuts in again. 'I never really told you I love you.'

I hear Nan sniff. She doesn't say anything for ages. 'I love you too,' she says eventually. 'We argued too much. I wish I could go back and change it.'

A pause. The tape clicks as it plays.

'Me too,' the voice says. 'We parted on bad terms. That was wrong.'

There's a long silence. I look at Mum. She raises her eyebrows.

'How's the baby?' the voice says.

It takes me a couple of seconds to realise which baby they mean. A lump appears in my throat. He must mean me. He must do. When this tape was made, I was a baby. He can't mean anyone else.

'Summer?' Nan says. 'She's lovely. She's a ray of sunshine. She's just like you were as a baby.'

I want to cry. I don't know what to think. Mum squeezes my hand again. I look over at her. She has tears in the corners of her eyes. She dabs them away with her free hand.

'Sky's growing up fast,' Nan says. She still sounds nervous, like she's struggling to keep it together. 'She's a little lady. You'd be proud of her.'

More silence. Mum takes her hand away to dry her eyes.

'I'm sorry I'm not there for you all,' Dad says. 'I was selfish.'

And then it's silent.

'What do you mean? What happened that day, James?' Nan says. She sounds more hesitant, more nervous than ever. 'The accident?'

Silence. It stretches on for ages. My heart thumps. My palms are sweaty. Beside me Mum fidgets and I sense that she's not sure whether I should hear this.

'Accident?' Dad says.

There's a stunned silence on the tape and in our front room. I look at Mum. She avoids my eyes.

'James? *James?*'

'I'm sorry, Jean,' the medium says. 'I think we've lost James now.'

'Oh,' Nan says. She sounds shocked, deflated, empty. 'Can't you get him back? I want to know what he meant . . .'

There's no answer from the medium. The tape hisses for a little longer before there's a loud clunking noise, like someone switching the microphone off. Mum and me both sit there and listen for a couple of seconds, not sure whether it's the end of the recording or not. Mum looks shocked. The tears are gone from her eyes. She looks like she wasn't expecting that, like she doesn't know how to deal with it. Which is just how I'm feeling.

'Well . . .' she says. Then she lets out a long, slow breath. 'I think that's your lot.' Her expression is somewhere between a smile and a grimace, confused.

I sit on the sofa and try to take it all in. That wasn't what I was expecting at all. I want to say something to Mum, but I don't know what.

Mum shifts in her seat. I keep hoping that she's gonna say something, but she doesn't either. Instead she goes over to the tape deck and switches it off, takes the tape out. She walks to the coffee table and puts the cassette back in its box.

'It was weird hearing Nan's voice again,' I say, because I can't bear the silence any more.

Mum smiles sadly. She comes and sits on the sofa. 'Yes. That was quite nice, wasn't it?'

'Kind of. It was horrible in a way as well,' I say. 'She sounded desperate.'

Mum nods. 'You have to remember that she was devastated when your dad died. I mean, we all were. It was so sudden. But Jean took it really badly. She kept looking for a reason. And the truth is that there is no reason for what happened. It was just bad luck, bad timing.'

'What did he mean when he said, "Accident?" like that though?' I say.

Mum doesn't say anything. She shrugs.

'Do you think he meant it wasn't actually an accident?'

Mum looks at me. 'I don't think it was your dad talking, Summer. Don't read too much into it.'

'But if it wasn't Dad's spirit talking, how did it know all the other stuff? About me and Sky?'

Mum sighs. 'I'm sure your nan would have told the medium that sort of thing before she started the session. The medium was just telling her what she wanted to hear. Besides, even if that was your dad's spirit on the tape, there was an inquest at the time. It was an unfortunate accident, nothing more sinister than that.'

Anger wells up in me. 'How can you say that? It *was* Dad's spirit.'

'Listen, Summer. All I'm saying is that a lot of people think that mediums just use the information they've already been given to make it seem like a spirit is telling them something. What you heard probably had nothing to do with your dad.'

I feel so annoyed at her. And what makes it more annoying is that she could be right. I just don't know what to think.

Johnny

I feel kind of nervous about this. The fact that it's a date makes me nervous enough to start with, but more than that I'm worried about coming here, to the spiritualist church. What if the Poisoned Dwarf's spirit turns up? I nearly texted Summer to change our plans. Nearly. But I didn't, so here I am – clammy hands and all – leaning against the wall in front of the church.

I'm not gonna say anything at all in there. Even if a spirit shows up asking for Johnny, I'll ignore it. That way I can't give anything away. And if Summer asks why I said nothing, I'll just pretend I was too scared to answer. No one's gonna make me say anything I don't want to.

I've been here ten minutes already waiting for

Summer. My fault mainly, because I was early, but I see her hurrying down the street towards me.

'Hey, Johnny,' she says. She smiles and then as she gets close, she leans in and hugs me and gives me a kiss that I wasn't expecting on the side of my face. 'You been here long?'

I shake my head. 'Just got here.'

Summer stands and looks at the church, and so do I. It doesn't look much like a church, more like a factory or an office or something. You wouldn't even know it was a church if it wasn't for the tiny sign stuck on the building saying, *Cottenham Spiritualist Church*, and a poster advertising tonight.

*The world famous Donald Howard, clairvoyant
and psychic consultant, exemplifies life after death,
communicates with loved ones and demonstrates
his psychic gift*

The first Tuesday of every month at 7.30 p.m.

Cottenham Spiritualist Church

Just reading the sign and seeing the picture of Donald Howard is enough to give me the creeps. He looks really smarmy and weird, like the people on TV that do this kind of stuff. He has a bald head, a long, white, braided goatee beard and scarily piercing ice-blue eyes. They must be contact lenses.

'Shall we go in, then?' Summer says.

Inside, there are ten or so rows of plastic chairs lined up in front of a small stage. There's a microphone set up on stage and a small table with a tablecloth, some flowers and a crucifix on it. I guess that must be the altar. Above all this there's a weird stained-glass window that looks like it's made from double glazing.

Summer and I sit in the back row. Maybe from here I can just watch this weirdness, take it all in and not be noticed.

Summer puts her hand on my arm. 'I feel nervous,' she says. 'Do you?'

I nod.

'I've never done anything like this before.'

'Me neither,' I say. 'I hope they don't call up anyone I know.'

Summer laughs. 'I hope they do call up someone I know. That's the whole point!'

The seats around us start to fill up. We say nothing. I feel petrified. This was a bad idea. I think about making an excuse and going home. Then the crowd, or the congregation or whatever you call it, applauds as the guy from the poster, Donald Howard, walks up on to the stage. He's tanned and dressed in a sharp, shiny suit but looks way older and wrinklier than on the poster. He smiles and waves at the audience and then takes the microphone from the stand.

'Thank you,' he says, and then he holds his arms out wide as though he's embracing the whole congregation. 'Welcome to Cottenham Spiritualist Church. My name is Donald Howard. Tonight we will make contact with the deceased.'

He takes a few steps around the stage as the audience murmurs excitedly. He doesn't look at the audience though. He's concentrating really hard on something, like he's trying to psych himself up. Maybe he's started contacting the dead already. Who knows?

I look across at Summer, who smiles slightly. She seems nervous and excited.

Donald stops still in the middle of the stage. 'It's time to begin,' he says. Suddenly the expression on his face changes to deadly serious. He looks upwards, as though to the spirit world. 'OK,' he goes on, 'I have a connection . . .'

The hall goes silent. All I can hear for a second is my own heart thumping. Donald closes his eyes, holds his hands out and then stands absolutely still. After half a minute he starts moving again. He talks quietly, so I can't hear what he's saying. I think he's talking to a spirit or something.

Eventually he looks back at the congregation. 'I have

someone who only wants to identify themselves as G,' he says, staring at the audience.

There's a murmur of excitement as people talk to each other.

'G is a woman,' Donald says. He looks into the audience again.

He's silent and still for a while. He concentrates. He talks to the spirit so that no one else can make out what he's saying.

'G is looking for her great-niece,' he says. 'Is it a name beginning with T? Yes?'

Loads of people shake their heads and look at one another. I look at Summer. She raises her eyebrows and smiles. And then someone in the middle of the audience nervously puts her hand up.

Donald notices her almost right away. 'Do you think you know G, darling?'

The lady in the audience nods. She goes bright red. She looks nervous as anything.

Donald nods his head, like he knew the spirit was for her all along. He paces around the stage for a bit, then stops and swivels on his heels. He looks at the lady. 'What's your name, love?' he asks.

'Tina,' she says quietly.

'Tina.' He smiles at her. 'OK, now. Spirit, have you got a message you'd like me to pass to Tina this evening?' Donald nods his head as he concentrates, listening to the spirit in his head or whatever it is he's doing. 'Right,' he says, focusing on Tina. 'Now, G says there was something to do with a barrier. Does that mean anything to you?'

Tina looks at the woman who's sitting next to her. She looks shocked. She says something that I can't hear and nods at Donald, looking terrified. 'A wall,' she says. 'Is she talking about the wall?'

Donald takes his time and then nods. 'Tina, was there something to do with a dispute about the wall? I'm getting the sense of a dispute here.'

Tina's face falls. 'Yes,' she says. She looks at her friend again and shakes her head in disbelief.

Donald takes a deep breath and nods. 'Now, G wants you to know that whatever happened, no one was to blame. She says it's all forgotten and forgiven. Everyone needs to move on.'

Tina stares at Donald, looking like she's about to cry.

'She wants you all – the whole family – to know that she loves you very much. Don't ever forget that, she says. OK, Tina?'

Tina nods. She wipes tears from her cheeks and tries to smile. Her friend puts her arms round her.

Donald moves off around the stage. He stops still after a few seconds and does the whole thing again – closes his eyes, holds his hands out, channels a spirit.

'I have another spirit who has a message,' he says. He opens his eyes, looks over the audience and smiles. 'I have another lady here . . .'

The audience all stare back at him expectantly, waiting for more information. Donald stands there, smiling, his head slightly cocked as though he's listening to the spirit.

'OK,' he says, looking directly into the audience now. 'The spirit is nervous. She's not long passed into the spirit world.'

My insides lurch at the words. What if it's her? It could be. What if she really is haunting me? I shrink down in my seat. I look away from Donald, at my feet.

'She's reluctant to say too much, but I'm definitely getting a letter from her. The letter J.' He closes his eyes again, holds his hands out, concentrates. 'Is the J part of a name?' He waits a few seconds, his eyes still closed. And then he nods. Slowly, he opens his eyes and looks out across the audience. 'Her name begins with a J.'

A few people in the audience whisper to each other. That makes me feel slightly better. Maybe I'm being paranoid. The spirit is for someone else. It has to be. But if that's the case, why do I feel so nervous? I can't even bring myself to look at Summer. I can sense her sitting forward in her seat. I just know that if she looks at me, she'll sense my nervousness and she'll see right

264

through me. She'll know my secret. And she'll hate me for it. *I* hate me for it. So I alternate my gaze between my feet and Donald.

'I'm also getting the name of a place,' Donald says, eyes closed in concentration. 'Exminster.'

My heart feels like it stops beating. Exminster? This can't be a coincidence. Oh my God. I take a deep breath and try not to panic, try and stay as still as I can and avoid looking at anyone.

'OK. J wasn't sure about coming through tonight, but she has a message that she wants to pass on. It concerns a young man. Is it? Or for . . . ?' He pauses.

I gulp. My temples pulse inside my ribcage. I'm not being paranoid. This *is* about me. I know it. I close my eyes for a second. I can't draw attention to myself. I have to stay calm and pretend that this spirit is nothing to do with me. If I manage to ride this out no one will know.

'Now this might be quite shocking for someone, so be prepared, please,' Donald says. 'J wants someone to know that what happened wasn't natural. It wasn't an accident. There was foul play.'

There's a gasp in the audience. My heart practically jumps out of my mouth. Jesus. This has to be the Poisoned Dwarf. She has to be talking about what happened outside the shops. I feel Summer's hand on my arm, gripping tightly, but I just ignore her.

'She wants someone to put it right. To put right what was done.'

I shrink even further down in my seat. I want to get out of here this very second. I sit and stare at the back of the chair in front of me, pretend this is all happening to someone else.

'And she's gone,' Donald says.

I look up, relieved.

'I'm sorry about that,' Donald says. 'There was obviously some real hurt there, some raw wounds. J didn't want us to get too close.'

And that's it. Donald is off around the stage again, channelling the spirits, raking over the coals of someone else's life. But I can't concentrate on anything apart from what's just happened. J must be Jean. That was the name in the paper, the name spelled out in flowers by the side of the coffin. She must have sensed I was here tonight. And if she can tell where I am, then it must be her presence I've been feeling in my room. I shiver.

A hand on my arm makes me jump. I turn. It's only Summer.

'You OK?' she mouths.

I nod my head and try to force a smile. I need to snap out of this. 'Fine,' I say. 'You?'

She makes a face like she's not quite sure. 'Yeah, I think.'

Summer

When it's all over, Johnny and me walk out of the hall. Around us most people seem to be chatting excitedly about the spirits the guy just got in touch with. Me and Johnny are silent though. I'm still taking it all in. I feel like I'm in shock. I keep thinking about J, wondering whether it was Nan or not. Everything she said seemed to fit. She could have been trying to tell me something about Dad. It fits with what I heard on the tape.

When we're out in the little tarmac car park in front of the church, Johnny and I stop and look at each other. For an awkward moment neither of us speaks. I decide I have to say something even though I don't really feel like talking right now.

'Did you enjoy it?' I say.

Johnny, hands in his jeans pockets, shifts around uncomfortably, kicking at the tarmac with the soles of his trainers. 'Yeah,' he says. But he doesn't sound convinced. 'How about you?'

I shrug. I can't make my mind up. I feel kind of freaked out by it. 'Yeah,' I say. 'It was a bit weird though, wasn't it?'

He nods. He doesn't look at me. And I start wondering whether this was such a bright idea. Maybe I should have come here on my own. Maybe I shouldn't have invited Johnny. I've probably put him off me for good. He must think I'm completely mad by now. First date we go to a graveyard, and second date we go to a spiritualist church. I have to try and make this all a bit more normal. So I put my arm in his and we start walking.

'Do you think any of the spirits were there for you?' I ask as we walk out of the car park and on to the street.

Johnny immediately shakes his head.

'So your ghost didn't turn up with a message?'

Johnny turns and looks at me. He seems sort of startled. His eyes search my face. 'No.'

We walk on a few paces in silence. And I'm convinced I've messed things up. I've put out whatever spark we had. Even his arm inside mine feels uncomfortable, like he'd move it in a second if he wasn't so polite.

'Are you all right, Johnny?'

He nods his head slowly. 'Yeah, why?'

'You're not acting like yourself.'

He stops walking and looks at me. 'Sorry. I'm just thinking. It was weird in there, that's all – hearing what the spirits were saying and stuff. I'll snap out of it.' He smiles. 'Sorry, I didn't even ask you whether you think you heard from your dad?'

'No. I think I might have heard from my nan though,' I say. We start walking again.

'Really? Why didn't you say something to the medium?'

I shrug. 'I don't know. I was too scared, I s'pose. Besides, my nan didn't seem to want to talk much. She seemed as scared as I was.'

'So did she say anything important?'

We stop cos we're at my bus stop. We stand and face each other. I don't really want to go into what Nan said. I don't even know for sure what it means. It was confusing.

'I'm not sure,' I say. 'It didn't really make that much sense.'

We stand and look at each other. Johnny steps forward and puts his arms around me. And I feel so relieved – he can't think I'm a freak if he wants to be close to me.

'I'm sorry I brought you to a spiritualist church,' I say. 'Maybe it wasn't such a great place for a date!'

Johnny doesn't say anything, just looks into my eyes.

'We'll go somewhere more normal next time,' I say. 'I promise. You can choose.'

'That's OK,' he says. 'I don't mind as long as I get to see you again.'

I smile. 'Of course.'

He smiles back and looks deep into my eyes. And before I've even thought about what's happening we're kissing.

Johnny

I don't feel like sleeping in the slightest. I'm tired, sure. After being woken up every night for the last God knows how long, I'm dead on my feet half the time. But I'm too wired to sleep. My mind's buzzing.

So here I am, sitting on my bed, still in my clothes, staring into space, trying to catch hold of my thoughts as they race through my mind. Thoughts about Summer. About the kiss. About how right it felt. About the surge of energy I felt flow between us as we touched.

I've been thinking about what happened with the Poisoned Dwarf as well and what Mikey might know about it. The same thoughts as always. The same old questions. Still no answers.

The clock on my bedside table shows the time 12.14 a.m. I sigh. I'd love to be able to lie down, shut my eyes and lose myself in sleep. I'd like to fall into a deep, dreamless sleep and stay there for a long time. A week. A month. A year. And when I wake up, everything would be normal again. All the stuff with the Poisoned Dwarf would just have been a dream. I'd be back to being me. Johnny. Carefree. Normal. I'd get up and the world would be a bright and welcoming place, full of hope. I'd call Summer up and we'd get to know each other some more. We'd spend what's left of the summer together, without a care in the world, and who knows what might happen.

But it's not gonna happen. If I lay my head on the pillow right now, I know that my mind would still be buzzing. I wouldn't escape all these thoughts. They wouldn't just float away. Besides, even if I do fall asleep, I know for sure what's gonna happen when the clock shows 2.43 a.m. I'll be woken. And I won't be alone. The Poisoned Dwarf's ghost will be here, watching me.

And then it occurs to me. I make a decision. I'm gonna stay awake. I'm just gonna sit here and wait till 2.43 a.m. Because maybe that way I can see what really happens at 2.43 a.m. in my room, why I keep waking up. Maybe I can prove to myself that I'm not going mad, that I'm not imagining it all. Maybe I can take whoever it is by surprise.

Summer

I should be at home. I got on the bus in the right direction, even pressed the button when we got near my stop. But I didn't get off. Instead I watched as we passed the turning to our flat. I didn't know where I was going, but I just felt like I couldn't go home. I had too much on my mind.

I chose a stop at random to get off and then I started walking around the streets with my earphones in. Thinking.

I ended up here. On a bench. I don't know where I am exactly. Somewhere between Tooting and Streatham. Mum texted me a while back, asking where I was and when I'd be home, so I made up a white lie to keep her off my back. I'll go home when I'm ready. I have some thinking to do. About Johnny and the kiss, what happened at the church, the creepy medium guy, the spirits. My nan and what she said. Was she trying to say that Dad's death wasn't an accident? Foul play, she said.

It seems to tie up with what Dad said to Nan on the tape. Which makes me think I need to listen to the other tape. There could be more on there that would explain this. And if it's true, it would kind of account for why Grandad didn't want us to hear them. Maybe Nan wants me to listen to it though. Maybe she wants me to know what happened. That's why she turned up at the church.

I try and get straight in my mind what I know about Dad's death. I've always been told he died in a road accident. Dad was driving to work and his car was hit by a van. He got rushed to hospital, but he died. I don't know all the horrible graphic details of what happened to him. Nobody ever told me and I never asked. That's all I've ever known and I've never questioned it before. Why would I?

Perhaps I'm reading too much into it. Maybe all Dad and Nan meant was that dying in a road accident – having your life smashed out of you by a van – isn't natural. That could be all they meant. Simple as that. But then why would Nan's spirit seek me out to tell me that? I know all that stuff anyway.

I hear a noise. I look up and see someone shuffling along the pavement towards me. A man. I watch him. He looks like he's struggling to stay upright. He's scruffy. His hair's matted. His clothes are torn and stained. And as he gets closer, I can smell that he hasn't washed in a long while. He notices the bench and shuffles towards it. And then he notices me. He stops where he is, unsteady. He points a finger at me.

'Why are you following me?' he says. His voice sounds rough and drunk and mad and angry.

I freeze. I panic. My insides tie themselves in knots.

'What do you flaming well want with me?' he shouts.

I look away from him. I don't know what to do. I don't feel safe here.

'I know who you are!' he mutters. 'You're a spy.'

I get up from the bench and edge away from him. He watches me as I go. I keep looking back over my shoulder as I head across the road towards a bus stop.

'Spy!' he shouts at me. 'I know who sent you. I'll get you!'

Johnny

I hear the message tone on my phone. It wakes me up. I open my eyes and sit up in bed. The lights are still on. I'm lying on top of my duvet, still in my clothes. And yet again the window is wide open and I'm drenched in sweat. And there's a presence. Someone else *is* here, watching me. A spirit. The spirit. The Poisoned Dwarf. The previous evening floods back into my mind. The spiritualist church. I remember Donald Howard, the way he walked, the look of concentration on his face as he tried to commune with a spirit and the words he spoke as he communed with J: 'J wants someone to know that what happened wasn't natural. It wasn't an accident.

There was foul play. She wants someone to put it right.'

I lean over and grab my mobile from the bedside table, noticing the time as I do. *The* time. 2.43 a.m. Why is someone texting me at this time of night? I look at my phone. *1 new message*, it says, from *The Poisoned Dwarf*. I open it and read it.

It was you.

I stare at the message. I rub my eyes to make sure that I'm seeing it right. Who sent me this? It can't have been the Poisoned Dwarf. She's dead. Someone else must know what happened, but who?

I put my head in my hands. This is bad. This is very bad. I try and think things through. The only people who know what happened – who know what really happened – are me, Drac, Jake and Badger, and none of them would've sent this message. Besides, I have all their numbers and they would have come up when I received the message. There's Mikey, of course. He keeps hinting he knows what happened, but I have his mobile number on my phone. He could've used one of his mate's phones to text me, but that's hardly likely at this time of night. I have no idea who else it could be. None. If only I'd managed to stay awake maybe I'd have seen something. I feel scared, like I'm being watched, like I'm not alone.

'Hello?' I say. 'Who are you?'

There's no answer. My room is silent. The curtains flap in the breeze. Some papers flutter down from my table and land on the floor.

I get up from my bed. I go over to the window and close it. I need to get out of here and I also need to take a leak. So I go out of my room, across the landing and into the bathroom. I close my eyes as I do my business.

I don't want to feel like this any more. I want to feel normal. I want to sleep through the night. I want to feel like I'm alone when I'm on my own. This is driving me insane. And there's nothing I can do about it.

I finish. I flush the toilet and go over to the mirror to see how much of a wreck I am. As I look up at the mirror, my heartbeat quickens again. There's a patch of condensation on it. Written there in capital letters is one word. *GUILTY*. The letters look shaky, like they were written by someone old, someone desperate.

As I stare at the words, the condensation clears. The message disappears. I stare at the mirror. I feel a chill. I look behind me. There's no one there. Who is doing this? Someone must have been here just now. There's no other explanation.

Maybe I am mad. Maybe I'm creating all of this stuff in my imagination to punish myself. I step towards the mirror and breathe on it. Condensation forms around the word. *GUILTY*. It's definitely there.

I hear a noise. Scuttling. I look around me again, but the room is empty. No one is here. And the noise has stopped.

I rub my head. I don't understand this. I take a deep breath. I feel like crying. This is too much. What is happening? What am I meant to do? I need to find who's doing this to me. I need to make them stop. There's only one place I can think of to start.

I step out on to the landing. I wait a couple of seconds and then walk towards Mikey's room. I reach out, put my hand on his door handle. I feel sick, paranoid, confused as hell. I close my eyes and brace myself. And then I turn the handle quietly. I push the door open. It makes a noise as it brushes over the carpet. The smell of Mikey's room hits my nostrils. Old socks. Mouldering food scraps. BO.

The room is gloomy. I step inside, trying to make out the dark piles of clothes and books and God knows what else that lie scattered across Mikey's floor. I can hear him from where I am, breathing heavily in his bed. As though he's asleep. As though he's pretending to sleep.

I creep over to his bed and then bend low so I'm at his head height. I pause for a second, try to figure out whether he's really asleep, whether it was him that came into my room and opened the window. Whether he sent the text. Whether he wrote *GUILTY* on the mirror. Whether this is a sick joke that he's playing. Even though that would make me angry, I hope to God it is. At least that would explain it. I could understand that. If it isn't, then . . . Well, I don't even want to think about what that means.

Mikey's face is turned away from me. He's breathing in deeply and breathing out with a kind of rasping sound. I can't tell if he's really asleep.

'Mikey,' I whisper. 'You little idiot. I know you're awake!'

There's no reply. His breathing doesn't alter at all.

'I know you're awake,' I say slightly louder. 'This isn't funny, you little idiot.'

Still he doesn't stir.

I reach out my hand and I touch his back, give him a push. This time his breathing changes. He mutters something under his breath. His breathing becomes shallower. Then he turns and opens his eyes. A look of sheer terror engulfs him. He jumps up in bed and pulls his covers around him.

'Johnny! What are you doing?' he shouts after a moment. 'You maniac!'

I stand up immediately. And I realise I have no idea what to say. I can't explain this away. What on earth *am* I doing?

'Why are you in my room?'

'I know it was you,' I say. 'I know what you did.'

281

He stares back at me, confused and scared. 'What are you on about?'

'My window,' I say. 'The text. The message on the mirror. I know it was you.'

He shakes his head, looking even more confused. I still can't tell whether it's real or an act.

'I know what you're up to,' I say.

He just stares at me.

I start backing away, out of his room, stumbling over the piles of rubbish on his floor. 'I'll get even,' I say. 'You wait.'

He shakes his head again, like he has no idea what I'm talking about. 'You've lost it. You need help, J. Seriously.'

I leave his room, shut the door behind me and then stand with my back against it and take a few deep breaths. I go to my room, to my bed. I try and work out whether Mikey could have done it. Now that I've been into his room and seen his reaction, I'm not sure it was him. He looked properly confused. I'm not sure he's capable of acting so convincingly.

I lie in bed and stare up at the ceiling. And I wonder why I'm the one that's being haunted. I wasn't the only one there that day. I wasn't the only one who shot at the Poisoned Dwarf. What about Jake and Badger and Drac? Why not them? I decide I have to see them. I have to see whether this is happening to them too.

Summer

Mum told me off when I got home last night, said she was worried sick. She went on and on and on at me. I didn't say a word. I knew that if I got into an argument I'd say too much. I'd tell her where I'd been and what I'd heard. So I said nothing. I stood and took it all till she went off to bed, shaking her head.

Then I went to my room and cried. I don't know what about exactly. I just felt confused and hurt. I felt strange. Yesterday was a weird day. Too much stuff happened. Good things. Bad things. Things I don't understand.

I thought about listening to Nan's other tape. I went through to the lounge to get it, but it wasn't there.

Neither of them were. That was probably for the best. I don't think I could have coped with anything else last night.

Instead I decided to try out a trick that Mum once taught me. She always says that when things are worrying you, when you have way too much on your mind, you should write it all down somewhere. It's supposed to calm you down, to clear your mind and help you sleep. I sat up in bed and wrote down everything I'd been thinking of in my diary: what the medium said, everything I knew about Nan, everything I knew about Dad and everything I felt about Johnny and me.

By the time I'd finished writing everything down, I was more confused than when I'd started. I didn't get the best night's sleep. Everything still swirled around my mind. This morning I'm no clearer either. Just more tired. But I want to find out more. I need to find out more.

Johnny

Something strange is happening to me. I know this for sure. It's about the only thing I do know for sure. When I woke up this morning and last night came flooding back into my mind, I grabbed my phone and looked at the message again to see if I could find some logical explanation for it. Only, the message wasn't there. I went through all the messages in my inbox and the one that I got at 2.43 a.m. wasn't there.

I went into the bathroom, locked the door behind me and breathed on the mirror. But that message wasn't there either – there was nothing on the mirror at all. And I started to wonder whether those things really happened. Maybe I imagined them as a punishment to myself.

I tried to avoid Mikey when I got downstairs, but he sought me out. He had a real go at me – laughed at me, called me mad. I didn't say anything, but I kind of agree with him. I definitely am losing my grip on what's real and what's not. I feel like when you step off a boat on to dry land and you still feel like you're swaying with the waves.

Which is why, instead of going home after footy coaching, I came straight here, to Badger's place. We're in his lounge. The curtains are still drawn. Badger is in his boxers and a T-shirt, like he's just got out of bed.

I look down at my feet and take a deep breath. I want to get all this off my chest, but I realise that it could sound a bit mental. I decide to come straight out with it.

'Badger, I think I'm being haunted,' I say.

He looks right back at me. 'Haunted?'

I nod. I look down at my feet. 'It sounds mad, I know . . .'

'What? By a ghost?'

I move the edge of my foot along the grain of the wood in the laminate floorboards. I shrug. 'Dunno. I don't know if it's a ghost or what. I just know there's something there.'

I hear Badger blow out a deep breath. 'Jeez, man. Are you serious?'

I look up at him, look him right in the eye. 'Totally.'

He shakes his head, not like he doesn't believe me, but like he wasn't expecting me to say something like this.

'It wakes me up at the same time every night,' I say. '2.43 a.m.'

Badger looks at me again. His face doesn't give much away.

'Lots of little weird things keep happening,' I say. 'Like every night I know I've closed and locked the window in my room, but I wake up shivering and the window is wide open.' As the words come out of my mouth, I realise it doesn't sound as weird in the cold light of day as it does at 2.43 in the morning. 'And every time it happens I get this feeling like I'm being watched or something, like there's someone there with me. So I look around and I switch the light on, but there's never anyone there.'

I pause. Badger doesn't say anything. I look up at him. I can't make out whether he believes me or not. I decide to carry on.

'Last night I woke up. Same time. 2.43 a.m. My phone had just beeped to say I had a message. It said it was from the Poisoned Dwarf. It said, "It was you."

When I checked my phone this morning the message wasn't there. And when I went into the bathroom last night, there was a message written in the condensation on the mirror: *GUILTY*. I tried to breathe on it this morning to see if it was still there, but nothing.'

Badger nods. He shifts on the sofa, ruffles his hair. 'That's weird.'

And we sit in silence. I fidget, praying that Badger doesn't just think I've lost the plot.

'You sure it wasn't Mikey messing about?' he says eventually.

I shrug. 'I checked his room. He was fast asleep. Besides, I have his number on my mobile. It would have come up as his.'

Badger sighs. He shakes his head. 'You can't think of anyone else that would have done it?'

I shake my head. 'No way. They would have had to have been in my house at 2.43 a.m. every night for about the last two weeks. Who would have done that?'

'Weird, man. You sure you didn't imagine it?'

I shrug. 'I'm positive. And that's not all,' I say. I take another deep breath. 'I went out with Summer last night to a spiritualist church.' I stop because I can see the look of disbelief on Badger's face.

'A church?'

I nod. 'Summer's dad died before she was born. She

wanted to see if he'd send her a message through the medium.'

'Right,' Badger says, raising his eyebrows. 'Of course. And did he?'

'No, but a spirit spoke to me.'

Badger looks freaked out.

'I'm serious,' I say. 'It was a woman. She said she was from Exminster. She said that her death wasn't an accident. That there was foul play. She said that she knew who did it and that it needed to be put right.'

Badger stares at me.

'It was the Poisoned Dwarf. It had to be.'

'But she's not from Exminster. She's from Raynes Park.'

'Exminster Avenue.'

Badger's face falls. 'Oh. Right.' Badger looks almost as scared and confused as I feel. 'You sure?'

I nod.

'Did you let on that the message was for you?'

'Of course I didn't. I'm not stupid.'

Badger shifts again on the sofa. He ruffles his hair with his hands. 'This is mad,' he says. 'Something weird is happening.'

I don't say anything. I just sit there and realise I don't feel relieved. I thought sharing it would make things better, but I feel empty and confused.

'You think it's the old lady that's been opening your window and waking you in the night?'

I shrug. 'It makes as much sense as anything does right now.'

'So what are you gonna do?'

'I have absolutely no idea. What can I do?'

Badger shrugs.

'There's literally nothing I can do.'

Badger stares into space and screws his face up like he's thinking of a solution, but I know it's useless. He won't think of anything and neither will I. What are you meant to do if you think you're being haunted? Call the Ghostbusters? Get an exorcist? See a shrink? If only it were that easy.

He gets up from the sofa, goes over to the window and stares out across the estate through the gap where the curtains don't quite meet in the middle. 'Jeez, J, man. I don't know what to say,' he says. He turns back and looks at me apologetically.

'Me neither,' I say, 'but I'll tell you one thing for sure – if it doesn't stop soon, I'm gonna lose it completely. I'll go mad.'

Badger walks across the lounge. He doesn't look at me. 'I'm gonna get a drink. You want one?'

I follow him through to the kitchen and sit down at the small table as he opens the fridge and gets a bottle of cola out. He grabs a couple of glasses and pours us both a drink. He sits down and we both stare at our glasses for a bit.

'I don't think you should say anything about this to anyone else,' Badger says. 'Just in case.'

'Course,' I say. 'You know what I find weirdest though?'

Badger takes a gulp of cola, looks at me and shakes his head. 'What?'

'Why me? Why am I the only one that's being haunted? I wasn't the only one that soaked her. It wasn't all my fault, so why do I end up being the one that's getting woken in the middle of the night? Why do I get the spooky handwritten message and the text from beyond the grave?'

Badger doesn't answer. He takes another gulp and puts his glass down. 'Maybe you are imagining it.'

'Thanks a lot, Badger. So you think I'm just going mad? Is that it?'

He shakes his head and frowns. 'No. I don't mean it like that. What I mean is, maybe it's guilt for, you know, for what we did. I've been feeling pretty bad about it too, man. I've had nightmares and stuff. Guilt's a weird thing, J. It can make your mind play tricks on you. Know what I mean?'

Badger gets up from the table, scraping the legs of his chair along the floor. He goes over to the sink and rinses out his glass.

'Maybe you need to forget about everything for a bit, J,' he says. 'We should go out and get wasted tonight.'

Getting so drunk that I literally can't worry about anything sounds perfect.

'Yeah, let's do it. I'll text Jake and Drac.'

Summer

So this is the list I came up with in the early hours of the morning. The things that I know for certain about my dad. No opinions. No hearsay. Just cold, hard facts. Things that can be proven. It's in no particular order, just the order that things came into my brain.

- His full name is (was) James Michael Hornby.
- He was born in Kingston Hospital on 4th March.
- He had two daughters. Sky and Summer. He only ever met one of them. That *one* wasn't me.
- He thought of himself as a bit of a hippy.
- He was a vegetarian.
- He owned a clapped-out Ford Fiesta.

- He had blond hair and deep blue eyes.
- He married my mum at the registry office in Tooting on 6th September.
- He worked for Surrey County Council in Kingston, in the department processing applications for student grants or something.
- He died of head injuries which he got in a road accident at 8.12 a.m. on 21st October.

That's about as much as I know. I know nothing of who my dad really is. Who he was. I never even met him. So that's what his life can be broken down to: ten emotion-less bullet points. That's all there is left of him. That and the things I have in my memory box. His copy of *The Catcher in the Rye*. His favourite records and CDs. Some photos. One of his diaries. A scarf. That is what I have.

When I look at the list, it brings everything into focus. I really don't know who he was. All I know is what other people have told me. The closest I ever got to him was hearing his voice when I was in Mum's womb. And it's not like I can remember that.

I have memories of him which in my mind are real, but they must be built up from what I've been told about him. Events that I've heard about a million times. I've imagined what he was like, what he'd be like now if he was alive. That's the nearest I'm ever gonna get to knowing who my dad was.

And everything that I do know about him, everything I've found out, I've had to scramble around to find out. But I'm gonna find out more. I have to. I'll ask Mum and Grandad and Sky. I'll listen to Nan's other tape. And I'll find out whether the message from the spirit was anything to do with Dad's death.

Seeing as the tape isn't in the lounge, I decide to explore another avenue first. The archives of the local newspaper. I'm gonna look them up to see if there's anything from when Dad died.

As soon as my computer has warmed up, I go to the local paper's website and I put the date of his death into the search engine. I scroll through the results. The top story is about some MP I've never heard of and there's a story about how some school has banned Christmas. Halfway down the list of stories, there it is: *MOTORIST KILLED BY VAN.*

My stomach knots as I read the headline. Underneath, there's another sentence:

A thirty-two-year-old man was killed when his Ford Fiesta collided with a van in rush-hour traffic on Plough Lane on Tuesday morning.

I stare at the screen, hand on the mouse. I feel scared all of a sudden. I'm not sure I want to do this. Maybe Mum's right. Maybe there are some things I'm best off not knowing. Maybe it's best to keep making my own fake memories of Dad based on all the bland, nice things people have told me. What am I gonna get out of reading this other than upset and hurt?

But I hear the voice of the medium somewhere in the back of my mind. I remember the message that the spirit delivered, about how there was foul play, and I realise I need to do this. I have to find out the details about how Dad died because that might be what the spirit was trying to tell me. So I close my eyes and I click the mouse.

When I open my eyes, the screen has updated. And there, in big letters, is the headline again. Down the page a little on the right-hand side is a picture. I cover my mouth as I look at it. A part of me wants to close the page straight away. But I can't. I stare at the picture instead. You can't see much, just a policewoman standing in front of some police tape, and behind that there's a police car and an ambulance parked next to a van and a crumpled car. Dad's crumpled car. The van that killed my dad. Fortunately you can't see anything else. You can't see Dad. There's no blood.

I don't want to, but I start crying. The tears appear slowly, but soon my eyes are so full of tears that I have to wipe them with my sleeve. My chin starts to wobble. I close my eyes and bury my head in my arms and sob. It's stupid, I know. It happened sixteen years ago.

There's nothing that can be done about it now. But seeing the picture just makes it seem real. It makes me wonder whether Dad was still there when the picture was taken, whether his body was lying on that bit of road just the other side of the crumpled car, or whether he'd been taken away already, whether he was already dead. I wonder whether Mum or Nan or Grandad or Sky even knew he was dead at the time the picture was taken. They were probably just carrying on in blissful ignorance as if everything was normal. I imagine the moment that someone had to break it to them. How on earth did they break it to Sky? What would she have been? Three? Four? How do you tell someone that young they'll never see their dad again?

The sobs recede a bit. I take some deep breaths, wipe my eyes on my sleeves and then after another minute or so, I sit up. This time I don't look at the picture, but I read what's written there:

A thirty-two-year-old man was killed when his Ford Fiesta collided with a van in rush-hour traffic on Plough Lane on Tuesday morning. The crash occurred at the junction with Durnsford Road at about 8.10 a.m. It is believed that the motorist, from Tooting, drove through a red light before being hit by the van. It is also believed that the driver may not have been wearing a seatbelt at the time of the collision.

A police spokesman said: 'The driver of the Ford Fiesta was treated by paramedics at the scene, but sadly died as a result of his injuries on his way to hospital.'

The junction was closed for five and a half hours while police launched an initial investigation into the cause of the crash.

Police would like to hear from anyone who witnessed the collision or was in the area at the time and may have seen the Fiesta or the van. Anyone who can help should contact Sergeant Alan Ryder at Wimbledon Police Station.

When I've finished reading, I stare at the screen. I don't know what to think. The story makes me feel empty. It makes me feel sad that they didn't even mention Dad's name, that it was a tiny news story one day and then fish-and-chip paper the next. I mean, it's not like I was expecting to read some long, involved story about him, about all his achievements and how he'll be sadly missed, but the whole story feels so matter of fact.

And there are things in the story that no one has ever mentioned to me. Like the red light. Nobody ever mentioned he jumped the lights. Or that he wasn't wearing a seatbelt.

I sit and stare at the screen for ages in disbelief. I'm not sure whether I feel better or worse or what.

Eventually I snap out of it though and search for the

298

following week's newspaper. Another list of stories appears on the screen. I scroll through them, scanning them for a mention of Dad or the van or a dead motorist or anything. But there's nothing. So I try the next week. And then the one after that. Nothing.

That's it. That's all Dad's life was worth in the paper. One story. A hundred or so words and a picture. Not even a mention of his name.

I switch my computer off and stare into space. I wonder why Dad would have skipped a red light. Why wasn't he wearing a seatbelt?

And now, in my mind, I have an image of a grey road, closed off, blue lights flashing, and my dad being cut from a car. Dying. Eyes glazing over. Every time I think of it, all I want to do is cry.

Johnny

It feels wrong, the four of us being here, not more than a couple of metres from where the Poisoned Dwarf had the heart attack that we caused. A shiver runs down my spine.

I wonder whether she can see me right now, whether her spirit's hovering around close by. I can imagine what's going through her mind if she is here, watching me hang around the place where it happened as though I don't have a care in the world, about to go and buy enough booze to get utterly wasted. She'd probably think I don't have even a trace of guilt, that I have no conscience whatsoever. She couldn't be more wrong. I get an urge to shout

out to her spirit to let her know I'm sorry, that I didn't mean to do it, that it was just a stupid joke. A joke that went totally, disastrously wrong. But I don't. I just turn on my heels and look at the spot where her car was parked.

'Oi, J! Cough up.'

I turn. 'What?'

Drac looks at me, raises an eyebrow. 'What's the matter with you?' he says. 'You look like you've seen a ghost.'

I sigh. 'Yeah,' I say, looking back at the parking space. 'I wonder why that is, Drac.'

'Jeez,' Jake says. 'You're not still on about that, are you?'

I don't answer. I just look at him, my eyebrows raised, thinking that he should be on about this as well, the idiot, because we gave someone a heart attack.

'You gotta let it go,' Jake says. 'There's nothing we can do about it, man. It was an accident, that's all. Get over it.'

I look at Badger. He raises his eyebrows – in solidarity, I think. At least *he* feels bad for what happened too.

'Look, are we gonna get wasted or what?' Drac says.

Everyone nods.

'Right, cough up, then. Fiver each.'

I reach in my pockets and take out my wallet, get five pound coins and give them to Drac.

He takes them and smiles. 'I'm getting cider, OK?'

We all nod.

Drac goes into the shop. There was no question of anyone else going in, seeing as he looks way older than the rest of us. Drac's the tallest and he's the only one that needs to shave more than once a week.

I nervously pace around on the pavement. I can feel someone watching me. The Poisoned Dwarf's spirit is here somewhere, I'm sure of it.

I look up at the building site across the road and wonder again whether anyone on site would have seen what happened. There's an enormous crane, for God's sake. They must be able to see everything that happens from up there.

I sense someone next to me. I look round. It's Badger, hands in pockets. He looks over at the building site too.

'You OK?' he says quietly.

I shake my head. 'Not really,' I say. 'I can't get it out of my head, not like Jake and Drac seem to have done.'

Badger kicks his heels on the pavement. 'Me neither.'

I turn and see Drac coming out of the shop. He swings the blue plastic bag in his hand as he walks over to us. I nudge Badger.

'I need to forget everything for a bit,' I say to him. 'I think I'm gonna get very, very drunk indeed.'

We head to the park. The warden has already locked up so we climb the fence and head across the grass to the crazy golf course. When we're all sitting around on the walls of the sixteenth hole, Drac reaches into the carrier bag and takes out a big bottle of cider.

He unscrews the lid and takes a swig and then passes it round. One by one we take it and drink. When it gets to me I gulp it down. Almost straight away I get a warm feeling in my guts. I can feel the kick of the alcohol. The edges of the world feel less sharp, fuzzier.

We sit there, not really talking about much. Drac and Jake are laughing and joking about something, but I don't particularly want to hear it at the moment. So I drink instead. Before I know it, the first bottle is empty and I can feel a warm glow inside me. My cheeks feel rosy. Everything feels a bit better. Drac raises his eyebrows at me in surprise. He reaches into the plastic bag and grabs another bottle.

My phone vibrates in my pocket. I take it out. It's a text from Summer.

Hey, Johnny. I'm feeling sad. U want 2 meet up? S x

I reply to her. **Sorry, can't right now – out with friends. 2moro?** I hesitate for ages, wondering whether it's a bit soft to put an 'x' at the end of the text or not. In the end the cider decides for me and I put one on and send it.

'Who you texting?' Drac says.

I shrug. I take a swig of cider. 'No one.'

'Oh yeah?' He taps his nose and winks. 'I know what you mean. Would it be a female no one by any chance?'

I put my phone back in my pocket. I think for a second about whether I should tell him or not, but my head is already fuzzy. Stuff it. I nod my head.

'Wahey!' Drac says, throwing his hands up in the air. He nudges Jake in the ribs, taking him by surprise and nearly knocking him off the wall. 'You hear that? Johnny's only gone and got himself a girlfriend!'

I sigh inwardly. I take another swig of cider. Badger catches my eye. He rolls his eyes and smiles.

'Is she fit, then?' Drac says.

How do I even answer a question like that? Say yes, and I'll get a load of hassle, get asked to describe her every physical detail – details that I don't even know yet. Say no, and I'll never hear the end of it. So I just nod my head and take another swig.

'Do we know her?' Jake asks.

I shrug my shoulders. 'Doubt it.'

'So where did you meet her?'

I try and think of an answer. Where did I meet her? 'On the bus.'

Jake smiles. 'When?'

'Ages ago. A month, maybe. You and Drac were acting like a pair of chimpanzees, throwing paper balls at her.'

Jake grins. 'Oh. I remember that. I remember her. She was all right, wasn't she? Grumpy, but fit.'

I drink some more and stare into space.

'But you didn't even talk to her or anything,' Drac says. 'Did you pull her using telepathy?'

Jake and Drac laugh.

I turn and look at him, raise one eyebrow, like I think he's being thick. 'I didn't speak to her on the bus, Drac, no.'

'So when?'

I stand up from the wall and throw my arms up in mock exasperation. 'Christ. What is this? The Spanish Inquisition? What else do you wanna know?'

Drac laughs. Then it's quiet for a second, before he says, 'What's the Spanish Inquisition?'

I shake my head. I pace around. I feel a bit unsteady. The cider is definitely taking effect. 'It's a saying,' I say. 'It's what people say when they're bored of some idiot asking them a million questions that are none of their business.'

Drac smiles. 'Oh,' he says. 'You should have just told me to shut my face in that case.'

I turn and give him a sarcastic smile. 'Shut your face!'

Drac laughs. He shuts up, but not for long. 'Have you . . . you know . . . yet?'

I laugh. You have to admire how thick his skin is even if he is an annoying idiot. 'Like I'd tell you!'

Jake smirks. 'So you have?'

I shake my head. 'No,' I say. 'And even if I had, it would be none of your business.'

They let the subject drop. I take a swig of cider and pass it on to Drac.

Drac looks at the bottle and then at me. He smiles. 'Slow down, J. You're gonna be wasted.'

I nod. 'That's the idea.'

Drac smiles. He holds up the bottle. 'Cheers, J,' he says. 'To your new girlfriend!'

Summer

Mum's on the sofa, holding a glass of wine, as I walk into the lounge. The TV's on, but she isn't really watching it. She looks up and smiles as I walk over to the sofa.

'You OK, Summer?'

I don't answer, I just shrug.

Mum leans forward and puts her glass of wine down on the coffee table. She turns so she's looking right at me. 'You're not OK, are you?'

I don't answer or even look at her.

She puts a hand on my shoulder. 'What's up?'

'I feel strange,' I say.

Mum nods. 'Strange in what way?'

'I don't know. About Dad mainly.'

Mum sighs. She picks up the remote and switches the TV off. She takes her wine from the table, takes a sip and puts it down again. 'Go on . . .'

'I just feel confused. I don't know what to think.'

Mum looks at me with a sympathetic expression on her face – though I can sense a bit of '*I told you so*' on it as well. 'What's got you thinking about this? This is because of the tapes, isn't it?'

I shrug. 'Partly, yeah.'

'I knew it wasn't a good idea to listen to the tape,' she says, almost like she's saying it to herself rather than me. 'Your grandad warned us. They've stirred up things that were probably best left alone.'

Neither of us says anything for a while. Mum takes a sip of wine.

'Mum, was Dad wearing a seatbelt when he had the car crash?'

Mum looks at me, shocked. She doesn't say anything right away. Her face searches mine. 'Summer . . . What? Where did you find that out?'

'I looked at the online archive of the local news-paper from the day Dad died.'

'Summer, I don't think –'

'Was he wearing one?'

Mum shakes her head and then looks away from me.

'Why not?'

Mum breathes in and out really deeply and slowly. 'I don't know, Summer. Really, I don't.'

And I feel bad. I've upset her.

She takes a gulp of wine.

'Did he jump a red light at the traffic lights as well?'

'Yes,' she says really matter-of-factly. Abruptly.

It's obvious I've hit a raw nerve, that she doesn't want to talk about this. I feel awful, but I have to know. I also have to know why nobody ever told me.

'How come I didn't ever get told this? Why did I have to find this out for myself?'

Mum takes a while to answer. She's searching for an excuse. 'I don't really know,' she says.

'Don't you think I have a right to know? He was my dad . . .'

Mum doesn't look at me. She stares down at the coffee table. 'How would telling you any of this have helped, Summer?'

I shrug. 'I don't know,' I say, 'but what harm could it have done?'

Mum sighs. 'Summer, there are some things best left –'

'Why?'

Mum bites her lip. For a second I think she's gonna

cry, but then she turns and looks at me. 'None of this will ever bring him back, you know.'

'I know. But I want to know the truth.'

Mum looks away from me, across the room.

I get the feeling I'm still being fobbed off. 'Is there anything else I should know about Dad's death?'

Mum shakes her head. 'No.'

The room's quiet for a while. Mum picks her wine up and drains the glass.

'Can I listen to the other spiritualist tape, please?'

Mum looks back at me. She shakes her head. 'I don't think that's a good idea. It won't help. It won't bring him back. All it'll do is upset you.'

'What if we listen to it together?'

Mum shakes her head again. 'No.'

'Why not? Have you listened to it?'

Mum shakes her head. 'No, I haven't. I'm not going to and neither are you.'

I stand up. 'Why?' I say. I can hear anger in my voice.

'Calm down, Summer,' Mum says.

'No.'

Mum reaches her hand out towards mine and tries to hold it. I pull my hand away.

'Summer, you need to stop thinking about all these things. It won't do anyone any good.'

'What would you know?' I mutter. I turn and start walking towards my room.

'Summer, please . . .' I hear Mum say.

I ignore her. I go into my room and slam the door behind me.

Johnny

It's late. I'd tell you what time it is, only, whenever I try and look at my watch, my eyes won't focus properly. I try to stand up. My legs almost buckle underneath me. Drac laughs at me. I try again and concentrate really hard on standing up straight.

'J, you're wrecked,' Jake says.

I turn in his direction. 'Good!' I laugh. 'That's exactly how I want to be.'

Badger shakes his head disapprovingly, like he's my dad telling me off. 'How much have you drunk?'

I shrug and it feels weird, like I'm not properly in control of my body. 'Don't know,' I say. 'Don't care either. I want more. Have we got any more booze?'

Drac shakes his head. He holds up the empty bottles and then lets them fall to the ground. 'All gone!'

I feel a bit of dribble trickle out of my mouth and down my chin. I laugh. I'm completely wasted. If my parents saw me like this, I'd be in a whole heap of trouble. But so what? For the first time in weeks I feel normal. I haven't got any worries.

'Let's go and get some more drink,' I say.

Jake laughs. 'It's half eleven,' he says. 'The shops are shut.'

'Is it?' I say. I hold up my wrist to look at my watch. It takes a while to stop the watch-face swimming in front of my eyes and even then I can't work out what time it is. I give up and look at the others.

'I'm going home,' Badger says. He walks over to me. 'You gonna be OK getting back?'

I nod my head and laugh for God knows what reason.

'You sure?' Drac says. 'Can you even remember where you live?'

I nod my head and again I can feel that my movements are exaggerated. '24 Sidmouth Avenue, Raynes Park, London, SW20 0HY.'

I watch as Drac shakes his head slowly and rolls his eyes. I can't help but laugh.

The others are silent for a second. They stare at me like they've never seen a drunk person before, like they're not drunk themselves at this very moment.

'What you looking at?'

No one answers me. I turn away from them and stare into the darkness for a while. I feel a hand on my arm.

'Right,' Jake says. 'Let's get you home.' And he starts leading me towards the fence.

'How much did you drink?' Jake asks me when we're out of the park, walking along the road, and Badger and Drac have gone their own ways.

I shrug. 'Who cares? Loads.'

'J, I've never seen you like this before. You're scaring me, man.'

'What's that supposed to mean?'

Jake stops. He looks straight at me. 'Nothing,' he says. 'You just don't usually get wasted like this. You usually know when to stop. You're being a bit of an idiot, mate.'

'I can do what I want,' I say, and I start walking along the road without him.

I hear Jake mutter something under his breath, but I can't make out what it is so I let it go. He catches me up and we walk along in silence for ages, turn left on to the main road.

'You're gonna have a killer hangover tomorrow,' Jake says as we walk towards the parade of shops and the turning to our houses.

I start thinking of a reply, but by the time it gets anywhere near coming out of my mouth, the words have evaporated from my brain and I'm just left open-mouthed. Dumb. Stupid. Drunk as a skunk.

A police car cruises along the road towards us. It slows down as it gets close. Me and Jake stare at the police inside and they stare back at us. Everything I've forgotten for the last few hours – the Poisoned Dwarf, Mikey winding me up about the police, the ghost – comes flooding back. I wonder if they're on the lookout for us, whether they're gonna arrest us. But then they look away from us and the siren starts wailing. The car turns in the road and roars off in the direction it's just come from. I stand where I am for a second or two, watching as the flashing blue lights disappear up the road.

And all of a sudden, I feel sober. Did they slow down to look at us? Do they know what we did? Or were they just checking us out because we're out late at night?

I feel a tug on my sleeve. Jake. 'Come on,' he says. 'I wanna get home some time this century.'

I start shuffling along again, getting closer and closer to the spot where . . . Well, the spot.

'Have you ever seen a ghost, Jake?'

Jake turns to me and rolls his eyes. 'Not this rubbish again, J,' he says. 'Are you serious?'

'Yeah, I am.'

'Ghosts don't exist,' Jake says. 'We've already had this conversation.'

'They do though.'

Jake turns and looks at me like I've gone mad.

'What?' I say. 'They do.'

There's silence for a second. Jake stares at me like he's trying to work out if I'm taking the mickey or not. I don't know why – must be the cider or something – but I smirk and then laugh. Jake sighs and then turns, starts walking home.

I follow. 'They *do*. I should know. I've got one all of my own. I'm being haunted.'

Jake doesn't even bother looking at me. 'Give it a rest, J.'

We turn left, on to the top of Exminster Avenue. Jake marches off ahead as fast as he can. He doesn't want to talk about it. He wants to bury his head in the sand. But I have to talk about this. So I think of something that I know will get his attention.

'It's the Poisoned Dwarf,' I say. 'She's been haunting me for weeks.'

Jake stops walking. He doesn't turn round immediately, but stands still. Then, slowly, he turns. And even though I know I shouldn't, even though I don't know why I'm doing it, I smile.

'Shut up, Johnny,' he says. 'You're drunk. You don't know what you're saying. You need to go home and sleep the booze off.'

I shake my head. 'I'm deadly serious. I've felt her presence ever since she died. She's been watching me. She wakes me up in the middle of the night every night.'

Jake shakes his head. 'You've lost the plot. Go home.'

'I'm not. It's true. She's waking me up every night at 2.43 in the morning. It's driving me mental. I don't know if I can handle it any more. Why would I make something like that up?'

'You need to get home before you say something really stupid,' Jake says. He walks over to me and grabs my arm, like he's gonna lead me home.

I shake my arm away. 'This is serious, Jake,' I say. 'We killed someone.'

'Keep your voice down,' Jake hisses.

I lean in closer to him. 'She died because of what we did. You can try and pretend it didn't happen. But it did. And her ghost *is* haunting me, all right?'

Jake stares angrily into my eyes, but he looks scared too. He doesn't say anything for ages. I think that maybe the message has got through his thick skull at last. Maybe he's starting to realise how serious this actually is. But then he looks away from me.

'I'm going home now. You should too. You need to stop shouting your mouth off.' And then he walks away.

I watch as he walks along his road through the orange glow of the street lamps. When he's gone in through his front door, I walk home. I cross Exminster

Avenue so I don't have to walk directly past the Poisoned Dwarf's house. As I get close though I can't help but look. I stop in the street and stare at number fifteen. The curtains are all drawn. The house is dark except for one room upstairs. I imagine the old man up there, lying in bed, looking at the empty place next to him.

A shiver runs down my spine. I can feel the presence again. She's here somewhere. I look around me at the pavement and the road and up at the windows of the houses nearby. There's no one else here. Just me and the ghost. Me and the Poisoned Dwarf. The thought crosses my mind to tell her to get lost, to get lost and leave me alone. But I don't. I head off, take one last look at number fifteen just at the moment that the upstairs light goes off and the house is plunged into darkness.

Summer

I looked for the other tape this morning, but Mum must have it hidden somewhere. I won't stop looking till I find it though.

Right now, I'm sitting in the park, waiting for Johnny to turn up. I look at my watch. He was meant to be here by now. I blow a bubble with my gum. I let it pop and suck the gum back in. And then I see him so I get up from the bench to meet him. He's hurrying along the path, looking at the ground. He doesn't notice me for ages, till he looks up.

'Hey, Johnny.'

He smiles. He looks tired though. 'All right, Summer,'

he says, and he leans in and kisses me on the cheek. He smells kind of boozy.

We walk along the path away from the pond.

I look at Johnny. He's pale and tired – not that I can talk, but he really does look different from normal. The skin around his eyes is dark. He's still cute though.

'Did you have a good time with your mates?' I ask.

Johnny shrugs. 'It was all right, yeah,' he says. 'Don't feel so good now though . . .'

I nod. I feel a teeny bit jealous. I wish my friends were around and that we went out and did stuff like that. 'Hungover?'

He nods. 'Like you wouldn't believe.'

Which isn't difficult, because I've never had a hangover in my life. I've never been drunk. I reckon I must have led a pretty sheltered life.

'Shall we go to the café or something? My mouth feels like the Sahara Desert.'

I look at him and smile. 'Sure.'

So we walk through the park to the little café by the lake. Johnny pays for the drinks and then comes and sits down. He hands my hot chocolate over to me. It's got a large swirl of cream with some cocoa shaken on top. I pick up the spoon from the saucer and start spooning it into my mouth. I try and do it seductively, suggestively, licking the spoon clean. It's a trick I learned from Ness at school. Except when I look up to

320

try and give Johnny some eye contact, he isn't even looking at me. He's tapping the top of his can with his fingers. He snaps it open and then swigs loads of it down.

'You been up to anything exciting, then?' he says.

I stir my hot chocolate. 'I've been spending most of my time trying to find out about my dad.'

Johnny looks up. 'Yeah?'

'Yeah. It was the spiritualist church that got me thinking,' I say, but I'm suddenly aware that maybe I shouldn't be telling him this. I'm giving him another reason to think I'm some kind of morbid freak-job.

'What do you mean?'

I take a deep breath. 'I don't know. I feel confused about it all. When we were in the church and the medium was saying that stuff about the unnatural death and foul play, it made me think of my dad.'

Johnny looks at me. His brow furrows, probably cos he doesn't know what to say when I talk about Dad.

'So I looked into it. I looked at the newspapers from when he died, tried to find out if there was foul play, if the spirit was trying to give me a message about his death.'

Johnny leans in close. 'And what did you find out?'

'I read the newspaper report about his accident

online and I found out a couple of things no one's ever told me – he wasn't wearing a seatbelt when he crashed and he skipped a red light. But that doesn't change the fact that it was an accident, does it? Unless he wanted to die.'

Johnny shrugs.

'Anyway, I asked my mum about it and we ended up having a row.'

Johnny makes a sympathetic face.

'There was a photo of the crash scene in the newspaper as well. I'd never seen it before. And I wish I still hadn't.'

'That must have been rough.'

I nod. 'It was.'

'So do you still think it was about your dad, then – that message from the spirit?'

'Who knows?' I say. 'A lot of things the spirit said seemed to fit, but I guess it could have been anyone.'

Johnny takes another swig of his drink. 'I've been thinking about stuff like that a lot lately,' he says. 'I've been feeling kind of weird the last couple of weeks.'

'What, since you met me?'

He laughs and shakes his head. 'No,' he says. He blushes. 'I didn't mean that. Something else.'

Then he doesn't say anything for a while. He looks down at the plastic table top and moves the salt shaker around absent-mindedly. And I wonder what he's thinking.

He stops playing with the salt suddenly and looks up at me. 'I think I'm being haunted, Summer.'

I wasn't expecting him to say that. 'Haunted?'

He nods. He looks down at the table, starts moving the salt shaker again. 'Sounds stupid, doesn't it?'

'No, not at all. Why d'you think it sounds stupid?'

'Because there are no such things as ghosts, are there?' he says, looking up at me.

I shrug. 'If you're being haunted, surely that's proof there are?'

He looks at the table again. He starts playing with the grains of sugar that are on the table, sweeping them up into a pile with his fingers. 'I don't know for sure that I am being haunted though. I haven't *seen* anyone. I just have this feeling like I'm being watched the whole time. And I keep getting woken up at the same time every night.'

I sit and stare back at him. I wish I knew what to say.

'I've been thinking that I'm just going mad – you know, imagining it,' he goes on. 'But then, the other night, I got this text.' He looks up at me. His eyes are kind of pleading with me.

'What did it say?'

He looks down again and fiddles with his empty can. He shrugs. 'Nothing much.' Then he clams up. 'It was just from a number I didn't recognise. It was something that no one else would have known about apart from me and my friends and the ghost.'

'Are you sure it wasn't someone playing a trick on you?'

'I thought that,' he says. 'But . . . I don't know. That wouldn't explain the weird feeling I've been having, like I'm being watched.'

I nod. 'So do you know who's haunting you?'

He nods. 'I think so. An old lady.'

'Really? Why?'

Johnny's quiet for ages. He stares at the table, moves the salt shaker again. 'I don't know.'

I honestly don't know what to say to him now. Things have got too deep. Johnny looks kind of hunched up and uncomfortable. And it's my fault for starting this stupid freako topic of conversation in the first place.

I stir my hot chocolate. And we're silent. When I look up, Johnny's still looking at the table. I reach across and put my hand on top of his. Immediately he looks up and smiles.

'Sorry. I shouldn't have told you all that,' he says. 'It must be the hangover.'

I smile. 'That's OK. I like sensitive people.'

He smiles too. His cheeks flush for a second.

'Hey, there's a boating lake just over there,' I say. 'Do you fancy hiring a rowing boat with me?'

'Definitely.'

Johnny

I'm on my way back home from the bus stop. I feel rubbish. I don't know why I told Summer all that stuff. It just sort of spewed out of my mouth. Jesus, I think I need to curl up in a corner and sleep this hangover off, which is exactly what I plan on doing when I get home.

I go to cross the road so I don't have to walk directly past the Poisoned Dwarf's house. But then I stop and I think, why should I keep crossing? I need to get over this. I can't spend the rest of my life scared to walk on that side of the road, feeling guilty and trying to hide it. I have to face this or it's never gonna get better.

As I walk along the pavement, a car drives past. I look up. It's the Poisoned Dwarf's husband. And all of a sudden I don't feel so sure that I want to walk past his house. What if he's getting out of his car as I go past? What if he looks at me? What if he knows what I did? What if she told him? I steel myself though and keep going.

I get near number fifteen and I hear the engine of his car switch off. The driver's door opens and out he gets, right in front of me. He brushes his comb-over up and across his head and then he shuts the car door. He looks at me and nods and sort of smiles. I nod back, my heart beating like mad. Then he walks past me and goes to the boot of his car. And that's it.

I keep on walking, my heart still thumping. This is ridiculous. All I did was walk past him and I feel like this. I need to get a grip. I need some sleep. I need to feel normal again.

Before I'm twenty more steps along the road, I hear a shout. A yell of pain. I turn immediately. It takes a second to work out where it came from, but then I see the Poisoned Dwarf's husband lying on the kerb, his shopping scattered all over the place.

I run back along the pavement to him. He's got blood coming from a cut on his head. He tries to sit up as I get close, but he winces in pain. He moves his hand down to his foot and grimaces.

'Are you all right?' I say.

He shakes his head.

I crouch down beside him. 'What happened?'

He closes his eyes and his face kind of creases up in pain.

'Is it your foot?'

He nods, eyes still closed, face still creased. He takes a slow, deep breath and then opens his eyes. 'Misjudged the blasted kerb,' he says. He lets out a breath. 'Stupid old fool that I am.'

I panic. I'm not really sure what to do. Should I call him an ambulance? Pick him up? Or get on my way and leave him alone?

'Can you stand up?' I say.

He looks at me and nods his head. And I notice – God knows why – that his comb-over has fallen forward across the bloodied cut on his face. He tries to stand, but he can't. He grimaces again.

'Give me your hand,' he says.

I hold my hand out and he tries to stand again. He puts all his weight on me and I'm shocked by how heavy he is. He gets up to a standing position. I stay beside him, holding him steady. He tries to put his injured foot down and winces again.

'Help me over to the house, will you?'

I put my arm around him and walk with him slowly as he hops across the pavement. I open the gate and then help him along the path and up the front step to his porch. We stop. He puts his injured foot down and takes his keys out of his pocket. He hands them to me.

'Could you open up, please?' he says.

I look at the bundle of keys and try and work out which one to use.

'The long one,' he says.

I open the porch and then the front door and help him inside. I take him straight into the lounge and sit him down in an armchair, then go and shut the front door.

As I get back into the lounge, he's bent over in his chair, his trouser leg pulled up and his sock rolled down. He's got a pained expression on his face as he touches his swelling ankle with his hand.

'Are you OK?'

He shakes his head without looking at me.

'Is there anything I can do to help?'

He lets his trouser leg roll back down. He sits up in his chair and nods. 'In the kitchen,' he says, 'in the freezer compartment, there should be some frozen peas. Wrap the pack in a tea towel and bring it through, would you?'

I nod and go through to the kitchen. As I walk, I notice the pictures on the wall. Photos. Of the Poisoned Dwarf. She has that same screwed-up face in all of them, no sign of a smile. But I feel bad for even thinking it. I look away from the photos and walk to the door. I think about whether she can see me right now, whether her ghost is in the house.

I search the freezer for frozen peas, grab a tea towel from a hook on the wall and then turn to head back to the lounge. As I'm leaving the kitchen I notice a calendar. My heart starts racing. The handwriting on the calendar is identical to that on the mirror in our bathroom the other night. The same shaky capital letters. I run my hand through my hair and think about what that means. Whose handwriting is it? Is it the Poisoned Dwarf's or maybe her husband's?

'Are you OK in there?' the old man calls through.

'Yeah, just coming,' I call back. I stare at the calendar for a few more seconds before going through with the peas.

'I think I need you to call me an ambulance,' he says as I pass him the peas. 'I think my foot's broken.'

I nod my head.

'The phone's in the hallway.'

So I go and make the call, which feels a bit odd. I've never had to do something like that before. While I'm doing it, there's a photo of the Poisoned Dwarf and a couple of other people – family, I guess – staring straight back at me from the wall. Looks like it was taken a long time ago. I look away from it. I don't want to look at her. I don't want to be reminded of what I did.

When I'm done, I go back into the lounge. 'Do you want me to call anyone else?'

He looks up, takes the frozen peas off his ankle.

'Have you got any family or anything?' I say. 'I could let them know you're going to hospital.'

He shakes his head. 'No. I don't want to worry them. They've been through enough lately. I'll tell them when I'm out of hospital.'

That makes me feel awful. I look away – at the floor, at the window, at the walls – anywhere but at him. I want to get out of here as soon as I can.

'You don't have to hang around,' the old man says. 'I'll be all right on my own.'

I shake my head even though every part of my being is screaming to get out of here. 'It's OK,' I say. 'I'll wait with you. Let me get you something to clean up the cut on your head.'

The old man smiles at me. 'Thank you. I really appreciate what you've done,' he says. 'Not many kids your age would do the same.'

Summer

Mum may not be willing to tell me where she put the other tape. She may not want me to listen to it. But if she's gonna spend her whole life at work, there's not much she can do to stop me looking for the tape and then listening to it when I find it.

The tapes were hidden in her wardrobe. So now here I am, sitting on the sofa, listening to the second tape hissing and crackling and then the same medium's voice going through all the warning stuff and asking Nan if she's ready to start.

My heart races as I listen to the silence on the tape, waiting for someone to speak. A doubt flits through my mind momentarily. Maybe I should switch this off now. Maybe Mum's right and I don't need to hear this. Maybe it can only do harm. But then I hear the medium's voice change, like someone is starting to talk through her. I forget everything else and just listen.

'Hello, Mum?' the voice says. 'It's me. James.'

'James?' Nan says. She sounds even more nervous than she did on the other tape.

'Yes. It's me.'

No one speaks for a while. All I can hear is the hiss of the tape and then a clunking sound.

'What did you mean, James?' Nan says. 'The other week, you sounded surprised when I said it was an accident. What did you mean?'

There's silence again.

'What happened, James?' Nan says. She sounds desperate, upset.

There's no answer.

'James? Are you still there?'

There's more hissing and crackling, but no voices.

'Yes,' comes the answer eventually.

'What did you mean about the accident?' Nan says, her voice breaking.

A long silence. It's creepy. It makes my heart pound. I want to know what he meant. I have to.

'There was no accident,' the medium says in a husky voice. 'It was meant to be.'

'What do you mean?' Nan says.

'Nothing happens by accident.'

'Did someone kill you on purpose, James?' Nan says.

There's a long pause. The tape starts to click as it plays.

'I was angry,' the voice says. 'I was angry because of what happened the day before.'

'What do you mean, James?' Nan says, sounding terrified.

There's a silence that feels like it's going on for ever.

'The argument,' the voice says. 'I was still angry.'

'Our argument?' I'm sure I can hear tears in Nan's voice. She sounds distraught.

Another pause.

'Yes.'

'I didn't mean ... I'm sorry ...' Nan starts to say, but her voice is full of tears, so full that she has to stop.

There's another pause.

'I didn't mean to do it,' the voice says. 'It wasn't your fault. Don't blame yourself, Mum. I was selfish.'

Nobody speaks for a while. In the background I hear something that I think is Nan sobbing. And I feel like sobbing with her. This is horrible. I feel ill.

'It happened because I was angry. If it was anyone's fault it was mine,' the voice says.

Nan doesn't answer.

'I was stupid. It was a reckless thing to do,' the voice goes on.

Silence.

'Look after the kids for me,' the voice says. 'Make sure Rose is all right. I'm sorry.'

I hear a noise, like someone taking a deep breath. Then Nan's voice, like she's trying really hard to stop the tears. 'I will, James. I will.'

Then a long silence. All I can hear is the hiss and crackle of the tape till the medium speaks again, this time in her own voice.

'He's gone, Jean.'

Nan says something quietly to the medium, something I can't hear. I hear her blow her nose and then the tape clunks as it stops.

I sit where I am for ages after the tape has stopped. I'm too shocked to move. I don't know what to think. I'm not sure I wanted to hear those things. I kind of wish there was a way that I could delete what I've just learned from my memory.

My phone starts to ring. I look down at the screen.

It's Mum calling. I get a pang of guilt. I feel like I've betrayed her trust. How can I pretend that I've never heard what I've just heard? I take a deep breath and answer the call.

'Hello, Mum.'

'Hi, Summer. Listen, I'm just calling because your grandad's just phoned me from hospital.'

My stomach turns over. 'What's Grandad doing in hospital? Is he OK?'

'Yes, I think so, love. He had a fall. He's sprained his ankle.'

'Oh. Is that serious?'

'I don't think so. Hopefully not,' Mum says. 'Listen, I'm going to leave work now and go and pick him up from the hospital.'

'OK,' I say. 'Can I help?'

'There's not really anything to do,' Mum says. 'I just want to make sure he's OK, that's all.'

'Can I come and see him?'

'OK. Why don't you head over towards Raynes Park. I'll let you know when we're on our way.'

'OK. See you soon.'

I hang up. I sit on the sofa and stare into space for a while till my phone beeps. A text message from Johnny. I open it up immediately.

Sorry I went a bit weird on u earlier. Too tired! Wanna meet 2moro? J

I text him straight back and arrange to meet him tomorrow afternoon. Getting away from this flat and this family for a bit will do me good.

Johnny

Last night was the the best night's sleep I've had in weeks. I think I kind of stirred around 2.43 a.m., but it felt different. It didn't feel like anyone else was there and I went straight back to sleep. Maybe this is it. Maybe I'm starting to deal with it. The sun is shining. I feel good.

I pull the newspaper trolley along behind me, stopping at each house to post the free newspapers through the doors. But before I know it, I'm halfway up Exminster Avenue and the old feeling returns. Guilt. The knot in my stomach. I stop where I am. I can see the silver car parked on the road outside number fifteen still, in the same place the old man parked it yesterday before he tumbled over. There's a tin of baked beans I must have missed yesterday when I was tidying up, resting against the front wheel of the car.

I wonder how he is now. When I left yesterday, as the ambulance was getting ready to take him to hospital, he seemed all right. He was in a lot of pain, but the paramedics said he'd probably just sprained his ankle badly. Nothing worse than that.

I walk along the pavement, taking the newspapers and pushing them through the doors of the next couple of houses, till I get to number fifteen. I stand and stare at it. The porch is closed and so is the front door. The blinds are all drawn. I wonder whether he's here or whether they kept him in hospital. I wonder whether he has anyone – any family – to help him out.

I take a paper from the trolley and bend over to pick the can up from beside the wheel of the car. I open the little gate at the front of the house and walk up to the porch door. I feel nervous. I reach out and press the doorbell. I hear it ring inside. I stand and wait.

The doors remain closed. No answer. He must be in hospital still. They must have kept him in overnight. I look at the tin in my hand and wonder what I should do with it. I decide to give the doorbell another ring and if he doesn't answer the door, I'll just put the paper through the door and leave the can by the side of the porch. I reach up and press the doorbell again. Then I wait and I wait and I wait.

After a minute or so, I place the beans down beside the door, fold the paper and push it through the letter box. It falls to the floor. I turn and head back to the trolley. But as I'm closing the gate behind me, I hear the sound of someone putting keys into the front door. I turn and watch as the front door opens. The old man stands there, a big blue boot on his injured foot, resting his weight on a crutch. I feel bad that I made him come out. I go back through the gate, pick up the baked beans and wait for him to unlock the porch door.

Summer

I put my key in the front door and twist it. I push the door open and go inside. I'm just about to call out to Grandad to say I'm here when I realise there's a voice coming from the lounge. Grandad's voice. I think for a second that he must be on the phone to someone, till I hear another voice.

I walk through the hallway and towards the lounge. As I get to the doorway, I stop and stare. Grandad's sitting in his chair nattering to someone. He looks up at me and smiles.

'Hi, Summer,' he says.

'Hi, Grandad,' I say.

Then I look across the room at the sofa. And in that

moment the world seems to shift on its axis. Nothing seems to make sense.

'This is –'

'Johnny!' I say.

Johnny gets up from the sofa. He looks at me, confused, terrified. His mouth opens like he's about to say something, but no sound comes out.

'What are you doing here?' I say.

He looks down at the carpet and then across at Grandad. 'I . . .'

'Johnny is the lad that picked me up when I fell over yesterday,' Grandad says.

I turn and look at Grandad. He's got a wide smile on his face.

'He's a guardian angel,' Grandad says, beaming. 'This lad picked me up off the pavement and called an ambulance for me. He even cleaned up the cut on my head and got me some ice for my ankle. He waited until the paramedics turned up and everything.'

My mind spins. 'Wow,' I say. I turn to Johnny. He's standing there looking awkward. 'You did all that? For my grandad?'

Johnny looks down at the ground again. He shrugs. Why's he being so modest?

'He did. This lad deserves a medal,' Grandad says. 'Called in today as well to check I was OK.'

I smile at Johnny. I go over and wrap my arms

around him, squeeze him tight. But he just stands there, stiff and awkward.

'I take it you two know each other, then?' Grandad says, laughing.

I let go of Johnny and let out a little laugh. 'Yeah, we do. Don't we, Johnny?'

Johnny nods his head hesitantly.

'Small world, hey,' Grandad says.

Johnny moves forward. 'Listen, Mr Hornby, Summer, I'd better go,' he says. 'I should deliver the rest of the newspapers.'

'Oh,' I say. 'Right. Was it something I said?'

Johnny looks at me and shakes his head. He looks really shy, nervous. I wonder if it's because he's shocked or whether he feels nervous in front of Grandad.

'Thank you for checking on me, Johnny,' Grandad says. 'I really appreciate it. Summer, will you pass my wallet, please.' Grandad takes a ten-pound note and holds it out. 'Take this, Johnny, won't you? By way of a thank you.'

Johnny shakes his head. 'No, thank you,' he says. 'I couldn't possibly take any money.'

Grandad shrugs. 'Please,' he says.

Johnny shakes his head. 'Really, please don't. I don't deserve it.' He starts moving towards the door. 'Goodbye, Mr Hornby.'

I walk with him to the front door.

'I can't believe you did that for my grandad,' I say.

Johnny half-smiles. 'It's nothing, really.'

'You're like my knight in shining armour,' I say. I kiss him on the lips.

Johnny doesn't kiss back. He stares at me for a second, then turns towards the door.

'Are we still meeting this afternoon?' I say.

He turns back to me, looking like a rabbit caught in the headlights for a second.

I smile at him.

He nods. 'Yeah. Course.'

'Three o'clock?'

He nods. And then he opens the door and leaves.

Johnny

I grab the newspaper trolley and pull it behind me as fast as I can. There's no way I'm delivering the rest of the papers right now though. I can't think straight. I need to get home. My head's spinning round and round in circles. I'm struggling to think what all this means, what the repercussions are.

It feels unreal, like this should be an elaborate practical joke, like at any moment someone's gonna jump out from behind a bush and start laughing at how gullible I am. If only. This is real. And I'm the one that has to deal with it.

When I get back home, I leave the newspaper trolley out at the front of the house. I go upstairs to my room and shut the door behind me. I lie down on my bed, stare at the ceiling and start to think.

So, Summer is the Poisoned Dwarf's granddaughter. And because of me Summer's grandma is dead. Summer thinks I'm some kind of superhero for rescuing her grandad, but she has no idea what I've really done. And I don't know whether I can ever look her in the eye again.

Maybe I should say something to her this afternoon. Come clean. Tell her what I did. Tell her that her grandma would still be alive if it wasn't for me. That would be the bravest thing to do, wouldn't it? The right thing to do.

I hear footsteps thumping up the stairs and then across the landing. My bedroom door swings open and Mikey and his mate Asif bundle into my room, back from staying the night at Asif's house. They stop dead as they see me. I sit up on my bed. Mikey and Asif look petrified as they stare at me, but then they glance at each other and laugh.

'What the hell are you doing in here?' I yell at them.

They look at each other and laugh again.

'Nothing,' Mikey says. 'I didn't know you were in.'

'What? This is my room. You're not allowed in here whether I'm here or not. Understand?'

Mikey smiles. 'Yes, I understand. You have a lot of

secrets, Johnny. Sorry,' he says, his voice dripping with sarcasm, 'I just got confused and forgot which room was yours and which was mine.'

Mikey and Asif laugh, then they charge out of my room and back downstairs. I lie back on my bed. I need to decide what to do.

Summer

Johnny is late. I'm sitting on the bench, waiting. There's no sign of him. It's been ten minutes now. I take my phone out. I go to the text messages and check I have the right time for meeting up. I do. He's definitely late. I write a text and send it to him.

Am in the park. Are you nearly here? X

My finger lingers over the button. Should I send it? Is it too naggy? Actually, so what if it is naggy? I press the button and in the blink of an eye the message is sent.

I sit and I wait for him to reply.

Time ticks by. Seconds feel like hours. And every passing second fails to bring with it a message from

Johnny. Why isn't he here? If there was a good reason, like he'd missed the bus or something, he'd have called or texted, wouldn't he?

I look at my watch. Fifteen minutes late. I start to think about how long I'll give him. I'm not waiting here for ever, that's for sure. I decide on twenty minutes. If he's any later than that, he'll find that I've gone.

Johnny

I lay on my bed for ages deciding whether this was the right thing to do. I wanted to stay at home. I didn't want to come out and face Summer. I can't begin to think how much she's gonna hate me when she finds out.

It would have been easy to make an excuse about why we couldn't meet and to have kept making excuses till she finally got tired of me and went and found someone else instead. It would have hurt her feelings a bit probably, but nowhere near as much as I'll be hurting them when I tell her the truth.

I spent so long thinking about it that by the time I left the house it was almost time to meet. I'm such an idiot. I've heard my phone go already, felt it vibrate in my pocket, but I've ignored it. I knew it would be her, asking where I was. I couldn't look at it, I don't know why. Maybe because it might have changed my mind and I would have got straight on to a bus back home.

I hurry through the park, dodging in and out of all the people lazily taking a sunny afternoon stroll.

Up ahead, I see her. She checks her watch and then gets up from the bench. She looks like she's had enough – she's ready to leave. I bet she thinks she's been stood up. I rush over.

'Summer. I'm sorry I'm late.'

She gives me a look, raises an eyebrow, but then she smiles. 'Why didn't you text me?' she says. 'I've been sitting here for twenty minutes.'

I start racking my brain for an excuse, but I realise there's no point. I'm not lying any more, not to anyone. 'Sorry.'

She sighs. 'I'll forgive you,' she says, 'seeing as you came to my grandad's rescue.' She winks at me. And then she throws her arms around me and kisses me on the lips.

I freeze. This is wrong. I can't let her do this. I can't act like nothing is wrong. But I don't know how to stop this, how to take control. Should I kiss her back? Should I come right out and tell her the truth now? I mean, what's the point in delaying the agony? Why not tell her now so we can go our separate ways and start to get over it?

Eventually Summer lets go of me. She takes a step back and looks at me. She raises an eyebrow, like she's confused. 'Are you OK?'

I look down at the ground. This is the time. Right now. I need to tell her now. My eyes stay fixed on a spot on the ground. My mouth stays firmly closed. By my sides, my fingers ball up into fists. I have to say something *now*. Speak, Johnny.

'Johnny?'

I look up and smile at her. At least, I try to, but the way it feels on my face, I can tell it comes out more like a grimace. I take a breath and prepare myself to say it, to let it all tumble out. Only, when I open my mouth, the words are gone. I don't know where to start. How can I tell her this?

'Are you all right, Johnny?'

Say something, Johnny. Tell her. She has to know. Tell her and then go home. Don't make this even more painful than it already is.

'Johnny?'

I take a deep breath. 'Shall we walk?' I say.

Summer smiles and nods.

And I sense that the moment has gone. I'm a coward. I couldn't do it.

'I still can't get over it,' Summer says as we walk along the path. 'You helping my grandad up.'

I nod my head. 'Yeah.'

'What happened?'

I don't really want to talk about this. I don't want her to start thinking I'm some kind of hero when the truth is the complete opposite. 'I just happened to be walking past when he fell,' I say. 'It was coincidence, that's all. It could have been anyone.'

'It's amazing it was you,' Summer says, and she links arms with me. 'Don't you think? It's fate again, isn't it?'

'Maybe. Anyone else would have done the same though.'

Summer shakes her head. 'Don't be so modest.'

I don't reply. What is there to say other than the truth?

'You know, my grandad gave me the money you wouldn't take earlier,' she says. 'He told me to spend it on you.'

'That's kind of him, but he doesn't need to give me his money. He said thank you already.'

'*I* want to thank you though,' Summer says.

In my head, I imagine turning to her, telling her the truth and then marching off. In reality, I keep on walking, my arm awkwardly linked through hers, hating myself more and more with every passing second that I don't tell her the truth.

'We could spend it in the café?' Summer says. 'Or hire a rowing boat again?' She turns to look at me. She has a smile on her face. It looks kind of suggestive.

I shake my head. 'I don't feel like rowing,' I say. 'Not today.'

She looks slightly crestfallen. 'Right,' she says. 'The café, then?'

I nod my head. 'OK.'

Summer

Well, that was weird. I'm confused. Did I misread the signs and totally imagine there was something between us? Has my summer been so boring that I made all this up to make it more interesting? Or have I just put Johnny off me? Something definitely doesn't feel right.

As soon as I got home I started reading *Catcher* again, from the start. For the hundredth-and-God-knows-how-many time. The real world is way too complicated and confusing a place to be right now. I'd rather be in Holden's world, where nothing, no matter how rubbish, has any effect on my life, where nothing unexpected can come along and spoil everything. Holden's life may suck monumentally, but at least his life sucks in a cool kind of way. Mine just sucks in the stupidest, most lonely and boring way possible.

I can't stay in Holden's world for ever though. I have to rejoin the real world at some point. So after a bit I put my bookmark in and then pick up my phone. I start to write a text.

Hi, Johnny. It was nice 2 c u earlier. Hope everything's OK. Call me if you want to talk X

I send it. I keep my phone in my hand and stare at it, willing him to reply, to say something like, *sorry I was weird earlier*. I sit and stare at my phone for ages and no text arrives. He's ignoring me, I know it. So after a while I decide to go back into Holden's world.

Johnny

I'm walking down Exminster Avenue when I look up and see her. Summer. She doesn't see me though; she's looking in the other direction, back turned. I feel a tug of guilt in the pit of my stomach. A familiar feeling. How can I live with myself after what I've done? I killed the grandma and tried to seduce the grand-daughter. Really, does it get any lower than that?

My instinct is to run and never look back. I want to get so far away from her, from what I've done, that it'll never find me. I can't let the past catch up with me. So that's exactly what I do. I start running as fast as I can, legs and arms pumping, to the end of Exminster Avenue and then out on to the main road. I keep taking turnings as they appear – left, right, left, left – so that I'm difficult to follow, difficult to find.

After a few minutes I'm somewhere I don't recognise, running along roads I don't know. The houses by the side of the road start to thin and before long I'm out in the countryside, running past fields. I cut across one of the fields, run along a rutted track and end up in a forest. I dart through the trees, then follow the course of a river. I cover the ground effortlessly, almost gliding along, up a hill, along a ridge. The sky above me is a brilliant blue.

I chance a glance over my shoulder and, to my horror, there she is, Summer, keeping up with me without breaking a sweat. She looks amazingly beautiful. Her eyes bore into mine, like she can see inside me, right into my soul. She reaches an arm out for me. She calls me.

'Johnny. Don't run.'

But I have to. I have to get away from her. I try to quicken my pace, to pump my arms and legs more quickly, but I'm slowing, barely moving forward. Summer is catching up with every step, grasping distance away. I reach the top of the ridge and take a second to look down at the valley below. I take one last look at Summer, then I launch myself over the ridge. I open my arms, spread my wings and I'm soaring. It's peaceful up here. I can't hear a thing.

But then I sense something next to me. I turn my head and look. Summer is there, soaring like me, enormous black wings extended. She looks at me and smiles, then reaches out a hand and holds my arm.

'Johnny, where are you going?'

I open my mouth to answer, but my tongue ties itself in a knot. I can't speak. I can't tell her the truth.

Summer pulls me towards her, wraps me in an embrace, folding her wings around me.

'You're my hero, Johnny,' she says, and she kisses me tenderly on the neck. 'You know that, don't you?'

I freeze at her touch, at her words.

'What's the matter, Johnny? Don't you like me?'

I try to wriggle free from her grasp.

'Johnny?'

She holds me tightly. There's no way out. None at all. I'm stuck.

'What's the matter?' she says.

'I . . . It's . . .' The words won't come out.

Before my eyes, Summer starts to change. Her face begins to wrinkle, like there's a plughole in the middle of her face sucking the rest of her skin in. Creases. Liver spots. Moles. Warts. Grey hair. She's become her grandma. She is Jean Hornby. She is the Poisoned Dwarf. She fixes me with a look that bores straight into my soul and hates what it sees there.

'Murderer!' she says. 'You can't run for ever.' And then she plants her lips on mine and starts to kiss me.

As she kisses me, it feels like she sucks the life out of me. Around us the air rushes up as we start to plunge towards the ground. Down through the clouds. Down. Down. Down.

This is it.

I'm gonna die.

I wake with a start, sit up in bed and look around the room. I sigh. I thought this was over. I turn my bedside light on. The curtains are open and blowing in the breeze. The bed sheets are soaked with sweat. And there is someone here. There is some*thing* here. I'm sure. I'm not imagining it. I notice the clock. It tells me what I already know. It's 2.43 a.m. Of course it is. Beside the clock, my phone catches my attention. It's glowing. The message tone sounds to say I have a message. My heart thumps. Who is it at this time of night? I pick the phone up. A part of me knows that I shouldn't look at it, but I have to. There is no way I can *not* look at it.

There's a text message from the Poisoned Dwarf. I open it up.

Put it right or I'll tell the police what you've done.

I shiver. I look around me. How can this be happening? Who's sending me these texts? I read it over and over again. I run my hand through my hair and over my face and I try to think. Then I have an idea. I can find who's doing this. I hit the options button on the left of the screen and scroll down to call sender. I press the button and put the phone to my ear. For a second there's silence, then the phone starts to ring.

Duh-duh.

Duh-duh.

Duh-duh.

As it rings, I start to wonder whether I'm doing the right thing here. I don't know if I want someone to answer the phone or not. What would I say? Would I be too scared to say anything?

But the phone carries on ringing.

Duh-duh.

Duh-duh.

Duh-duh.

Nobody picks it up.

But I hear another noise in the house. I take the phone away from my ear and listen. I can hear a phone ringing. I sit and listen for a few seconds. It's coming from somewhere out on the landing. I feel a chill. Whoever's behind this is here now in the house with me.

I stay where I am, motionless, too scared to move. I don't want to know what's out there. I just want it to go away. I look at my phone. The screen glows in the dull light of my room and I think about hanging up. But what would be the point? Whoever texted me is outside my room now. They know I'm here. There's no hiding from it so I decide to do something about it. I get up from my bed and creep towards the door. With every step I take, the sound of the phone ringing is louder. I put my hand on the door handle and slowly turn it. I try and keep my breathing slow, try and stay calm.

I peek around the door. My eyes dart, checking out the landing. But there's no one there. The ringing isn't coming from the landing. It sounds more like it's coming from Mikey's room. I grit my teeth. I knew it was him. I quietly step towards his room. As I get close, the ringing stops. I reach my hand out and slowly close my fingers around Mikey's door handle. I count to three in my head, and then I burst into his room.

Mikey is out of his bed, crossing his room. He freezes. He stops and stares at me, terrified. He looks like he realises he's been caught. I notice his phone lying on the floor. He looks at me, then at his phone. He stoops down and grabs it.

'What the hell are you doing in my room?' he hisses. 'It's three o'clock in the morning, Johnny, you idiot.'

I stare at him. 'What am *I* doing? I'd like to know what you're doing, sending me messages in the middle of the night.'

Mikey looks confused. 'What are you talking about?'

'You know what I'm talking about,' I whisper. 'The text message. You sent it just now.'

Mikey shakes his head. 'What text message?' he hisses. 'I didn't send any text message. I was asleep till you phoned me.'

'It *was* you,' I say, 'because when I pressed call sender on my phone, your phone rang. I heard it. I know it was you.'

Mikey shakes his head again. He makes a circular movement with his index finger next to his head. 'You're mad, Johnny. Loopy. Messed up.'

I stare at him and anger wells up in me. He's been behind this all along. I've been thinking I've been going mad and all along it's been Mikey. How could I ever have thought it was anyone but him?

'You're imagining things,' Mikey says.

'Prove it then. Give me your phone,' I say. I hold out my hand. 'Let me check it.'

Mikey hides his phone behind his back. 'No. Go away. Get out of my room.'

I stare back at him. I move my hand closer to him. 'Give me the phone. If the message isn't in your sent items, I'll leave you alone and apologise.'

Mikey shakes his head. And for a split second he smirks. 'I'm not giving you my phone. It was *you* that was calling my phone in the middle of the night. Get out of my room.'

'Give me the phone,' I say slowly, quietly, forcefully.

'Get lost,' Mikey says.

And I lose it. Anger floods my entire being, surges through my veins. I lunge towards Mikey and knock him to the floor. He hides the phone underneath him and swings at me with his free arm. I try to turn him round to get to the phone, but he won't budge. So I punch him in the back. *THUMP*. The noise of the impact is hollow. I hear the air escape out of Mikey's lungs in one go. He gasps as he tries to re-inflate his lungs. I hit him in the back again. And again. This time the punches land with a *SLAP*. I get up off Mikey and pull him from the floor. He feels like a rag doll in my arms. He's no weight at all. He looks at me. He's struggling to get his breath back, but there's still a look in his eyes. Mocking. He's enjoying this. It was him. He's been haunting me, making me think that there's a ghost.

I feel my fingers form themselves into fists again. And I swing at him. Right fist. Left fist. They both land on his face. *THWACK*. *THWACK*. And Mikey collapses to the floor. I catch a glimpse of blood leaking from his mouth. He raises his hand towards it and dabs at it.

'Give me the phone!' I shout.

Mikey shakes his head. 'You're . . .' He pauses to get his breath. 'You're gonna get in so much trouble for this.'

I kick him in the ribs. He doubles up in pain. The phone falls from his hand and I grab it before he has a chance to.

I go straight to his sent messages. I flick through them. There it is. Sent at 2.43 a.m. **Put it right or I'll tell the police what you've done.**

I stare at Mikey. He looks back at me, blood leaking from his mouth. He looks scared. Worried. For once he's not smirking.

'You little freak,' I say.

'What?' Mikey says. His words sound wet, like he's spitting the words at me, like they're coated in blood and sweat and saliva, but they're defiant.

I stare at him. I don't understand him. I can't begin to understand what's going through his brain.

Mikey dabs the blood at his mouth. He looks at his hand, then shakes his head. 'You need help, Johnny. You're not normal.' And then he clutches at his ribs and winces.

I toss his phone towards him. It hits him on the head. And then I turn on my heels and leave his room. He's right. I have lost it. I am mental. I don't know what's real any more. I don't know who I am. I don't know who anyone is. I'm paranoid. I'm scared. I'm angry. I'm crazy. I don't like it. I don't like me. And I don't like Mikey. I hate Mikey.

Just then I hear movement from Mum and Dad's room. I have to get out of here. I rush back across the landing to my room, pull on some clothes and throw some things into a bag.

As I leave my room, Dad comes out of their bedroom, pulling his dressing gown on.

'What's all the noise?' he says.

I stand where I am, frozen. 'Nothing,' I say.

He realises something isn't quite right though. 'Why are you dressed?'

'I'm going out,' I say. 'There's something I have to do.'

'It's the middle of the night,' Dad says.

But I'm already walking down the stairs.

'Johnny,' he calls after me. 'It's the middle of the night! Come back here!'

I ignore him. I'm halfway down the stairs. I run the rest of the way. I hear Dad starting to come after me, Mum coming out of her room and Mikey talking to her.

I open the front door and step out into the night. And then I start running.

Summer

My phone wakes me at about seven. I have no idea who could be texting at that time in the morning, so I ignore it for a while, turn over and try to go back to sleep. It doesn't take long before my curiosity gets the better of me though and I sit up in bed. I reach over to my bedside table and grab my phone.

A text from Johnny. I open it right away. **Hi. Can I see you today? J**

And that's it. I text him right back and say yes.

I start to wonder why he's texting me at this time of the morning asking me to meet him. I try and work out whether it's a good thing or a bad thing. He was acting weird yesterday. Maybe he wants to apologise. Or maybe I'm reading too much into a text message.

While I'm thinking, my phone buzzes again. Another message from Johnny. **Meet me in the park @ 9?**

I reply. **OK. I'll be there.**

I think about what the time is now and I realise I better get up and get showered.

Johnny

I couldn't stay in the house, not with Mum and Dad awake. Not after what had just happened. I had to get away. I was so angry and confused and embarrassed. I didn't know what to think or what to do.

As soon as I closed the front door, I started running. I didn't know where I was going. I just knew I had to get away and I knew that Dad might try and follow me. So I took a route he wouldn't be able to predict, weaving through a maze of streets. To begin with, I was filled with adrenaline. My jaw was clenched. I felt like lashing out at anything that was in my path and I did – litter, leaves, traffic cones all got kicked.

I didn't think about where I was heading – I was just trying to get away so no one would find me. But I soon realised that I was heading in the direction of Wimbledon. I kept going. My phone rang as I was walking. I looked at it. For a mad moment, I thought it was gonna be the Poisoned Dwarf. But it was Dad calling. I ignored it. He left a voicemail, which I didn't listen to. I switched my phone off and kept walking.

There was no one around. I guess there wouldn't be at three in the morning. A couple of cars cruised past. A police car slowed as it saw me. The officers inside looked me up and down and it made me completely paranoid. I wondered whether Dad had called the police to let them know I'd run away, but the police car kept going, cruising through the night. An empty night bus trundled along the road. A few drunk people wobbled along the pavement on their way home.

As I walked, the birds started to sing and light gradually crept into the sky. I didn't want it to because if it started to get light, it was the beginning of another day and that would mean that soon the streets would start filling with people going about their normal everyday lives. And I couldn't cope with that. I wanted the night to go on and on and on, to hide me away from the world. I needed time to be alone, to think.

I walked for about an hour. And as I slowly calmed down, I thought things through. What I'd done and how I felt and whether this mess could ever be sorted.

I drew a line right there. I started to work out how I was gonna make things better and I realised that although it's gonna be difficult and painful and messy and horrible, I can do it.

From now on, I'm gonna make the right decisions.

I stopped walking eventually. I sat down on a bench in the park. And I started working on the future. I switched on my phone and deleted all the messages which Mum and Dad had left, and I wrote some of my own.

Summer

I smile as I see him. He sees me too, but he doesn't smile. He gets up from the bench and walks hesitantly in my direction, not making eye contact. I'm not getting good vibes from him.

'Hi, Johnny.'

'Hi.' He tries to force a smile, but I can tell he doesn't mean it.

Then we stand awkwardly for a while. He doesn't look directly at me or say a word.

'Are you all right?'

Silence. He looks at the ground. I don't know what to say to him.

'Let's go somewhere quiet,' Johnny says eventually. 'We need to talk.'

I nod, but I have a sinking feeling. I don't like this. It's never good news when someone says, 'we need to talk.' Nobody ever 'needs to talk' when it's good news.

We walk to the café in the park. There are loads of mums with their babies and their buggies in there. We get our drinks without saying a word and find a place in the corner, away from everyone else. The whole time Johnny doesn't look at me. He seems odd. Twitchy. Nervous. Like he's thinking about something secret. I'm guessing that whatever he's thinking about is the thing we need to talk about.

Even when we're sat down, Johnny doesn't say anything. He hunches over the table, cradling his drink, wiping the beads of moisture on the outside of the can with his fingers.

'So?' I say.

Johnny looks up at me as though I've just startled him. He closes his eyes for a second and sighs. 'I don't know how to say this . . .'

Those seven words are enough to make me want to run from the café crying. This is how it starts. This is the start of the end, I know it. 'How to say what?'

He sighs again and looks at his can. 'I think we should stop seeing each other.'

373

He catches my eye for a second, then looks away. I stare at him. I knew that he was gonna say that. There was no way he was gonna say anything else. But still I'm shocked to hear the words come out of his mouth. I feel tears start to form in the corner of my eyes. 'What? Why?'

He hunches over even more. He doesn't say anything.

'Don't you like me?'

He closes his eyes. 'Of course I do,' he says. He opens his eyes again and bites his lower lip with his teeth. He looks like he's about to cry. 'I think you're amazing, but . . .'

'Then why?' I say. 'I thought there was something between us. A spark.'

Johnny closes his eyes. He sits there for maybe ten seconds, eyes closed, breathing deeply, before he opens them again and looks up at me. 'There is,' he says. 'But I can't do this. There's something about me that you don't know, and when you find out you're gonna hate me. We can't see each other again . . . I'm sorry.'

What is he talking about? 'Are you seeing someone else?' I say.

He shakes his head, tears in his eyes.

'Then what?'

Johnny stands up. He puts his hand into his bag and

takes a piece of paper out. A letter. 'I'm sorry,' he says. 'I didn't mean for any of this to happen.'

He places the letter down on the table. He looks at me. I can see that he's trying to stop the tears. Then he looks away and walks off through the café.

I stay where I am. Frozen. Shocked. I stare at the letter. My name's written on the front. For a second I feel like ripping it up without reading it, getting up and running after Johnny. But the moment passes and all I do is sit and stare at my name written on the piece of paper.

Johnny

I start running as soon as I'm outside the café. I don't want her to come after me or catch me up. I don't want to see Summer again for as long as I live. I know what she's thinking of me this very second. She knows what I did to her grandma and she knows how much of a coward I am. She hates me. She has every right to. I hate me. How could anyone not hate me?

After a couple of minutes, I'm out of the park so I stop running. I switch my mobile back on. Immediately my message tone sounds a couple of times. More messages from Mum and Dad. I delete them. I don't want to read what they have to say or hear their voices right now. I write them a text of my own instead.

I'm sorry for what I did to Mikey. I'm OK, but I'm not coming home. I have something I need to do. You'll understand soon. Sorry. I love you.

I linger over the send button for a few seconds. It seems like a melodramatic thing to send to them. What are they gonna think when they read that? But then what else am I meant to write to them? I'm not gonna tell them what's really going on – they'll find out soon enough. Before I can change my mind, I send it.

I start to write another message. To Badger and Drac and Jake. Only, I don't know what to write, how to explain it to them in just a few words.

I can't keep this secret any more – it's been eating away at me. Don't worry – I'll keep your name out of it. J

I look at it for a few seconds, then I press send. As soon as the message is sent, I delete it from my sent items. I switch my phone off and look for a bus stop.

Summer

Johnny's letter is still sitting on the table in front of me. His can of drink is there as well. He didn't even take a sip from it.

I'm still tempted to put the letter in the bin without reading it. Listening to Nan's tapes from the medium didn't make me any happier or any less confused. And it's gonna be the same with this letter, I know it is. I mean, what can it possibly say? *I didn't realise how much of a weird, morbid freak you are. I don't like you enough, so this has to end. I think I can do better. It's not me, it's you.*

I know I'm not gonna put the letter in the bin though. I have to know what it is that's made him behave like this. Maybe he's overreacting. Maybe we can sort it out, whatever it is. Everything seemed to be going fine. Weird, maybe, but only in a good way. At least, that's what I thought till yesterday, till I saw him at Grandad's. Johnny seemed different then. He'd changed somehow.

I have to know. I have to see if we can make it right. I lean forward, take the letter from the table and open it.

Dear Summer,

I'm really sorry that I'm writing this to you. I'm too much of a coward to tell you to your face. I hope one day you'll be able to forgive me, though I know I don't deserve it. The truth is, we can't see each other any more. It's not because of anything you've done. It's not because I don't think you're the most amazing person I've ever met – because you are. It's because I've been keeping a secret from you and I can't keep it any more.

There's no easy way to put this, Summer. I've been sitting here for hours trying to think of a way I can explain this and I have no clue. All I can say is that I'm not proud of what happened. I'm ashamed. A couple of weeks ago, I was on my bike in Raynes Park when I saw someone sitting in a car with the window wound down. I didn't know at the time, but it was your grandma.

Me and my friends had our water pistols with us and I suggested we shoot them at her through the open window. I can't begin to justify why we did it. It was a stupid thing to do. It was meant to be a joke. We didn't mean for anyone to get hurt. I wish I could go back and change things, but I can't. It was a really stupid decision. That's all it was. But it cost your grandma her life. If it wasn't for us, she would never have had a heart attack and she would still be alive today.

I know my apologies won't make it any better, but I am sorry. I couldn't be more sorry.

I only realised it was your grandma yesterday when I saw you at your grandad's house. I'm so sorry for the hurt that this will cause you. Please believe me when I say that the last thing I wanted to do was hurt you.

I'm going to the police station right now to tell them what happened. I can't live with myself any longer. I don't know what will happen to me, but I promise I'll stay away from you for ever.

Love,
Johnny

I fold up the piece of paper and place it back on the table. I stare into space. I don't know what to think.

Johnny

I get off the bus and look up at the police station. I get a strange, nervous feeling in my stomach. My heart is thumping and I have sweaty palms. This is it. There's no going back. I have to go in there and put it right.

I cross the road and walk slowly up the steps. As I get closer to the door, I think maybe I'm gonna chicken out. I could turn around, get on a bus and leave. I could take all the money out of my bank account and spend it on getting as far away from this mess as I possibly can. I could run away. I reckon I'd be able to get a long way from here. Out of the country, probably. I could go somewhere no one knows me, where no one knows what I've done, and start over again. But I know that's just idle thinking. I'm not gonna feel any better if I run away cos I'd feel just the same way I do right now. The only way to feel any better about this is to face up to it, to take responsibility at last.

I open the door and step inside. I look around me. It looks just like the waiting room of a dentist or something – a few brown chairs in one corner, a load of posters on the wall and some leaflets. Over on the right-hand side there's a booth with a screen, kind of like in banks. Behind the screen there's a policeman in a white short-sleeved shirt. His head is down, lost in paperwork.

I take a deep breath and walk to the counter.

'Excuse me,' I say.

The police officer looks up from his papers. 'Can I help you?'

I pause. I try and think of the right way to say this. 'Can I speak to someone?' I say. 'I've committed a crime. I killed someone.'

Summer

I open the front door and go straight through to the living room, where Grandad's sitting in his chair.

'Hello, Summer,' he says.

I sit down on the sofa without a word. I've been thinking about how to say this all the way here, but I'm totally clueless. I don't want to hurt his feelings, but I need to know the truth.

'Are you OK, Summer?'

I shake my head. 'No. I'm not.'

Grandad stares at me, like he wasn't expecting that answer and doesn't know what to say.

'Grandad, how did Nan die?'

Grandad's eyebrows raise and then furrow in one

movement. He takes a deep breath. 'Summer . . .' He stops.

'Did she die because of the heart attack she had the other week?'

Grandad shifts uncomfortably in his seat. 'Well, yes. I –'

'What caused it?'

Grandad looks down at his lap.

'Did she get shot at by some kids on bikes?'

Grandad looks up at me suddenly, like I've taken him by surprise.

'Did she?'

Grandad nods and sighs.

My head's filled with a confusing mix of emotions. I can't work out whether I'm disappointed or confused or angry or what. 'Why didn't anyone tell me?'

'I honestly don't know, Summer.' He breathes deeply and stares into space.

'Didn't anyone think that it was important? Didn't anyone think I'd like to know?'

Grandad just looks back at me. He looks sad and old and shrivelled. 'I'm sorry, Summer. I suppose we didn't think it would help you to know.'

'What?'

Grandad looks down at his lap. 'Nobody meant to upset you.'

I can't help but let out a snort. I feel angry. 'So yet

again the adults decide that I can't be trusted to know the truth? Is that it?'

Grandad's eyebrows furrow. 'No,' he says. 'Not at all. Why do you say that?'

I snort. I feel too angry and frustrated to say anything.

'Would it have made a difference to have known what caused the heart attack? She still died, whatever anyone said or didn't say.'

I sigh.

'What's brought this up, love?' Grandad says quietly.

I take a deep breath. 'I know who did it. I know who shot at Nan.'

It's difficult to read the expression on Grandad's face – it's surprised, angry and sad all at the same time.

'You know the boy that did it as well, Grandad,' I say. 'Johnny. The boy who picked you up off the pavement.'

Grandad stares at me in disbelief. 'Are you sure?'

I nod. 'Positive. He just wrote me a letter confessing and apologising.' I hold the letter up, wave it in front of Grandad's eyes. 'He's handing himself into the police this morning. He thinks he killed Nan.'

Grandad closes his eyes for a second and shakes his head. Then he looks at me. He sighs. 'Nobody killed your nan.'

I'm confused. 'What do you mean?'

'No one killed your nan apart from herself.' Grandad looks down at his hands. He looks like he doesn't want to tell me this. 'Your nan hadn't been happy for a long time, Summer. She hadn't been well for a long time.' He doesn't meet my eyes as he talks; it's like he can't bring himself to. 'To be frank, I think she gave up on life. She stopped taking her heart pills a long while ago. I tried nagging her, but . . . Well, you know how stubborn she could be.'

I'm shocked. I always knew Nan hated having to take so many pills – she always used to moan and make a big drama out of it – but I never thought she'd just refuse to. 'Really?'

Grandad nods. 'She took the medication when she was in hospital to keep the doctors happy, but as soon as she came out of hospital she refused again. It was a matter of time, Summer. We had an argument the night she came home. I tried to persuade her to take her medication, but I couldn't. She passed away in her sleep that night. I think that was what she wanted – she'd had enough suffering for one lifetime. She got her own way in the end.'

'Why? Why wasn't she happy?'

Grandad scratches his cheek and stares into space. He takes another long, sad breath. 'Lots of reasons,' he says. 'Mostly because she never got over the death of your dad, I think.'

I stare at Grandad. I can feel tears in my eyes.

'She was never the same after he died.'

I close my eyes and try to stop myself from crying. I have to hold it together cos I need to find out more. 'What happened, Grandad?' I say. 'What really happened to Dad?'

Grandad shifts uncomfortably again.

'Did Nan and Dad have an argument before he died?'

He nods his head slowly and reluctantly, then closes his eyes.

'Why?'

'It was about money. Can you believe it?' Grandad says. He opens his eyes and looks at me. There are tears in his eyes as well now.

I look back at him, not sure what to say.

'We'd lent money to him and your mum,' he says. 'Your nan wasn't happy about James owing us that money because he seemed to be spending money like it was going out of fashion. She never liked the fact that he spent most of his money on drinking and smoking. Things came to a head one afternoon when he was round here. They talked about money, your nan had a bit of a dig at your dad and he took offence. Then things escalated. Your nan demanded he pay the money back. She gave him a month to find the money. They had a blazing row and your dad said some things

387

he didn't mean and so did your nan. Your dad decided he'd had enough and stormed off.'

I nod. I feel a tear leak from my eye and roll down my cheek.

'He went out drinking that night and didn't go home until the early hours of the morning. He was steaming drunk. And then he started arguing with your mum.'

Tears are running down both my cheeks now.

'He drove to work the next day,' Grandad says. 'Of course he was still well over the alcohol limit. He wasn't thinking straight. He skipped a red light and got hit by a van. The silly fool wasn't even wearing a seatbelt. He didn't stand a chance.'

I sigh, but it comes out a bit like a whimper.

'Your nan blamed herself every day for the last sixteen years, Summer. The truth is that it was no one's fault, but she wouldn't accept that.'

I close my eyes.

Johnny

I have no idea what time it is or what's going on. Things have been happening around me and I don't seem to have any bearing on them now. I'm powerless and lost and confused. I wish I could curl up in a corner and go unnoticed.

All I know is this. When I came to the police station and admitted killing someone, they didn't handcuff me immediately and throw me in a cell like I thought they would. Instead they asked me what my name was and where I lived and how old I was. They asked me to turn out my pockets and they wrote down all the things that I had on me and then took them away in a clear bag.

They said they wanted to interview me under caution, but that I needed an 'appropriate adult' with me – a parent or guardian. I shook my head, mumbled that I didn't want anyone else to know. The thought of admitting what I'd done in front of the police was bad enough, but having to admit it in front of Mum or Dad as well was too much.

While we waited for my parents to turn up, I sat in the front office. I was expecting some grey cell with graffiti scratched into the paintwork – at least I would've been hidden away if I'd been in a cell. Instead I sat on my own, watching people come in and out of the police station. I was terrified and nervous and empty. I started to doubt that I was doing the right thing. The police had told me I was free to go at any time.

I have no idea how much time had passed, but later Dad turned up. He looked like I felt. Shocked. Scared. Disbelieving. Out of his depth. A solicitor turned up too. We talked, I answered questions, but I really have no idea what was said – the words just washed over me. It was like it was happening to someone else, like I wasn't there.

Eventually I was taken through the corridors to another room. An interview room, grey, with strip lights, empty except for brown office furniture and a tape recorder.

They told me that I was being interviewed under caution, that I wasn't under arrest and that I was free to leave whenever I wanted. Then they asked me what happened.

I told them the truth. At least, a version of the truth. I left out the fact that there were three other people involved in the drive-by soaking. Neither the police, the solicitor nor Dad seemed to doubt what I said. The police just asked me a few questions, picked up on a few details, asked whether I'd shot at other people with the water pistol. I told them the whole truth then. And as I spoke, I kept watching their faces for a reaction, to see what they thought of me. There was no reaction though. I could've been ordering a burger and chips for all the emotion on their faces. When the interview was over, I went back to the front office and waited. And waited.

And then, suddenly, the solicitor is in front of me, talking, telling me that the police aren't bringing any charges against me, that it isn't in the public interest to investigate it further. I listen and nod and struggle to take it in. This is meant to be good news.

The sergeant speaks to me before they hand all my things back. He gives me a telling off, like I'm back at school and I've thrown a rubber at a teacher or something. I stand and listen, wanting to be anywhere else but here. The last thing he says is, 'I don't think you'll be doing anything stupid like that again, will you?'

He sounds really patronising, but he's right. I won't.

I guess I should be feeling relieved. But I'm not. I feel hollow.

Dad thanks the police, looking about as embarrassed as me. Then we walk through the front door of the station, out into bright daylight. The rest of the world is going on as normal, oblivious to what I've done. It feels like the world should have stopped turning, like there should be TV cameras thrust into my face, broadcasting my guilt around the globe. Everyone should know what I've done. I shouldn't be allowed to get away with this. But everything is as it always was.

We walk in silence down the steps to the car. We drive home in silence. No radio. No talking. Just the hum of the engine as we drive through Wimbledon and into Raynes Park.

As we pass the big houses along Worple Road, I will Dad to say something. To start shouting at me. To call me an idiot. To tell me I'm grounded for the rest of my life. To get angry or upset. Anything. But he doesn't.

We cruise through Raynes Park and he doesn't say a word. I feel like I'm in a dream. Nothing feels the way it should.

We take a left at the lights at the end of the high street. I look out of the window. The parade of shops is just up ahead. There are no cars parked out there today. No silver car. As we get closer, I notice two people come out of the shop and grab their bikes. Jake and Drac. They look up as the car approaches. I see the look of recognition as Jake works out whose car it is. And then he spots me. He sits on his bike and stares at me, a look of disdain. He shakes his head slowly.

We turn right and then on to Exminster Avenue. We go past the Poisoned Dwarf's house, past the parked silver car. I imagine her husband inside the house, sitting in his chair with his broken ankle. I wonder whether he knows what I've done. I wonder whether Summer told him, whether she's there now.

In a second the house is behind us and we're into Sidmouth Avenue. Dad pulls into the parking space outside our house and switches the engine off. He undoes his seatbelt, but he doesn't move to open his door. So neither do I. I can feel it in the air – a lecture is close.

'We need to talk about this.'

I nod my head.

'But not right now – you need to get some rest,' he says. 'When we get inside, you do need to apologise to Mikey though. Do you understand?'

I nod again.

There's a long moment when neither of us does or says anything. Then Dad opens his door.

As soon as we get inside the house, we go through to the lounge. Mikey's not there for a change. Mum is, though. She looks at me and then at Dad. Her face is a mixture of sympathy, concern and disappointment.

'Are you OK, Johnny?'

I nod. It's easier than telling the truth.

Mum gives me a hug. And when that's done, I stand there, not sure what to say, where to look, what to do.

Dad tells me to sit down on the sofa, so I do.

'Mikey, come down here, please,' Dad calls up the stairs.

Moments later he clumps down the stairs and comes into the lounge. He looks shamefaced. He has cuts around his mouth and his right eye has swelled and closed up a little. As he sits down in a chair, he feels his side, like he's in pain. I get the impression he's acting a bit. But I feel bad. I feel embarrassed. I did that to him. I lost control.

'Mikey?' Dad starts, standing in front of the TV. 'I think you have something to say to Johnny . . .'

I feel confused. This isn't what I expected. Why am I getting an apology?

Mikey folds his arms. He doesn't look at me. He has a look of contempt on his face. He shakes his head.

Dad shifts on his feet. 'Pardon?'

'I'm not apologising to him,' Mikey says. 'He's a

394

psycho.' He points to his face, then lifts up his jumper and points to some marks on his side. 'Look at what he did to me.'

Dad sighs. He shifts on his feet again. 'Look, Mikey,' he says, 'Johnny *will* apologise to you. He knows that what he did to you was wrong, don't you, Johnny?'

I nod my head.

'But that doesn't change the fact that you were also in the wrong,' Dad says.

Mikey huffs in his seat. He turns his body away from me.

There's silence. Dad stares at Mikey. Mikey stares at the fingernails on his left hand. Mum stares at Dad.

'Well, Mikey?'

Mikey takes a deep breath. Then, in the most reluctant voice I've ever heard, he mumbles, 'Sorry.'

Dad nods. He looks relieved. 'Johnny?'

I look down at the floor. 'I'm sorry.'

And that's it. The end of the conversation. It doesn't feel like any kind of closure to me, but it's as good as we're gonna get.

We don't sit around in the lounge for much longer. As soon as I can, I come up here to my room and lie on my bed. I feel tired, but I don't feel sleepy. I still feel wired and weird and uncomfortable. I take my mobile phone from my pocket and switch it on.

A flurry of messages come through. From Mum and

Dad and Jake and Drac and Badger. I don't read any of them. I don't know if I ever want to know what they were thinking of me this morning. Maybe I'll delete them.

But I look through the contacts instead. Sure enough, there's the Poisoned Dwarf. I open the contact and look at the details. It's Mikey's mobile number. I delete the entry from my phone.

Another text message comes through. From Summer. I stare at my phone for ages. I don't know whether I want to read it or not. My thumb hovers over the buttons. Read or ignore? Read? Ignore? Do I want to know what she thinks of me? Don't I know already?

I press read.

Hope u r OK. I read ur letter. I think we need to meet. I have something to explain to u. S

I'm about to reply, when my bedroom door opens. I put my phone on my bed and look up. Mikey comes into my room.

'What do you want?' I say.

Mikey doesn't say anything. He comes over and lies down on the floor next to my bed. He reaches his arm out underneath my bed and rummages around.

'What are you doing?' I say. Ordinarily I'd get up and drag him out of my room, but that obviously isn't the right thing to do at this moment. So I just watch what he does.

'Got it,' he says a couple of seconds later. He pulls his arm out from under my bed, then sits up on his knees. In his hand he has a digital watch. 'Whoops. The alarm's been on all the time it's been under here. Hope it hasn't disturbed you.'

He stands up and walks towards the door. As he leaves my room, he turns and winks at me.

I lie back on the bed, roll over and shut my eyes.

Acknowledgements

Huge thanks to my contact in the Met, Linda Kernot, for her expert legal knowledge and for helping me find my way round a police station.

Apologies to the Timpsons and Browns for borrowing and changing stories here and there.

My Inspiration for DRIVE BY

In my first summer at sixth form, I remember an urban legend going around the common room. During a free period, a group of lads was messing about, soaking each other with pump-action water guns on the school field, when they had a bright idea. One of them had recently passed his driving test and they all got in his car and cruised around the sleepy streets of the small market town where our college was as though they were gangsters, soaking bystanders with their water pistols. A drive-by soaking. The story went that a police car (it must have been the only one in town) happened to be watching the boys as they brandished their water gun at their car window. The police thought it was a real gun and immediately gave chase, with their lights flashing and the siren shattering the peace. The car chase didn't last long. As soon as they realised the police were after them, the boys pulled over. Needless to say, the police weren't too happy when they searched them and discovered that the 'weapon' was a water pistol. I'm not sure who was more embarrassed. Whether that story has any basis in truth is debatable, but it has stayed with me all these years.

I wondered what might happen if somebody were to do something seemingly innocuous but the consequences turned out to be tragic. What if you shot at someone with a water pistol and instead of simply getting a bit wet, they had a heart attack and died? Would you own up or keep quiet? Would it be manslaughter, murder or just a tragic accident?

That's how *Drive By* started. However, while the book originally grew from that urban legend, new characters turned up to complicate things, most notably Summer, who brought along her own tragic back story. Much of Summer's story – deaths, spiritualists and all – was inspired by real-life events. If you'd like to read more about my inspiration for the book, be sure to stop by my website – **www.JimCarrington.co.uk**.

I hope you enjoyed the book.

Jim Carrington

Check out the **Jim Carrington Fan Page** on **Facebook**

Read on for a taster of
Inside My Head
also by Jim Carrington . . .

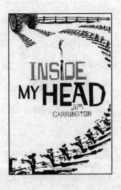

PAUL KNAGGS looks forward to school.
Because at school he can rip Gary Wood to shreds.

And GARY just takes it – usually.

DAVID is Knaggs's friend.
He does what Knaggs says – usually.

ZOË has moved from London to the middle of nowhere.
As far as she's concerned, life is over.
And then she meets the school loner, Gary.

GARY – KNAGGS – DAVID – ZOË.

When their stories collide, things get messy.

David

I'm already on question four as the bell goes.

'Hand in your books when you've finished,' Mr H calls over the noise. 'Then you can leave.'

Mills and me hand our books in and walk out of the lab, to the cloakroom.

About thirty seconds later, Knaggs joins us. 'D'you see Wood?' he says. 'I thought he was gonna start blubbing!'

I nod my head. 'Yeah, I know,' I say. 'He looked like he was gonna explode.'

'Leave it now, though,' Mills says. 'You know what he's like.'

I nod.

Knaggs shrugs. 'He won't do anything.'

No one answers him. I avoid Knaggs's eyes.

We all set about looking for our blazers and bags on the floor of the cloakroom. I find my blazer, brush the dust off it and start looking for my bag.

Then there's a noise. *SMACK!* Loud and shocking.

The whole place goes silent and we all turn to look. Knaggs is lying on the floor of the cloakroom, holding the side of his face. His mouth is open. He looks stunned. For a second, I'm confused. But then my brain starts to fill in the missing parts and I look around for Wood. But he's not there. The door out of the cloakroom swings shut.

We all crowd round Knaggs.

Mr Moore comes and gets me out of literacy, next lesson. He doesn't say what it's about. He just walks me through the empty corridors in silence. But it's obvious what he wants me for.

When we get to his office, I expect to see Knaggs sitting there. But he isn't. Neither's Wood.

'Take a seat, David,' Mr Moore says. He points at a comfy green chair.

I sit down in it and sink back. But I feel awkward, so I sit up straight instead. My hands are sweaty. My heart's pounding.

Mr Moore starts off, going on about how I'm a responsible boy and that he trusts me to tell the truth and all that stuff. I just sit there feeling weird. See, I know what he's gonna ask me to do. He wants me to point the finger. He wants me to grass someone up. Knaggs or Wood. It's what teachers always want – some mug like me to make their job easier. I have a decision to make, I know. I can tell him the truth and keep the teachers' rules. But the thing is, then I'd be breaking the kid rules. I'd be breaking the biggest kid rule of all: grassing up my best mate. Or I can lie. It's the kind of choice where I have no choice.

'Tell me what happened in the science lab, David,' Mr Moore says.

I sit and think for a moment. The truth's easy. I know exactly what happened. We were messing about all lesson, like normal, and Knaggs started taking the mick out of Wood. The rest of us just encouraged him to do it. But Knaggs pushed it too far. Anyone could see how angry Wood was getting – he was about to explode. And then Wood went mental. But I can't say any of that, not the stuff that actually happened. Knaggs would get into trouble. I'm gonna have to lie, bend the truth a little. Otherwise my life won't be worth living. I shift uncomfortably in my seat. I've got a nervous guilty feeling in my stomach and I haven't even started lying yet.

'Was there an argument, David?' Mr Moore says. 'Tell me what you remember . . .'

I look up at him. He's looking straight at me, almost smiling but not quite. I take a deep breath. 'It started when Gary came into science late, sir,' I say. No lies yet but my heart's still beating like crazy. 'Gary and Knaggs – I mean, Paul Knaggs – well, they were having a laugh, taking the mickey out of each other, just winding each other up.' My voice is shaking slightly. It doesn't sound like me talking.

Mr Moore picks a notebook up off his desk and then a pen. He writes something down. And then he stops and looks up at me again. He smiles. 'It was both of them, you say?'

I nod.

Mr Moore makes more notes. Then he looks up at me. 'OK. How were they winding each other up, David?'

I look down at my feet. 'Don't know. Just the usual, really. They always do it. Just calling each other names and that. It was nothing serious, sir. It was just a bit of give and take.'

I look up. Mr Moore's writing more things in his notebook and nodding his head. Over his shoulder I can see a signed cricket bat and an old photo of the school team. I stare at them. God, I wish I was outside playing cricket instead of sitting here.

'Go on,' Mr Moore says.

I look back at him with a start. I must look guilty as hell. So I look at my shoes again. See, I'm a rubbish liar. People can see it in my eyes straight away. I can't hide it. 'Well, then we all got on with our work. Tried to get it all finished before the end of the lesson. Except Gary. He just sort of sat there and stared at the desk. He looked angry. And then he tried to start it all up again,' I say. And I hate myself for saying it. I think of Wood sitting there in the lab, with that angry face, taking it all. I should be telling Mr Moore about that. But I can't. I can't grass on Knaggs. That's the rules. The kid rules. He's my mate. I have to stick up for him. 'Gary kept trying to start it all off again, calling Paul short and that. And so Paul took the mickey back a bit. And that's when Gary started to look *really* angry, like he couldn't handle it any more.'

Mr Moore raises his eyebrows. 'I see,' he says. 'Can you remember exactly what was said?'

I stare back at him. The 'sort of' smile has gone from his face. He looks serious now. I feel like he's about to rumble me. I shake my head. 'Not exactly, sir,' I say. I look up at the cricket bat again, to avoid looking in his eyes. 'Gary was taking the mickey out of Paul for being short. And Paul was taking the mickey back, saying Gary's head looks like a cheese puff. And then Gary just got really angry. He said he was gonna kill Paul – that sort of stuff.'

Mr Moore raises his eyebrows again and notes something else down in his book. He underlines it three times, then looks back at me. 'You're sure that's what he said, David . . . ?'

I nod. 'Yeah.' My heart's thumping so hard I can hear it in my ears. I feel sick. I want to be out of this room.

'Absolutely sure . . . ?'

I take a breath. 'Yes.'

'Thank you, David,' Mr Moore says. And then he shows me to the door.

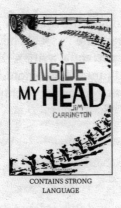

CONTAINS STRONG
LANGUAGE

AVAILABLE NOW

www.JimCarrington.co.uk

Praise for **Inside My Head** by Jim Carrington

'I loved it and you should go read it'
Bloggers Heart Books

'A thought-provoking read'
Bliss

'Witty and hard-hitting dialogue and a compellingly
written storyline'
Irish Post

'Claustrophobic and unbearably tense, it's extremely
compelling and gives a good deal of pause for thought'
Bookbag

'One of the most thought-provoking and compelling books
I have read for a long time . . . This book is utterly believ-
able . . . and it is so perfectly written that you actually feel
the sting of every taunt. There should be a copy of this
book in every secondary school library'
Book Zone 4 Boys

'A thought-provoking novel . . . Well written and
worth a read'
Chicklish

'A very, very pacy and unputdownable contemporary
novel . . . Very much in the style of Melvin Burgess and
Kevin Brooks, this is a powerful debut novel'
Love Reading 4 Kids

'Easy to relate to and impossible to put down'
Armadillo